# TO CATCH A CATFISH

*A Love, Lies, and Catfish Novel*

## JOI JACKSON

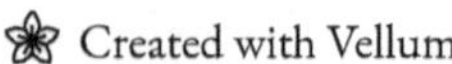 Created with Vellum

*To my husband*
*Thank you for allowing me to run random ideas and scenarios by you. While the ninjas and car chases you suggested didn't make it into the final draft, thank you for your patience and male point of view. I couldn't have finished this book without you!*
*Love you forever,*
*Joi*

# CATFISH DEFINED

*A catfish is someone who creates a false online identity. Catfishing is common on social networking and online dating sites. Sometimes a catfish's sole purpose is to engage in a fantasy. Sometimes, however, the catfish's intent is to defraud a victim, seek revenge, or commit identity theft.*

*-From whatis.com*

❦ 1 ❦

# LONDON

L ondon Lewis saw the yellow note on the door before she reached her office.

*London, please stop by my office when you get in – Aja*

STICKY NOTES FIRST THING IN THE MORNING WERE never good news. They never said things like "Cake in the break room for breakfast!" or "Happy Friday! Leave a couple hours early today." No. Yellow stickies first thing in the morning meant there was some urgent need from someone higher up the food chain.

Grabbing the note, London sat her laptop tote on her desk while scanning the message from her cousin and boss, Aja Lewis. Hoping to snag a cup of tea and breakfast from the café downstairs, London had arrived a few minutes early for once. *So much for that*, she thought as she read the note again. Direct and to the point. Typical Aja. No wasted words. London squared her shoulders, preparing to walk to her cousin's office.

The walk was brief. The headquarters of Exposé, the company Aja started four years ago to help people find out if they were the victims of catfishing, was one of those office suites that catered to small businesses that needed to look more established than they were.

Their space had four offices, or cubicles with doors, as London liked to call them, a conference room that boasted of holding eight people when five was really the max if everyone wanted to sit down, and a compact break area with a long table and bench. London passed the second office and break room on the way to Aja's office.

Aja had probably been in the office for at least two hours. A typical Type A go-getter who personified Black girl magic, she commanded all of the attention in any room she occupied and carried herself like she was 6'2" even though she was only a little over five feet tall.

As London approached Aja's office, she heard her cousin's voice.

She paused, waiting to hear whether Aja got a response. There was a hushed answer, but London recognized the other voice as Aja's best friend and new business partner, Zaria Laurent.

London didn't know why Aja wanted to talk to her but it didn't feel like good news.

Knocking quickly to announce herself, London smiled and proceeded towards the empty low-slung white chair in front of Aja's matching desk. Aja had infused her personality into her office; the furniture was modern and beautiful but London dreaded sitting in the uncomfortable chairs, wondering if Aja had done that intentionally to keep anyone from lingering too long in her space.

Aja had a killer wardrobe and London always liked to see what mood Aja was in by the clothes she selected that day. Normally in edgy styles, Aja was more conservative in a black pantsuit, tomato red blouse, and her signature sky high pointy black stilettos. Aja's conversation with Zaria stopped abruptly when London entered, confirming they were discussing her.

London found herself comparing the two women. Where Aja was petite and brown skinned like London, Zaria was tall, statuesque and fair. Zaria had recently gone blonde with a faux hawk she wore curly. A vibrant blue scarf knotted like a turban at the top of Zaria's head coordinated with the royal blue and black shirtdress she wore.

"London, please have a seat." Aja glanced over at Zaria, who nodded quickly.

London tried to read each woman's face for clues but came up empty. The professional look on Aja's face was the one she used when she had to deliver unpleasant news or correct a client's assumptions.

"Good morning, London," Zaria said as London folded herself awkwardly in the chair. She smiled and nodded at Zaria in response.

"Cute top, is that another one of your vintage finds?" Zaria asked, tilting her head toward London.

*Where was this coming from?* Zaria hadn't socialized with London beyond standard greetings since London started working at Exposé two months ago, and now she was all smiles and asking about her wardrobe? Her stomach clenched. Were they trying to soften her up to deliver bad news?

Was Aja about to tell her she was fired? And why was Zaria in the room? Zaria was in charge of sales as far as London knew.

"Thanks." She touched her collar, reminding herself which top she wore, a semi-sheer black lace high neck blouse with ruffles that ran down the front along with a pair of wool trousers. The blouse was typical of her style: vintage, frilly, and feminine. "No, this one came from the mall. Maxie clawed the vintage one I had." London played along for now and kept up the small talk.

Aja made a face. "Uncle Gene still has that crazy stray cat? I thought my dad said he was going to put her up for adoption?"

"Nope. He said she's grown on him and now she's a member

of the family. It's like having an evil stepsister. She doesn't appreciate that I have moved into her house, and I've never been a cat person so we can't stand each other." London shifted her position in the chair, trying not to wince but feeling as if she was practically sitting on the floor.

She waited a beat. "Are you going to fire me? I know I've made some mistakes in the case note system, I always forget to log out but I..."

Shaking her head, Aja cut her off. "Of course not. Why would I fire you?" Aja frowned at London. "You're doing a great job; plus I would never hear the end of it from my dad or yours."

That was certainly true. Their fathers, identical twins born minutes apart, were close and had conspired to convince Aja and London to mend their broken fences and work together. London assumed they had to work much harder on Aja than they did on her as she had recently moved back to Atlanta from DC broke, broken, and jobless.

When her father suggested talking to Aja about a job, she was hesitant since they weren't close any more. After he'd confided that Aja needed the help more than she was willing to admit, London resolved to get over her pride and embarrassment and just broach the subject.

Glancing at her smart watch, Aja continued. "Anyway, the reason I called you in is that Zaria had a suggestion we wanted to discuss with you." She seemed to be measuring her words carefully, as she glanced at Zaria, who nodded enthusiastically at both of them.

London frowned slightly. Zaria hadn't gone out of her way to make London feel welcome since she'd started at the company, giving London the distinct impression that Zaria was avoiding her. Not that London could blame her given their history.

She couldn't imagine what Zaria had in mind for her. She was generally leery of people in sales. Most of the time that sales personality was an indication they were good at manipulating people into doing whatever they wanted.

Aja continued. "The business is doing well. We're on track to double our revenue from last year and I plan to expand. But that means we need more cash. I'm looking for an angel investor who can help us take the next steps."

While that all sounded great, London wondered what they needed from her. Currently, London's job was to take the information gathered from the client, such as social media accounts they used, how they met the person they wanted Exposé to investigate, anything they knew about the other person and figure out the real story. Then London put all details and a conclusion into a report that was submitted to the client.

Aja turned to Zaria. "Yes, London, we were thinking you could start onboarding clients." After dropping that bombshell, Zaria rushed on. "We think you'll be great at it. You have good technical knowledge and we think you'll be able to establish rapport with clients. If you do the onboarding, Aja is free to do more promotion of the company."

London held up her hand as if she was back in elementary school asking for a bathroom break. "When you say onboarding, what exactly is that?"

"Right, glad you asked. After a new client signs up, we interview them to understand why they think they have a catfishing situation and try to find out as much as possible about the relationship. We then outline the process and let them know what to expect," Aja answered.

Zaria pressed on. "You will still do the research you normally do, which is your superpower, but instead of passing the research off to us, you'll present it to the client yourself. It's a great opportunity. And we need your help."

Zaria stopped, glancing back at Aja. *Another mic pass to Aja,* London noted.

Aja nodded. "It's not hard, I promise. I'll help you and answer any questions you have. You can do this! Your research reports are more thorough than any of those done by the contractors, so you will still do that, but moving forward, as Zaria said, you would be their point of contact when clients sign up." She placed her elbows on the desk and clasped her hands together. "London, you can totally handle this."

London chewed her lip, considering their words while her inner introvert screamed in protest. They were really trying to sell her on this promotion and she wondered what the catch was.

*Client facing? Ugh.* London loved that she didn't have to deal with the public. Since starting at the company, she had only worked two cases which were super simple to crack. She was pretty sure that was intentional so she wouldn't give up and quit as a couple of previous researchers had.

Aja leaned back to close the deal. "Your ninety day review is coming up. If you agree and all goes well, I'll give you a salary bump."

Normally, London wasn't driven by money, but she had to consider her current circumstances. She was living at home with her father and his evil cat in her old princess purple bedroom with a bank account that was barely covering the minimum balance needed to keep it active. She could definitely be bought.

"Ok, I'll do it. What do I need to do?"

*It couldn't be that bad, right?* While she was definitely more comfortable sitting in front of a laptop by herself, she wasn't going to hiss and claw at approaching strangers. Surely, she could be a charming onboarding person, or whatever her new title would be.

She turned to Zaria, who looked like she might shake London's hand now that they'd sold her on the job. "What exactly do you call people who do onboarding?"

Aja glanced at her watch again then at Zaria. "Good question...maybe Client Account Liaison? It's a new position so we'll come up with an impressive title." She rose from the desk, a signal that the meeting was over. "I'm expecting a call in a few minutes, but we'll talk later."

Zaria rose smoothly from the low chair then strode to the door, smiling at London. "This is going to be a good move for you. I think you'll enjoy working with clients." She turned to Aja. "I'll call you later; I'm off to the airport."

London watched Zaria leave. An attempt to propel herself easily from the chic chair from Hell as she'd just seen Zaria do ended with London's legs splayed like she was ready for a pelvic exam. Readying for another try, London only caught part of Aja's next comment. "Wait, what?"

"I was optimistic you'd agree so I went ahead and scheduled your first client at 2:00 today."

London struggled then scooted to the edge of the seat to right herself. She tried to keep most of the panic out of her voice. "Today?"

Before Aja could respond, her phone rang and she waved London out, repeating her promise to talk later.

⚜

THE PROMISED "TALK LATER" HAPPENED AT A QUARTER to one, five minutes before London's new client walked in.

London and Aja were in London's office where Aja was bent over walking London through pulling up the New Client Questionnaire on her laptop when the outer door chimed. Aja's head swung to the time displayed on the screen.

"Oh, he's early." Aja swore under her breath, which caught London by surprise. Unable to help herself, she snorted a laugh. Her cousin, the consummate professional, dropping an F bomb, was hilarious.

Aja turned to London with an expression that made her quickly drop the grin. "His name is Donovan and he's here about his grandmother. Just follow my lead. I'll ask the questions and you can take notes on the questionnaire." She stood up straight and adjusted her suit jacket, her game face fully on. "You ready?"

Attempting her own game face, London managed a sickly grimace, prompting Aja to frown and ask if she was all right.

London dumped the game face. She would just smile instead. She followed Aja to the receptionist area where the client was waiting.

London's first client was tall, dark and, she realized, familiar. Ok, she had to admit, he was also very nice looking. She gauged his height at a couple inches over six feet as she had to look up a bit to see his face. He had the lean, muscular body of a distance runner with locs that grazed his broad shoulders.

London assumed he had come from an office as he was wearing the standard casual office uniform: dark slim cut jeans, striped blue shirt and sports jacket that fit like it was custom made. London studied his face. Smooth brown skin with dark brown eyes and lashes most women would kill for coupled with full lips. She knew his face but couldn't place it.

Why was this beautiful stranger so familiar? He didn't give off model or professional athlete vibes so that wasn't it. She was racking her brain when she heard Aja call her name.

"I'm Aja Lewis, we spoke on the phone last week, and this is London Lewis. She's going to be handling your inquiry. She's our best research analyst."

London felt a quick elbow jab from her cousin, causing her to jump. Aja wanted her to say something, she guessed. "London, this is Donovan Willis."

Donovan shook her hand. "Same last name, Lewis. Any relation?" London saw his eyes dart from her face to Aja's and land on hers.

"We're cousins." Aja smiled, poking London again. "Our dads are brothers. Keeping it in the family, right, London?"

As Donovan spoke, London realized even his voice was slightly familiar. Her brain went into overdrive scanning for where she'd seen and heard him before. Although she often forgot a name seconds after hearing it, she was good with faces and voices.

Suddenly, London snapped her fingers and gasped. "You won the World Cyber Games Tournament when you were younger. You were on the news because you got to go to South Korea and everything. That's where I know you from!" London pushed at his arm enthusiastically, fangirling big time now. "Your scores were amazing."

As soon as London touched him, Donovan jumped back as if threatened. London quickly dropped her arm, letting it hang awkwardly at her side. She hadn't meant to get so handsy with a man she just met. "Sorry."

"No worries." Donovan lifted a brow. "You saw me on TV back then?" London saw another realization hit him. "So you must be a gamer then?"

"Yes, I loved all things Quake back in the day. You've done a few of the QuakeCons too, right?" London asked, referring to a gaming conference for a popular first-person shooter video game.

Donovan nodded, stroking his chin. "Yeah, I went in 2003 but I came in like sixth place. The competition was crazy that year." He pointed at London. "Did you go?"

"Please, my father would have banned me from the computer if he'd known I was playing a shooting game. So, no tournaments or conferences for me. Do you still play?"

"Not as much these days. Since I work in game development now, I have this annoying habit of analyzing the games and finding design flaws which kind of ruins the fun of it. Do you play much?"

London happily chatted about the games she played now and how she missed some of the old school games from her childhood. Donovan agreed and added some games of his own. London glanced over at Aja catching her roll her eyes ever so slightly. Aja wasn't all that into video games when they were kids and London imagined she certainly had no interest in gaming now.

Aja clasped her hands together. "Let's head into the conference room to talk. London, can you grab your laptop?"

London excused herself and Donovan gave her this wide, slightly gap-toothed grin that tapped her in the pit of her stomach. Flustered, she practically ran to her office.

Reaching her office, London took a deep breath. What the

hell was wrong with her? Ok, so the man was amazing at a game she loved as a kid. So what? Not a big deal and certainly no reason to act as if he was a celebrity. She was a professional and would conduct herself as one.

She took an aggressive gulp of water from the bottle on her desk, almost spilling it, and grabbed her laptop, working on her game face.

When London entered the conference room, Aja was sitting at what was considered the head of the five-seat table and Donovan sat to her left facing the door. They were chatting about the stock market, causing London to roll her eyes as Aja did earlier.

Donovan quickly rose and held out a seat next to him for her. Trying to recall the last time any man held her chair, she awkwardly sat down, thanking him. London planned to sit on Aja's right making it easier to look at the client while taking notes, but now she would have to turn to the right to address him. She was also close enough to be very aware of his scent, a pleasing combination of spice and citrus, which made her want to close her eyes and breathe it in fully. There was just something enticing about a man who smelled good.

Once London was settled and ready to take notes, Aja gave him some background on the company. "Donovan, this is a very straightforward process. We will take the information you give us and start researching your inquiry. Expect a weekly report from us at minimum, but we'll keep you posted more frequently if there are major developments. If we conclude that the probability of a catfish is very high, we'll notify you. We will not contact either party; we leave that up to the client's discretion."

She smiled and leaned in, tenting her fingers like a trusted therapist. "Why don't you tell us about your grandmother and what brings you in."

Focused on her new client, London watched as Donovan exhaled then placed his elbows on the conference room table.

"My grandmother's name is Emmaline Roberson and she

lives here in Atlanta." He rubbed his chin. "I guess my grandmother started using that dating site for seniors, Silver and Sexy, about eight months ago. She told me one of her friends found a husband through the site and she decided to give it a try. I didn't really think she was going to go through with signing up."

London clicked quietly on the keyboard taking notes as Donovan continued. "We're close and she's told me about some of the men at church who hit on her, but she's been very secretive since she signed up for that site. Silver and Sexy has an app for your phone that allows members to send direct messages to each other. She had me help her set that up on her phone and now she's on it all the time. I can tell when she gets a message from him because she gets all flustered."

Donovan leaned back in his chair.

Aja tucked a stray lock of hair behind her ear. "How old is your grandmother? And why do you think the man isn't who he says he is?"

Donovan rubbed his chin again. "She's seventy-five."

London could tell he was considering the second question carefully. "I think it's the secrecy that's bothering me. Normally she shares with me what's going on in her life. I don't know for sure that the man is up to no good, but I wonder why she hasn't told me about him. Why is she hiding someone she clearly likes from her family?"

Feeling for him, London really hoped this investigation turned out to be a case where Donovan's grandmother didn't tell her family because the relationship was too new to share.

Looking up from her notes, London asked, "Does your grandmother know you have concerns or that you've hired us?"

"No, and she can't know any of this. She would kill me." His head slumped forward. "This has to stay between us." Their eyes met and London saw the internal battle he struggled with for going behind his grandmother's back. She wanted to rub his shoulders and tell him everything would be ok.

Aja nodded, clasping her hands like she held his secret within them. "Of course. We will do our digging discreetly and let you know what we find. If the man is who he says he is, and we certainly hope that's the case, she need not ever know."

Dropping his hands back to his lap, Donovan's lips parted slightly as if he wanted to speak then thought better of it.

"Was there anything else you wanted to tell us?" London asked gently.

"So, most of your cases, are they actually catfish?"

London leaned back in her chair. Since she had so little history with the company, Aja would need to take this one. London recalled her cases were both catfish. One was a middle-aged married man who was masquerading as a single woman in her twenties and the other was a prison inmate pretending to be a dancer on tour with Rhianna.

"People come to us because they feel there's a problem in their online relationship. Unfortunately, most of the time their feelings are correct," Aja said softly. "But your case is unique. Usually, the person in the relationship hires us. As I said though, we will treat your inquiry with kid gloves and your grandmother will never know."

The interview continued. London learned that Donovan's grandmother was retired and now wrote a foodie blog with videos of her cooking and gardening. London was impressed with this woman already; compared to her life at thirty-two, Emmaline's life at seventy-five was far more interesting.

London stopped typing as she thought about a blog she might start and felt eyes on her. Snapping out of her daydream, she glanced around to find Donovan and Aja looking at her expectantly.

Desperately, she blurted the first question that came to mind. "Did you say your grandmother hasn't met this man in person yet? How do you know?"

Donovan shrugged. "It's just a hunch. I can't explain it, but my gut says she hasn't met him in person and that something's off. If I find out this man is married..." He let the words trail off and London wondered what he would do when he found out the truth.

Chances were good this man was at best, not who he claimed to be and at worse, out to do harm. Men preyed on women online all the time.

"As I said earlier, we'll give you all the info we find, but if this person turns out to be a catfish, we don't recommend confronting him. The best course of action is to give the info to your grandmother and let her end things."

Aja stood and handed Donovan an info packet. "London's business card is in here as well as mine in case you need them. We'll get started on our research and send you updates, but don't hesitate to call either of us if you have questions or find out something that could be useful."

Donovan stood, tucking the packet under his arm. He shook Aja's hand then turned to London, shaking her hand and giving her an appreciative look that had her wanting to fan herself from the heat it caused.

❦

"THIS INVESTIGATION IS PERFECT FOR YOU!" AJA SAID, her eyes lighting up. "Let's talk strategy." Back in the conference room, Aja had London connect her laptop up to the large flat screen monitor mounted on the wall so they could review London's notes together. She stood near the monitor, ready to point out aspects of her notes that London needed to focus on. London felt almost like she was back in college attending a lecture.

Scanning the beginning of the questionnaire, Aja put a hand on her chin. "What was your initial impression of our client? Does he seem trustworthy to you?" She paused, pursing her lips. "Beyond the fact that he plays games as an adult male."

London guessed Aja saw that as a negative. Go figure. As an occasional gamer herself, London found that part to be rather charming, but that was just her. "Well, if I remember the news story correctly, they interviewed his grandmother along with him because she took him to South Korea. I'm wondering if it was the same grandmother. If so, they have to be super close, and I'm thinking he wouldn't have asked for help if he wasn't legitimately concerned."

"Ok, but here's a question for you. He's a game programmer, right?" Aja hobbled back to the desk chair nearest the monitor and flopped into it. "These things are killing me. I hate breaking in new shoes."

Kicking the sleek pumps off one by one, she continued. "So, he knows more about technology than the average Joe, right?" She didn't wait for a response. "Then why do you think he hired us? He could probably find out everything he needed to know on his own, for free."

London considered the question. "Maybe deep down he doesn't want to share her with another man and this is a good way to say, 'See, I told you there were no good men out there.' And we provide irrefutable proof instead of him just telling her that meeting men online is dangerous."

Aja tucked her feet under her legs. "Good point. You might ask him about that next time you talk." She pointed at the screen again. "Donovan also said his grandmother was using a dating app. I think the quickest way for you to start looking into this man she's dating is to download that anti-cheating app I told you about last week."

Nodding, London made a note. The app Aja referred to scanned all of the major dating apps and sent any activity or messages to the mate's phone. Even though she worked in technology, London was in awe of some of the tools and apps that had been created in the last few years.

"You'll need to install the app on the grandmother's phone." Aja clasped her hands and rested her head on them, thinking. "That might be a challenge."

*How on earth was she going to do that?* London hoped to dig into the woman's relationship from the comfort of her desk. She eyed her cousin. "Might be? She's not going to just hand me, a total stranger, her phone and say 'Sure, young lady, install anything you want on this. I trust you implicitly!'"

Aja's response was an eye roll and deep sigh. "There's an art to getting things done that I must teach you." She held up a ballet pink fingernail. "Donovan could get her phone and install the app for you. You two seem to have hit it off. Ask him."

"Well, that could work," London said reluctantly. *Why didn't she think of that?* She wondered if she was truly ready for this. "Are you sure I should take this one? There's so much I don't know yet. Maybe I can just work on the research." *Where it's safe*, she added silently.

"London, of course you can handle it. You've already established trust with the client and since he's tech savvy, you can get his help with access to her devices if you need to. That app should help out a lot though. You should be able to get the man's screen name. We're assuming it's a man, but it could be a woman; that might be the reason she doesn't want the family to know."

Aja glanced at her watch. "I've got a call with a client in a few minutes. Anyway, you can get the other person's screen name, use it to find out their identity, and dig into their background. This one will be a piece of cake."

London should have known better.

❦ 2 ❦

# DONOVAN

Donovan reviewed the specs for a video game scene he was tasked with redesigning. The game needed a refresh for the latest version but he wasn't sure what the team wanted. He had been given vague directions from senior leadership to 'make it ten times better than the last one'.

He glanced at the time on his laptop monitor. Almost time to call it a day. After working on the same scene all day, unable to get the feel of it just right, he was tired of looking at the screen. Maybe he would review the current version once more and try to come up with new ideas, and if that didn't work he'd pack up then try again once he made it home.

"You look like you need a drink." Valtreece Turner stuck her head into Donovan's cubicle and peered at his screen. "You still working on that same cave scene?"

Val helped herself to the seat next to Donovan's desk. She put her elbow on the desk, still vying for Donovan's attention, much like she'd done since they were in elementary school.

"Damn, you made me lose my train of thought." Donovan glared at the screen then turned to face her. "What do you need?"

"Hey, friend, it's good to see you too, I'm great, thanks for asking." Val crossed her arms over her chest. "I was trying to see if you wanted to hit the gym tonight, but you seem to be in a mood." Val's tone was testy. Her arms still crossed, she sat back in the chair.

Donovan sighed, frustrated. He was pretty much done for the day; he might as well go hang out. "Nah, I'm cool. We can go to the gym. I've been messing around with this scene all day and it just doesn't look right. It's driving me crazy." He pushed away from his desk. "I'll work on it when I get home."

"You work too much. Let's hit the gym for about forty-five minutes then head to Twinz so you can get some ass." Val smirked then raised her eyebrows, wiggling them suggestively.

Donovan scowled at her.

Why were the women in his life always trying to put him out there? If his grandmother wasn't doing her not-so-subtle matchmaking, Val was trying to get him to go out and make a fool of himself in front of women who were in it for the tips.

He didn't even like the food at Twinz, a local eatery with attractive waitstaff who wore low-cut tee shirts and tiny shorts which Donovan suspected was to distract patrons from the bland menu choices. Despite the food, the place was wildly popular among Donovan's coworkers.

He waved her off. "You just want to see if that server with the red braids is there. You know she's too young for you."

Val scoffed. "Too young! She's gotta be at least twenty-one to work there, right?"

"Um, remember the twenty-four-year-old poetess from Decatur? You said you needed to find someone self-aware enough to not share every random thought she had in the moment." He stretched his arms above his head and glanced at the time again.

She waved a dismissive hand. "That was a lapse in judgment on my part. So, gym tonight?"

"I'll go to the gym, but I'm heading home after that." He gestured toward his laptop. "I gotta figure this out."

Donovan glanced at Val's khakis, light blue golf shirt and loafers. "You're not dressed for the gym."

She rolled her eyes. "I know. I was coming to see if you were still going. No sense in changing if you wanted to hit Twinz."

Donovan scowled.

"I'm kidding." Val hopped up from the chair. "Ok, I'm going to change; I'll meet you out front."

Donovan watched as she strode back toward her desk. He had to admit she lightened his mood. He'd been ready to throw something at the monitor in frustration. But she was right, he did work too much and stepping away from the problem was best.

Val was a good distraction and he was glad she was dragging him to the gym.

Two years ago, when Val came out and then divorced her husband, Donovan was one of the few people who supported her decision. He was able to get her a job at his company when she'd decided to get into game development and he was proud of all she had accomplished.

Packing his laptop and power cord into his backpack, Donovan headed to the men's room to change.

❧

In the lobby, Val was dressed in basketball gear, tapping her foot impatiently. "You are slower than molasses in January. Let's go!"

One of the perks of working at a game development studio was paid membership at a local gym just steps from their office in Midtown Atlanta. The downside was if you were planning to go to the gym, you might as well stop into the office to work. Val was one of the few employees who lived close enough to take the train to work, so she generally was in the office two to three days a week.

As they crossed the street to the gym's main entrance, Val kept up a steady stream of chatter while Donovan, still working through the problems with his design, only half listened.

"You know they let Candy Crush Chuck go, right?" Val kept

her ear to the ground in the office and liked to share all the juicy gossip with Donovan, who couldn't understand how a firm full of mostly male geeks managed to keep so much drama going on.

"What? When? I just saw him this morning." Donovan stopped in the middle of the sidewalk and got scowls from a group of women in yoga pants and sports bras vying for the gym.

He jumped out of the way of the yoga mob and held the door for Val once they were clear.

Val hoisted her gym bag onto her shoulder and led the way to the basketball court. "Yep, it was right after he got back from lunch. I guess playing Candy Crush all the time was fine until he got caught watching porn on company time."

At the court, there was a game in progress, so they added their names to a sign in kiosk and sat on the benches to wait their turn.

Donovan's mouth dropped open and Val reached over and pushed his chin up. "Are you serious, he was watching porn at the office? When?"

Val leaned in so only Donovan could hear her. "Last night, from what I heard. Chuck was in the office when I left around six, and apparently he was supposed to be working on some analytics for the senior leadership team. Taking a break to eat, he went downstairs to get his takeout order and his manager stepped in his office to drop off something and got an eyeful because Chuck forgot to lock his machine."

She sat back, smug. "Rule #1, if you're gonna watch porn in the office, always lock your screen."

Chuckling, Donovan put his elbows on his knees. "Wow, I thought he could do no wrong. Can't say I'm sorry he's gone. He was always stealing people's ideas."

"Yep, good riddance. Hey, did you ever call the number I gave you for your grandmother?"

"I actually went to their office yesterday, it's close to ours. I hired them." A thought occurred to him. "So how did you know about Exposé?"

"Dude, there's this tool on your phone or laptop called the internet and you can use it to search for stuff."

Donovan flicked Val's shoulder and she drew back in mock horror. "Hey now, I'm just sayin', there are ways of getting information. What happened?"

"I called and talked to the owner, this woman named Aja and she tried to get me to sign up online but I wanted to go into the office to make sure it was legit. Their service is not cheap...anyway, I met the owner and she brings her cousin in, both of them fine AF, but the cousin," he tapped Val on the arm. "Val, she remembers me from way back in the day when I was on the news for winning that tournament in South Korea."

Val raised an eyebrow. "I'm impressed. Was the cousin Beyonce though? Because you are looking like a starstruck fan."

Donovan covered his mouth then rested his chin on his hand. He wasn't star struck. Just, well, impressed she remembered him. That's all. It wasn't every day attractive women went out of their way to recognize him, especially attractive women gamers. He had a right to be impressed.

"Val, she's a gamer. And I'm not..." Donovan defended his reaction to Val as much as himself, but he stopped when he saw that Val's attention was elsewhere.

"Oh, that's us, let's go." The current game wrapped up and Val motioned to the player who called her name.

After their game, the players all dispersed, leaving Val and Donovan alone on the court. As she bounced the ball, Val picked up the conversation. "A sexy gamer, huh? That's like your high school fantasy. Is she single? You ask her out? You know it's high time you got some action."

She chest passed the ball to Donovan. He caught it, glaring at her as he held it. Val raised her hands in surrender. "I'm just sayin'. Truth hurts."

"No, I didn't ask her out. What do I look like, one minute concerned about Gram and then the next, trying to push up on the woman like some horny old politician? They probably would have thrown me out."

He tossed the ball into the net with more force than necessary. "I need to find out if this man Gram is seeing is legit and make sure he's not some pervert or ex-con trying to pull a fast one on her. That's the only goal."

Val jogged after the ball. "I get that, but just see what else you can find out about the sexy gamer. Keep your options open. Like I said, you need a good..."

"Valtreece." Donovan said with a warning glance. "Can you not put all my business in these streets, please?"

"Can you not use my government name in these same streets?" she shot back and tossed the ball to him. "This is real friend talk. How long has it been? By the look on your face, too long. Not every woman you're interested in is like your loser ex-wife, you know."

Donovan scowled, not wanting to admit the truth in Val's words. Logically, he knew this but deep down, the fears lay in wait, appearing when he found himself getting too attached.

They played another full court game, joining a small group of thirty-something frat bros who needed two people to round out their game. The guys were soft and not much of a match for Val who had played in college.

Donovan waved them off when they asked to play one more game. He was sweaty and feeling all of his thirty-five years. Pulling his locs up into a handful and sliding an elastic band over them, he told Val he was going to hit the shower and head home.

She was barely sweating, he noted as she jogged over to him. "Can I get a ride to the train station?"

He nodded and they agreed to meet at the membership desk after getting showered and changed. Donovan was still scowling as he readied himself to take a shower. He hated public showers but he hated being sweaty in his car even more, so he sucked it up and used the gym shower.

As the warm shower water flowed over him, Val's words ran

through his head. It hadn't been that long since he'd had female company, had it? He thought back to the last woman he'd dated. Hell, that was last year.

Earlier this year, his grandmother had worn him down and he'd finally agreed to go out with a woman from church and that lasted exactly one date. Since then, not much. Donovan frowned. He'd recently been promoted to lead designer and put in a lot of hours at work, especially during crunch times.

Freshly showered and with a new idea for enhancing his cave scene, Donovan repacked his bag and glanced at his phone.

There was a message from Exposé. They couldn't have found something this quickly, he assumed. He normally just read the text of any voicemails he received. This time he actually listened to the message as he left the men's locker room to meet Val.

"Hey, Donovan, this is London Lewis, your research analyst from Exposé. Hope you had a good day. I have a question for you. If you could call me back when you get a chance, I'd appreciate it. Oh, you can also text me back at this number. It's my cell. Thanks, talk to you soon."

*London Lewis.* He even liked the way her name sounded.

He almost wanted to replay the recording just to hear her voice again. She hadn't said anything even remotely sexy, but it was the sexiest voicemail he'd gotten in a long time. Maybe Val was right. Donovan was staring at the phone when Val walked up. He looked up at her, realizing too late that she'd asked him a question. "Huh?"

"I asked if you'd be in the office tomorrow." Val attempted to look at his phone. "What's got you in a daze?"

"Ah, I don't think I'm going in tomorrow. Friday traffic is the worst so I'll be home. Anyway, London, the woman from Exposé called me." He knew he probably looked smitten and braced himself for Val's teasing. He shook his head, attempting to focus.

"Yo, did they find something already? What did they say?" She motioned him over to a bench.

As they sat, Donovan stared at his phone as if it held answers.

"I don't think so. She said she had a question for me and asked me to call her. Or text her." He started to type a text and Val snatched the phone.

"Nope. No texts. Call her. Right now." She handed the phone back and crossed her arms.

"What if I don't want to call her in front of you? You could be breaking client privilege." That was a stretch, but he had to say something.

"Are you going to talk dirty to her?" Val asked. Donovan pursed his lips in response. "Well then, and she's not your lawyer so what you just said is BS."

He glared at Val, who glared back, waiting. Clearly, he was going to have to make this call now, in front of her.

Donovan sighed and called London's number. With each ring, his heart beat a touch faster.

London picked up after three rings. "Hey London, this is Donovan. You called? Is this a bad time?"

Was he back in middle school calling his first crush? He cleared his throat. "What's up?"

Val was practically in his lap staring him down. He turned away slightly.

"Thanks for calling me back so quickly. I was wondering if you have access to your grandmother's cell phone?" London sounded breathless, like she had run to answer the phone.

Donovan nodded, then remembered they weren't on a video call where she could see him. "Yeah, um, I can access it. Why?"

"Ok good, there's this app that will scan all of the dating sites and log any activity from them where you can see it from your device. The catch is we have to install it on her phone."

Donovan interrupted. "We can't do that; she'll notice a new app. She's only got a handful on hers."

London spoke while Donovan panicked. "It's undetectable. She won't know it's there and it won't use up a lot of battery power. We've tested it on our phones and it's good. We just need a few minutes with her phone to install it, then I can sync it with my phone to read the messages or you can use your phone."

"Send the messages to your phone. She might see them on mine." Donovan normally didn't worry about his grandmother looking at his phone, but he was taking no chances.

He glanced at Val, who was making hand gestures. He turned away, missing London's question. "Sorry, say that again?"

"I asked if you had any ideas on how we could get her away from her phone to do this."

Shaking his head again, and ready to say no, Donovan remembered his grandmother's church was hosting a singles event at Top Golf, an entertainment venue featuring a golf driving range, this weekend.

She'd hounded him to go but he'd refused. Now he could tell her he would go and would be bringing a guest. *Perfect.*

"Actually, I have an idea." He told London about the singles event. She agreed it was a good idea and they made arrangements to meet in the parking lot to strategize on a plan to get the phone.

Donovan ended the call and turned to Val. "We're going to basically tap my grandmother's phone."

"Ha, you better hope she doesn't catch you." She crossed her legs on the bench and put a hand under her chin, grinning at him. "So, you are taking a date to Miss Emma's singles event?"

"No, she's not a date. She's going to install an app on Gram's phone so we can see the messages she's exchanging with this man and hopefully find out what he's up to."

He ran his hands over his head. Saying their plan out loud made it real. And exposed the holes. How would he explain London's presence? Donovan knew his grandmother. She would spend the evening probing London's suitability as a wife and mother like a high-priced lawyer with a client facing death row.

Val seemed to read his mind. "If she's not a date, what is she? Miss Emma is gonna want to know and you know you aren't the best liar; so how is all of this going to work? Hmm?" Val crossed her arms, waiting.

Sighing, he weighed his options. "Maybe you should come too and say she's your friend." Donovan gave her a hopeful look.

Val snickered. "Oh yeah, hell no. Your grandmother is still mad at me for giving up 'that good man' for women. Can you imagine if I showed up at her singles soiree with a date? No sir, I do believe I'd take a bullet for you first. Sorry, you're on your own."

He gave her his best puppy dog eyes. She shot him a glance then looked skyward, thinking. "How about this? Just say she's a new coworker from out of town. Keep it simple."

Donovan considered the idea. "That could work."

Hopefully London would go along with the ruse. Wait, what was he thinking? Why wouldn't she? The whole reason was to steal his grandmother's phone and install spyware on it. The event might actually be fun now that he had a covert mission to complete. And spending time with London was appealing, though he wouldn't admit that to Val. She would take that info and run with it.

"I take it you don't know if she's married? Or an atheist? Oh man, Donovan brings an atheist to the church singles event. That would be the best singles event ever." She snorted, clearly enjoying the thought. "I might risk Miss Emma's wrath to see that drama unfold."

"I told her it was a church sponsored event. She didn't hiss or curse the church so I'm guessing she's ok with church in general."

"That's a good sign, I guess." She checked the time. "Let's go, I'm going to miss my train." Val rose from the bench and they headed back toward their office where Donovan's car was parked. "Well, I'm gonna want a blow by blow of the singles soiree on Monday so be ready to talk."

Donovan had a feeling he'd have plenty to tell Val after the weekend was over.

# LONDON

London made a quick right turn into the Top Golf parking lot. She had three whole minutes to spare, thanks to typical Atlanta traffic snarls. She scanned the rows of cars, found an empty spot, and whipped her car into the space.

Two minutes.

Slapping the visor down, London opened the lighted mirror to check her face. She had taken more care with her makeup, using YouTube to create what the makeup artist called a natural no-makeup look. Problem was, she didn't own most of the brushes and products the YouTuber used and had to improvise. London's dark skin now had a rosy glow which gave her a more polished look. The woman in the video chose a nude matte which looked nice on her lips, but having nothing close to that color, London had gone with a glossy red.

*I should do this more often.* Taking an extra second to admire the look in the tiny mirror, she immediately dismissed the notion. Unless she rose an hour earlier each day, her new look was not sustainable. Briefly, she wondered why she felt compelled to take such care with her looks on that particular day and decided she would chalk it up to having clients to impress.

Getting out of the car, London ran quick hands over the light wrinkles on her poplin cropped jumpsuit and slipped on her shoes. She scanned the entrance as she approached, her wedge espadrille sandals giving her a few inches of added height. She already regretted her shoe choice. While they made her legs look amazing, she'd pay for her vanity with sore feet.

Donovan stood at the bottom of the stairs to the entrance, alternately glancing at his phone and the parking lot. London assumed he would be more casually dressed for the event but she wasn't complaining. His mid washed jeans and checked button down shirt that exposed his muscular arms looked good on him. She wondered if he owned any of those low slung sweats she'd seen modeled in fashion magazines. Yep, a pair of heather grey sweats and no shirt, she decided, then shook her head quickly to clear those thoughts. She wasn't going to lust after her client.

"You made it." He saw her and tipped his head in greeting. "Been here before?" Donovan asked as he led the way up the stairs. London silently sent up a prayer of gratitude there were only five stairs to the entrance. Her cute shoes were definitely not a good idea for golf.

Grimacing at the thought of being in the shoes for the next few hours, London forced a smile when Donovan looked at her. "No, but I heard it's fun. Full disclaimer. I know nothing about golf."

"Don't worry about that. I can teach you how to swing." Donovan smirked at her.

London paused. Was he flirting with her? She was pretty sure he was but in case he wasn't, she kept her mouth shut. She had never mastered the subtle art of flirting, so she'd probably end up saying something that sounded sexy in her mind but transformed to cringy as soon as it left her mouth.

They stopped at a counter height table to the side of the main entrance where Donovan held out London's chair for the second time since she'd met him and passed her a menu. "My grandmother isn't here yet. I wanted to meet a little early so we could come up with a plan to get her phone away from her."

Nodding, London put the menu aside. "What if we say you forgot your phone in your car and you need to use hers to make a call?"

"Won't work. I've already talked to her and told her I was here." Donovan scanned the menu of bar food and cocktails then looked at London.

"Maybe I could pick it up thinking it was mine. Or you pretend your phone is lost and ask her if you can use hers to call it and listen for it." London picked up one of the paper coasters for drinks and studied it. She had to say something that had been bugging her since Aja brought it up.

"You know, you could install the app on her phone yourself and probably figure out what's going on. It would save you some money."

He turned his head slightly, studying her as if he didn't understand what she was talking about.

"Not that I don't want to help," London said quickly, "but since you work in tech, you could DIY this."

Donovan rested his elbows on the table and sighed. "You're probably right. But if my grandmother is sexting," he shuddered, "I don't want to know any of the details. This is where you come in. You can see all the graphic stuff, if there is any, and I stay blissfully unaware of my grandmother's sex life."

*Good point.* London's grandparents on her mother's side had been married forever and she had no desire to know what they did behind closed doors. "Fair enough. I was just curious."

"My friend, Val, who referred me to your cousin, asked the same thing. I told her what I just told you and she told me to hire professionals."

He passed London his phone. "I like the idea of using her phone to 'find' my phone, so put this in your purse and I'll tug my ear when I want you to go outside and I'll bring her phone out with me."

London had just dropped his phone into her clutch when she heard a voice behind her. "There you are!" She and Donovan jumped at the sound of his grandmother's voice. She hadn't realized how much she and Donovan had leaned into each other, ostensibly to strategize for their mission, until they both quickly leaned back like they'd been caught. London slid back in her seat, then turned to introduce herself.

London gawked a little, staring at a woman who could only be described as *golden*. Like what London imagined actress and singer Vanessa Williams would look like in her seventies. She was taller than expected, about 5'8" or 5'9", trim, with smooth golden skin and eyes and a short bob with golden highlights.

She turned to London after greeting Donovan. "You must be Donnie's coworker. I'm Emmaline Roberson."

"Hi, Mrs. Roberson, nice to meet you, I'm London." The piercing amber eyes held London's like she was waiting for more. "And thank you for allowing me to crash the party." London put on her best smile.

Emmaline's smile didn't fully reach her eyes. London willed herself not to squirm uncomfortably.

"Please call me Emma." She turned back to Donovan. "Donnie, would you go see if our space is ready? It's under the church's name."

As soon as he was gone, Emmaline focused on London. "So, I hear you're new to Atlanta? What brings you here?"

London swallowed, reminding herself she wasn't on trial. The woman was just trying to get to know her. "Ah no, actually I grew up here and moved to DC after college. I just moved back to Atlanta a couple months ago. So many things have changed since I left...it almost feels like I'm a new resident." London realized she was babbling and closed her mouth.

Emma nodded. "I assume you aren't married? Any kids?"

Her gaze moved over London, stopping at the bare left hand. London resisted the waves of disapproval rolling off of the older woman. "No, ma'am, never been married, never had kids. But I would like both."

"Kids are a blessing, but they change your life in ways you could never imagine. My daughter, Donnie's mother, was the typical rebellious child. She tried me every chance she could get and she was really her father's child. I don't know where that stubborn streak in her came from. Anyway, she's grown up to be a successful, independent woman, so I guess we did all right." She paused. "When she got pregnant, I assumed the baby would be just like her, but Donnie was just the sweetest baby ever. We bonded the first time I held him."

*Ok, I get it.* Anybody who wanted her grandson would have to go through her first. She was glad she had no plans to date the man. She was content to admire him from afar like a museum showpiece.

Judging by her tone when she mentioned her daughter, London was willing to wager they didn't get along. Family dynamics tended to be messy. She wondered if the rift between her and Aja was obvious to outsiders.

She needed to focus on her current situation, but she was curious. Was Donovan a mama's boy as well as a grandma's boy? "I was telling Donovan that I remember seeing him on the news when he won that gaming tournament in South Korea. Did he go with you?"

Her eyes lit up. "Oh, my goodness, you have an excellent memory. That had to be over twenty years ago."

Emmaline smiled at the memory. "But yes, when he told me he qualified to go, I said, well, pack your bags, we're going!"

She leaned in like she was sharing a secret. "I had never been that far away from home and had no idea what to expect, but I wanted him to have that experience. I think I was more nervous about the competition than he was. He kept telling me to chill out."

Chuckling, Emmaline asked, "How did you remember that? The news story was maybe five minutes."

"Well, I was into gaming big time growing up, but my dad wouldn't let me play because he thought the games promoted violence. I snuck around playing at the houses of different friends.

Emmaline gave her a knowing glance and London continued. "I was obsessed with that game and when I saw not only was the winner from Atlanta but he was also African-American, I don't know, it was like validation for me." She shrugged, feeling self-conscious. "Someone who had a similar background to mine was into something that I was always told I shouldn't be into. I wasn't encouraged to like technology. I was supposed to be playing with dolls, I guess."

London hadn't intended to reveal so much about herself to this woman whose life she had been hired to dig into, but once she started talking, words just kept flowing out of her mouth. She'd never really shared these thoughts with anyone and was surprised she chose Emmaline to talk to.

Emmaline patted London's arm. "Well, I'm glad you didn't listen. More women need to get into these technical jobs; this is the future. Since you're working with Donnie, I know you're smart. You just make sure they're paying you what you're worth. I had to fight for equal pay back when I was working."

London was speechless.

Rarely did women of a certain age understand or even have interest in what she did. Her own grandmother would only shrug and say "something with computers" when anyone asked her about what Aja and London did for a living.

Fascinated and curious, London wanted to ask the older woman what career she retired from, but Donovan, and a slender, leggy attractive woman in heels that put London's three-inch wedges to shame, walked up to the table to announce that their party could start their golf rounds.

"Hey Trina! When did you get here?" Emmaline rose and greeted the woman with a hug then looked back at London with her arm linked through Trina's. "This is my favorite Sunday School teacher, Trina. Trina, this is one of Donnie's coworkers;

I'm sorry, tell me your name again?"

London smiled as brightly as she could. "It's London. Nice to meet you."

Trina did a little finger wave as Miss Emma went on. "I'd always hoped that Trina would become part of the family. But that's up to Donnie." She beamed at him.

"Gram, let's go play golf," Donovan said, resignedly. He turned to London, apology in his eyes, stepping away from Trina and his grandmother. "Ready?"

London smiled so hard she felt like her face would crack. She didn't know their history, but Emmaline seemed to be laser focused on pairing Donovan and Trina up, whether they liked it or not. Not that she knew Donovan well, but she wouldn't have pegged Trina as his type. As if any of this was her business.

The four of them joined a group of people chatting together. There were fifteen people including London's group playing at three different bays all in a row. Donovan, Trina, another twenty-something woman whose name London didn't catch and her were in the second bay, while Emma, two other older women, and three men dressed like they were going to play real golf played in the first bay.

London glanced down at the last bay and counted three men and two women in their group. Excluding London, the ratio of women to men was pretty even. She was impressed. Maybe the church would bring together a few new relationships before the night was over.

Each bay had its own table and she selected a seat facing the green to await her turn while doing one of her favorite activities: people-watching. To her left between the table and the putting area, there was a container with all of the clubs for the bay arranged by size and gender.

London watched Trina pull each club out of the container, examine it like she was hitting the green at the Masters, and then motioned for the other woman in their group to take a picture of her posing with the club. After several variations of the same basic pose, the women switched places and Trina snapped away.

Bored with the Instagram moments, London looked around, wondering where Donovan had slipped off to when she heard the scrape of the metal chair on the floor as he slid into the seat next to her.

"Did you decide what you wanted to order yet? I'm going to find our server." Donovan looked at London expectantly.

"Uh, no. Just a glass of water, please." London caught him watching Trina and her friend as they continued to pose and post. "So, that's who your grandmother has chosen as your future wife?"

He rolled his eyes and shook his head.

"Yeah, that was news to me." Donovan huffed. "She's going to be waiting a while on that. I've known Trina since high school. We didn't run in the same circles and she basically ignored me. She's always set her sights on snagging a professional athlete, so of course that means I'm not even in the running. Not that my heart is broken."

He leaned in and lowered his voice. "My grandmother doesn't know this, but I heard she's only teaching Sunday school because one of the guys who plays for the Falcons belongs to Gram's church and likes to take his daughter to Sunday School during off season."

*God, he smelled good.* Today's scent was a spicy woodsy cologne that wreaked havoc on all of London's body parts.

She gasped in mock horror. "Are you gossiping about the church people? Maybe she's trying to do her part because she believes the children are our future?"

"Oh yeah?" Donovan tilted his head toward Trina so that London would look up.

They watched the Sunday School teacher bend seductively over the golf club, blowing kisses to her virtual audience. When Trina glanced their way, they ducked behind menus to hide their laughter.

A server approached the table and took their orders. London was starving but this wasn't her cheat day so she selected a salad and a sparkling water.

Between traffic battles and her other time management issues, she hadn't had time to eat much, but suddenly she found she had no appetite. Her nerves and jitters were getting to her and she wasn't sure why.

With the menus gone and Trina attempting to swing at the golf ball, Donovan turned his attention to London. "So. Tell me about London Lewis."

*Ugh.* She hated when hiring managers asked that question during job interviews. She shrugged, turning back toward the game. "Is this my second round of interviews? You already hired us. What else do you need to know?"

"A lot, but I'll start with the basics. Is some huge no-neck bodybuilding world heavyweight champion type going to storm in here looking for you and beat me down for talking to his wife?"

London put her elbows on the table, resting her chin on her hand. "Is that your not-so-subtle way of asking if I'm married?"

"Are you?"

She glanced at the scoreboard, not meeting Donovan's gaze. The subject of marriage was still a sore one. "Nope." To avert any further questions about her, she tossed the question back to him. "You?"

Immediately London felt silly for asking. Of course he wasn't married. His grandmother was trying to push him and Trina down the aisle.

"Divorced," he responded then said, "Is that same huge dude going to come storming in here to beat me down for talking to his girlfriend?"

Picturing her ex, storming in anywhere looking for her, made London want to laugh. He had expected her to do that for him. Never the other way around. He'd generally treated London like she should consider herself lucky he'd chosen her. "No. "

"Why not?"

"Why not what exactly?"

"Why isn't he coming?"

"Who? My big burly heavyweight champion boyfriend?"

"Yep."

"Well, he doesn't exist. But," London saw that it was her turn and rose to pick up a golf club, "if you see a single man fitting that description, you can send him my way." With that, she did what she hoped was a sexy saunter over to take her turn. Naturally, it took two swings to even hit the ball and when London did finally hit it, it fell far short of the first target.

London hung around near the putting area, waiting to see her score. No surprise, the score was low but at least she was on the board. Donovan was next, approaching the putting area, with his golf club seated on his shoulder like a baseball bat.

When he neared London, he leaned over and whispered, "If I see such a man, I'm sending him Trina's way."

They both glanced at Trina, who was attempting to dig the cherry out of her cocktail without putting her whole hand into her glass and grinned at each other.

Watching the other players in their party getting into the game and laughing together, London realized she was enjoying herself.

The weather was perfect, warm with no chill in the air, dusk was approaching, giving the green where the balls landed a natural glow. Yes, technically, she was working but she was having a good time. She wasn't on a date, so there was no added pressure to be what the other person was looking for.

Their conversation flowed naturally, mainly due to Donovan's perceptive observations about all of the other church members in attendance. London found his comments were spot on and hilarious.

Everyone took a break to eat after the first round. Being the consummate hostess, Emmaline made the rounds, visiting with each table. As it turned out, they didn't need their elaborate plan to get her phone; she left it on their table when someone from another table called her over to ask her a question.

London saw her chance. She caught Donovan's eye and tilted her head slightly towards Emmaline's phone.

He gave her a quick "I'm on it" nod, then got up from the table and asked the rest of their group a question about the scoring while London slipped Emmaline's phone into her purse, leaving Donovan's on the table in its place.

They had the same type of phone; Donovan's was several models newer and a little bigger, but it might buy London some time if Emma thought the phone was hers. London then rushed off to the ladies' room to install the app and sync it with her phone.

When London entered the restroom, it was empty, allowing her to grab the first stall. She locked the door, then put the toilet seat lid down and sat on it so that she could rest both phones on her lap.

Emmaline's phone had no lock on it and London was able to quickly open the app store then download the app she needed.

While waiting for the app to install, London heard the outer door open and distinct voices coming closer. She recognized one to be Miss Emma's. London panicked for a moment, trying to figure out what to do.

She needed to test the app before she returned the phone and staying put seemed to be the best option. She raised her legs so they wouldn't show if someone glanced at the bottom of the stall while she quickly verified she could see messages from the app on her phone.

One of the stalls further down shut and locked as a voice called out. "I think everybody is having a good time. I never would have thought I would be golfing at seventy though." London stayed perfectly still, afraid to make any noise. Her legs were fairly strong from the boxing and kickboxing classes she took, but she didn't know how long she could hold them in that position.

"Yeah, this was a good idea, Emma! The young people are having fun. Speaking of young people, who is that girl with your grandson? I thought you said he was hanging out with Trina?"

Emmaline responded. "The big one? She's one of his coworkers. She just recently moved back here from DC or somewhere."

Judging by the voices, London estimated there were three women in the room. If she heard all three go into stalls and lock the doors, she figured she could hustle out without being seen. She didn't want to hear any more of their conversation.

She waited but no more doors closed.

Ms. Emma and the other woman were there for moral support, she guessed. She would have to stay put until they left. Luckily, she saw the stall doors had no gaps so no one could see in her stall and she couldn't see out.

"Hmm...they looked kind of friendly when I saw them. Your grandson was feeling her, as the kids say."

"Her? No, she's not Donnie's type. Too dark and definitely too big. She must weigh 250."

"Emma, please! Men like thick girls these days. And she's a pretty girl." The other woman in the stall finished and flushed then London heard the door latch move and the stall door creak open. "Yeah, Em, she's cute for her size," the woman said over the sound of water pouring from the faucet.

Emmaline made a snorting sound but said nothing else. Next, a hand dryer roared to life, drowning out any further conversation, then all was quiet as the women left and the door closed behind them.

Lowering shaky legs, London sat in the stall, shellshocked and near tears. She'd sensed the woman didn't like her. When they first met she saw Emmaline's disdain all over her face, but she had no idea it was due to her size. London couldn't imagine what kind of fat shaming Emmaline was capable of had she known London when she lived in Atlanta before. Back then, London weighed significantly more than she did now. When London got engaged the year before, she committed to taking control of her health and body so that she could feel beautiful and strong in her wedding dress.

London fumed. She weighed less than Emmaline thought, thank you very much. And her skin tone was too dark? *Too dark for what exactly?* She shook her head, trying to make sense of Emmaline's words. Did she truly believe that skin tone correlated to a person's worth?

She opened her purse, seconds from tossing the woman's phone into the toilet. *We'll see how many calls that old bitch gets now.* But she knew she couldn't do that. Emmaline Roberson's shallowness was not worth losing her job. Those painful words just kept playing over and over in London's head, like a corny meme. "Too dark and definitely too big. Too dark. Definitely too big."

London didn't trust herself not to say something to Emmaline, but she knew she had to get the woman's phone back to her. Not wanting to face anyone, including Donovan, London sat in the stall, unable to move. She felt like she was back in high school, drowning all her feelings in sweets and fried foods and the urge to return to the bar and order one of everything on the menu was strong.

So much for having a good time. She should have known better. She frowned, stroking her favorite hoop earring. Her job was technically done. The mission was complete. She could just go home. If she dropped the phone off at the bartender's station and told them someone left it in the restroom then she could leave. She'd send her regrets to her client via text, which she knew was a coward's way out, but leaving now was for the best.

London dropped the phone off at the bar and was steps from the exit when her phone buzzed. She checked her text messages.

**Donovan: Where r u? I'm upstairs looking for Gram's phone. Come up?**

**London: What's upstairs?**

**Donovan: Rooftop terrace. Come on up.**

The exit door beckoned. So close. London could respond

saying she didn't feel well. If she hurried, she could be home on the couch in thirty minutes. Another text came through.

**Donovan: Margarita or Moscow Mule? I can have one waiting for you**

*Say no. Say no. Say no.*

**London: Margarita pls**

Against her better judgment, London headed for the elevator and away from the exit, making a deal with herself. She'd have one drink, confirm with Donovan that the app had been installed, then head home.

Normally, London would have taken the stairs to get some extra steps in but that was out of the question in the uncomfortable wedges. As the elevator rose to the rooftop level, London's anxiety rose along with it. What if Emmaline was sitting with Donovan? She wasn't prepared to sit there and be cordial after she'd learned what Emmaline really thought of her. She knew what she'd do. If Donovan's grandmother was with him, London would feign a headache, then excuse herself as fast as she could. She straightened her spine, bracing for the worst and stepped out of the elevator.

❦   4   ❦

# LONDON

London surveyed the rooftop terrace and the view beyond it. The early evening sky still had some violet and dark pink hues that the lighting on the terrace complimented. There was a nice view of the Atlanta skyline and Donovan had picked a corner of the long sectional where they could enjoy the view.

Donovan raised his bottle of beer in a mock cheer and motioned to the seat next to him. London let her shoulders drop in relief at seeing him alone. As soon as she sat, a server dropped off an ice-cold margarita. London thanked the server, glancing around the space. There were a few groups of people at the bar and surrounding tables, but no sign of his grandmother. Maybe she could put Emmaline's rude comments behind her and enjoy the rest of the evening.

Attempting to sit as gracefully as she could on the low sectional, London said, "Thanks for the drink. You left everyone downstairs?"

"Anytime." Donovan grinned and London relaxed. "Yep, my grandmother thinks I'm looking for her phone. Did you get the app installed?"

Taking a long sip of the cold drink, London nodded. It was

stronger than she expected but just what she needed. "I gave it to the bartender downstairs."

He nodded, picking up his phone. "Let me tell her."

London opened her mouth to remind him Emmaline wouldn't get the message, when she saw the exact moment he realized that calling or texting her wasn't going to work.

He ran a hand over his locs. "Dammit. Hey, did you want to play another round?"

*And spend time with modern day Evilene? Um, hell no.* "Nah, it's nice up here. I'll be ok by myself."

Donovan looked toward the doors leading back to the stairs and elevator then looked at London, like he might sit back down. The dutiful grandson won. "I'll be right back. I'm going to go act like it just occurred to me to ask the bartender and I'll be back once she has her phone. Don't go anywhere, ok? I'll just be five minutes."

London raised her glass to him as he'd done earlier. "I'll be here."

She watched Donovan hurry towards the stairs, enjoying the view. The man filled out a pair of jeans nicely. London fanned herself. She was getting quite warm and didn't think she could attribute all of the warmth running through her body to the alcohol or the warm September evening.

*Stop that, he's a client,* the rational voice inside said, as if London wasn't aware. *You aren't even six months out of the worst relationship of your life. You shouldn't even be thinking about dating anyone new.* Good point.

She downed the rest of the margarita.

*And,* the nagging voice continued, *his grandmother is horrible.* Another reason why she needed to get up from this-what was this thing she was sitting on anyway, a lounger? Get up from this lounger and go home.

But she didn't. Instead, the server came by and asked if she wanted another margarita. She shrugged. Might as well.

Picking up the second drink, London watched the sun retreat

and thought again about going home while she waited for Donovan to come back.

◈

LONDON BLINKED AT HER PHONE. WAS THAT RIGHT? According to the time on the phone, Donovan had been gone about thirty minutes now. Where was he? London knew she really should be heading home but now there was a tiny problem. She was on her third drink and feeling no pain. Between her horrible *cute* shoes and the three drinks she'd tossed back like shots, she wasn't sure she could get up and make it to the elevator, let alone drive herself home. Might as well get comfortable. She settled back into the lounger and waited.

Donovan rushed over as she was staring mesmerized at the skyline. "I am so sorry! I had to get one of the men a taxi and ..." He stopped. "London? Are you all right?"

London traced the skyline with her index finger then turned to him. "Hey, there you are!"

"Ah, how many drinks did you have?" He looked at the two empty glasses in front of her then studied her face again.

She beamed at him, ready to pinch his cheek and tell him how cute he was. Donovan turned slightly to stack the empty glasses where the server could collect them. "Well clearly you had at least two. I knew I should have called you."

Ignoring his question, London's tipsy brain decided it needed some answers. "Hey, your grandmother said that I'm not your type." She held up her fingers in quotes. "I wanna know, am I your type?"

His mouth dropped open slightly but no words came out. Then he frowned at her. "What?"

The rational part of her brain forced through the drunken haze. She needed to walk back those words fast. This was her *client*. "Ah, don't answer that. Just forget I said anything. I should go home. I need an Uber or something I think."

She groped around, looking for her purse which contained her phone.

Donovan put a hand on hers. There was that warmth again. This time London knew it had nothing to do with the alcohol or the warm night and she wanted to slow down and enjoy the feeling. "I'll take you home. Where are your keys?"

Her purse was right where she'd left it, on the cushion beside her.

"No, you don't have to do that. I can take an Uber." She giggled. "Maybe the Uber driver will let me drive."

"Yeah, no. I'll drive your car to your house. You are in no condition to..."

London cut him off. "To make decisions? You might be right. Hey! Can I call you Donnie?"

"Yeah, you've had one too many. And no, you can't call me Donnie." Donovan addressed her sternly using this no-nonsense tone that London found adorable.

Not like a cute bunny though with whiskers and pink ears. That image made her giggle.

She studied his face. No. Definitely more like a sexy bunny. But that wasn't right. He was a man.

In a bunny costume though?

A thought hit her. *Stripper bunny!*

She snorted, imagining Donovan in one of those stripper outfits: no shirt, cuffs and bow tie topped off with a pair of those bunny ears made for women.

Then her thoughts shifted as she watched him thrust his hand out for her car keys. She dropped the keys onto his palm. Donovan had large hands with long fingers. *What*, she wondered, closing her eyes slowly, *would those hands feel like meandering over her bare skin?*

"London, are you about to pass out?" Donovan's alarmed tone broke the spell. "Can you hear me?"

Reluctantly, London raised her head and opened her eyes, meeting Donovan's wide-eyed stare. She noticed that his eyes were only a shade darker than his grandmother's but a hundred times warmer and filled with concern. Too bad he was a client and she was done with relationships.

"I'm fine, Donnie! Could I have some water?" He shot London a warning glance then rushed toward the bar for the water while London tried to get herself together. Her head was fuzzy and buzzed, her hormones were on fire, and she was sure she was about to do or say something she would regret in the sober light of day. *Keep your mouth shut and your hands to yourself. Keep your mouth shut and your hands to yourself,* she chanted silently.

Donovan returned with water in a large to-go cup and a wrapped straw. "Keep your hands to yourself." London murmured to him.

"What? London, I didn't touch you. Here, drink some of this." He passed her the water and straw at arm's length, like he thought she might scream for help at any moment.

She covered her mouth with her free hand and giggled. "Oh, you thought...no, I didn't mean to say that out loud. That was meant for me. I didn't use my inside voice." she explained, pointing at her mouth.

London studied the straw and cup in her hand. There was no way she was going to be able to pull that wrapper off and put the straw into the drink. To her fuzzy brain, this seemed like the most complicated task in the world. Donovan stared at her, she assumed he was trying to figure out what was going through her head.

"*Donovan,*" London emphasized, drawing out the word more than necessary, "could you please take the paper thingy off the straw for me?"

"Yes, *London,* I will." Donovan slid the straw from her hand and unwrapped it, punching it into the water cup. "What exactly did you mean when you said keep your hands to yourself was for you?"

Sober, rational brain told London to say nothing. *Just drink the water.* Her eyes held his, then she looked away. "I should go home."

London fidgeted as he regarded her for a few minutes. "I guess you're not going to answer my question, huh? Ok, let's go. I told my grandmother you weren't feeling well and that I'd make sure you got home okay."

Nope, she wasn't going to say another word if she could help it. And technically what he'd told his grandmother was true. London was feeling all kinds of things, *well* being the least of them.

The ride home was quiet. London gave Donovan her address, and then watched him pull up the GPS app on his phone. Once the navigation started, they were whipping through downtown towards the interstate. Donovan handled her car like a pro and feeling confident he would get them to her house safely, London reclined the seat so she could rest her eyes. She heard him change the satellite radio station from hip-hop to National Public Radio and she mentally rolled her eyes. He *would* listen to NPR, she thought as she dozed off.

Sitting up as they turned into her subdivision, London directed him to her dad's house. It was almost midnight and the house was dark except for a motion detection floodlight that came on when they pulled into the driveway. London knew her dad had gone to bed a while ago. She shivered from the AC and yawned. "How are you going to get home?"

"I'll take an Uber." He turned the car off and reached for his phone. "It shouldn't take long." He glanced up at the large house. "Nice place."

"Thanks. I grew up in this house. I'm back home with my dad until I get back on my feet." She stifled another yawn, hoping he didn't see it as a hint that she was ready to go in. "I feel really bad that you don't have your car. You want to come in? We have a guest bedroom if you want to stay here and I can run you to your car in the morning."

"Nah, I'm good. I didn't drive to Top Golf so I can just get an

Uber home." He studied the phone. "I have about fifteen minutes till the car comes." Donovan stared at her with concern. "You ok?"

"I'm better. You must think I'm the most unprofessional person ever. I normally don't drink like that, especially when I'm supposed to be working."

Nerves had London babbling, the effects of the margaritas waning and allowing her sober mind to take control. "Thanks for making sure I got home. Oh, we have a porch swing in the back, want to sit there? I can get you something to drink."

He nodded and they piled out of the car. The craftsman style house had a wraparound porch that housed a porch swing big enough for two and a couple of ceramic tables. Donovan eyed the swaying porch swing. "Is that thing ok to sit on?"

"Yep, I usually sit here in the mornings on weekends and have my tea. It's really comfy and bigger than it looks. Have a seat and I'll be right back." London dashed into the house to grab drinks.

When she returned with two bottles of water and a can of Coke, Donovan was leaned back in the swing, trying to get comfortable. She set the drinks down on the table. "Try sitting with your legs crossed or to the side," she offered.

Trying to swing his legs to the side, Donovan lost his balance and almost fell face first out of the swing. London watched in amusement as he caught himself then finally gave up, sitting with his back on the cushions and his legs dangling. "So, you sit out here a lot?"

She nodded, holding up a bottle of water and the can for him to choose. He motioned toward the water and she sat it beside him. "Yep, my dad used to read me stories out here when I was little. This was like our spot." London settled into the swing, tucking one leg under the other.

London considered turning on a porch light but decided against it. She didn't want to give the bugs a spotlight for them. There was enough moonlight that they could see each other. He ran a hand over his locs, looking sheepishly at London but saying nothing.

An awkward silence settled over them as London waited. She could tell he had something to say.

He twisted the top on the water bottle. "I'm sorry for leaving you alone for so long. I went up there initially just out of curiosity. When I got up there, I saw that perfect area, and the thought popped into my head that I should see if you wanted to hang out with me there away from the rest of the group. Then when you came up, you didn't seem to be having a good time and I think I made things worse by leaving you alone." His shoulders slumped. "I feel like I ruined your evening."

"You know I was technically working tonight, right?" She took the other bottled water then opened it. "Therefore, you weren't responsible for my having a good time." London took a long drink.

"Right, I know that," Donovan said slowly, twisting the cap back on the water bottle. "I might have enjoyed the evening too much. I kind of forgot you were working."

Donovan scooted up closer to the edge of the seat, putting one long leg on the ground and setting the swing in motion. "You've had me in this state all day where I feel like I'm staring at you like some lovesick puppy. I wanted to spend some time alone with you but when I got the opportunity, I blew it. Especially when you told me to keep my hands to myself." London was holding her breath when his gaze met hers. "I thought you had read my mind because I was thinking about touching you at that very moment."

London felt a tremor course through her. *This was bad.* She should run into the house and lock the doors before she did something foolish like invite him up to her room.

Inches from each other, London could see her attraction mirrored in his deep brown eyes. "That wasn't directed at you," she murmured. "I thought I was using my inside voice."

He chuckled, his voice low. "Well, now I know how to get the truth out of you in the future. A pitcher of margaritas."

"I don't say everything I'm thinking when I'm tipsy, just a lot that I shouldn't." Crossing her arms over her chest, London attempted to act insulted. Donovan wasn't totally wrong but still.

"Umm hmm. I think you were beyond tipsy. I think I could have asked you anything at that point and gotten London unfiltered." His tone was teasing but her body reacted like he was talking dirty. She resisted the urge to close her eyes and lean into his voice.

The question slipped out before she had a chance to catch it. "What do you want to know?"

"I want to know if your lips are as soft as I've imagined they are. I want to know what you'd do if you decided you weren't going to keep your hands to yourself." Donovan moved closer, causing the swing to sway, his voice a low growl near her ear, sending chills surging through her. He moved in even closer. "I want to know if I should..."

London managed half a nod before their lips met. The kiss was hesitant at first, awkward as they adjusted. His lips were warm, soft and faintly cherry scented from the lip balm he used. Quickly they explored each other's mouths and their rhythm was soon fully in sync. The swing rocked gently and they took their time exploring this new territory. London ran her hands through his soft locs while Donovan tugged her closer, his large hands splayed over her back. She arched in response.

Donovan came up for air first. "I've been thinking about doing that since I met you," he said, playing with a loose curl that had worked its way out of her ponytail. "I thought, 'Man, she has to be the sexiest nerd I've ever seen' and you had on that black blouse..."

The mention of work set off London's internal warning bells which she ignored. Images of Aja's disapproving glare were swatted away. "You remember that? I didn't think you'd paid me that much attention." She'd have to wear that one more often.

"Oh, you had my undivided attention." He captured her lips again, making London want to moan when she heard the back door creak.

The porch light, bright and obtrusive, flicked on. London bolted back to her side of the swing and Donovan straightened up quickly as London's father stepped out of the house in a faded black robe that had seen better days with Maxie in his arms. He and Maxie both raised an eyebrow at her.

Like London needed the judgment of a stray orange tabby. "I thought somebody was trying to break in. London, I assume you're ok out here?"

"Yes, Dad, I'm fine," she muttered. Might as well introduce her father to this strange man she was locking lips with. "This is Donovan. Donovan, this is my father, Edward Lewis." London felt like a teen caught playing spin the bottle. She wanted to sink into the ground.

Donovan greeted her father, who tipped an imaginary top hat to them, winked at London then shuffled back into the house.

London sighed. "My family has a strange sense of humor." She scooted back into the porch swing. "Oh, I totally forgot, when is your Uber supposed to get here?"

He looked guilty. "I might have canceled it when you went in for the drinks." Donovan pushed up from the swing and stood, stretching. "I'm heading out before I get you grounded for a month." He smirked at her.

She tossed a throw pillow from the swing at him. "Ha ha ha. I can take you if you want. Where do you live?"

He described the area, which was about ten minutes away. "You sure you're ok to drive?"

"Yeah, between the water and the, um, other stuff, I'm awake." Translation: she was thoroughly aroused and couldn't sleep if her life depended on it. And she'd only experienced his kisses. If those were any indication of his seduction skills, London figured she was in deep trouble.

The slow, gap-toothed grin appeared. That grin, London

mused, was enough to make even the most prim, proper woman want to tug her bottom lip with her teeth, romantic comedy style. "Gotcha. I'm fully awake, too."

Shoving tired feet back into her espadrilles, London tossed the keys to her car to Donovan after locking the house up. On the drive to his house, they made small talk and tried to avoid the sexual vibes bouncing off of each other. The kisses earlier had ignited what was only a slow burn during the golf outing.

He pulled up to the driveway of a three-story townhouse in a newer subdivision and killed the engine. Donovan turned to her, passing the keys. "You remember how to get home? Take a left once you get to the front entrance."

London nodded, stifling a yawn. It had to be close to one in the morning.

He started to say something then stopped and looked towards his house. "Text me when you get home so I know you got in safely."

Telling him she would, London watched him exit the car and practically run to his front door. Her head hit the steering wheel in frustration. How many bad decisions can one person make in a day? Not only had she gotten drunk, she kissed her client like some desperate love-struck teen. Clearly he regretted the whole evening and she was sure things would be awkward between them as they worked on his investigation.

What was she going to tell Aja?

❀   *5*   ❀

# DONOVAN

On Monday afternoon, Donovan rubbed his eyes, fatigue from a long work day settling into his bones. He yawned, wishing he could take a nap, then rolled his head around to ease the tension in his shoulders. An envelope popped up on his screen, indicating he had a new email. He groaned and started to ignore it, until he saw it was his first status report from Exposé. Deciding he was done for the day, Donovan shut down all of his work apps and opened the email from London.

He pictured her at her laptop typing up the email. That first day they met, he noticed she furrowed her brows while she was typing and he found himself wondering if she'd done that while composing his email.

He ran a hand over his locs. This woman was dangerously close to getting under his skin which was not a good thing. Donovan had successfully kept the women he dated since his divorce at arm's length. That way he didn't set himself up for disappointment and heartbreak when they left.

Somehow, he knew with London, she wouldn't stay at arm's length. Hell, he was probably going to be the one to pull her in, despite his vow to keep things casual.

Rubbing his face, Donovan recalled Saturday night when London dropped him off at home. He'd been *that* close to asking her to come in. He hadn't asked because he was afraid she'd say yes.

Reading through the report, he noted London provided some initial intel on the mystery man his grandmother met on Silver and Sexy. In her notes, London named the subject Mr. Miami since she didn't yet know exactly who he was. She included both screen names the couple was using on the dating site.

*The unidentified subject has retired from the military. He's a widower living alone and has hinted about coming to Atlanta to see your grandmother, but nothing has been planned yet as far as I can tell.*

*The subject, referred to in the rest of the report as Mr. Miami, hasn't displayed typical catfish behavior such as asking for money or mentioning large expenses which is a good sign. I was able to verify the date they started talking, which correlates with the dates you gave us during the initial consultation.*

*Also, based on my observations of the messages, E. Roberson hasn't been contacting anyone else on the app. As we don't have access to Mr. Miami's profile, I am unable to determine if he is talking to anyone else on the app.*

Donovan closed the report, thinking about what he'd read. The man said he was a widower but he could be lying and just because Mr. Miami hadn't yet asked for money didn't mean that wasn't his end game. And what exactly did the man think he was going to do once he came to Atlanta? The quicker they exposed this man, the better. Donovan decided to go see what his grandmother was up to. He could do some digging while he was there now that he knew for sure she was seeing someone.

Donovan used his key to open his grandmother's front door.

"Hey Gram, it's me!" he yelled, glancing around the house where he'd spent the majority of his life. The house spelled faintly of bleach, but not of cooking. He slumped his shoulders. No chance of a random recipe experiment tonight.

"Donnie, you don't have to yell, I'm not hard of hearing yet." She strode into the living room, holding her phone, the other hand on her hip.

"Just making sure you knew it was me. Wouldn't want you to pull that pistol on me."

"Well, if you were breaking in, you'd be the loudest burglar I've ever heard." She chuckled. "And how do you know about my gun?"

He waved a dismissive hand. "Gram, everyone knows you keep that thing in your nightstand."

Donovan saw her carefully put her phone face down on the coffee table before she took a seat on the couch. Did he interrupt a conversation with Mr. Miami? Why was she being so secretive about him?

"What're you doing?" He slumped on the couch beside her, picking up a deck of playing cards that lay on the table. "You been playing Solitaire?"

"Yep, I don't like to play on the computer. Can't give myself any hints that way." Emmaline looked closely at him. "What's wrong with you? You look like you've got a lot on your mind."

He shrugged, tossing the box from hand to hand. "Nothing, long work day."

"You want to talk about anything? I have chocolate cake and milk like I used to give you when you were little. Or we can play a couple rounds of War. That was your favorite game after I taught you how to play."

He ran a hand through his hair. The woman sitting beside him was responsible for the man he was. When he was a kid, he would sit with her at the dining table where they had all their meals telling her about his day at school. She always gave him her full attention and he felt like he could ask her anything and she'd tell him the truth, unlike the other adults he knew. He did want to talk about her new boyfriend or whatever he was, but he wasn't willing to get into how he found out about the man.

"No thanks. I'm not hungry." He pulled the cards from the box then shuffled them. If he lost the first round, he'd admit he hired a firm to dig into her love life.

If she lost, he'd find an opportunity to check out her phone for himself.

He dealt all the cards.

Emmaline gathered her pile of cards, keeping them face down and making sure the stack was neat. "I meant to ask you, is your coworker doing better? What was her name? Lauren?"

"London." Donovan let out a breath. "She's fine. You ready?" He wasn't going to talk to his grandmother about how much he wanted to bed the woman he'd hired to dig into her love life.

She nodded and they both turned a card from their pile face up.

She frowned then slid her reading glasses on. "Well, she wasn't very social. She only played one round of golf with us then disappeared." She scooped up his card and hers, putting them face down in a new pile, "Is she the reason you're all bent out of shape? What's going on?"

Gram always had a sense about what was going on in his head.

He turned over the next card in his stack. "Nothing. She's a coworker. Even If I did decide to date her, we'd have to sneak around. Work has a policy against dating coworkers." He watched his grandmother closely. "Besides, I don't think I could keep a relationship secret. Especially from you."

If she caught on that his comment was directed at her, she didn't show it.

She turned her card over and again scooped up his card with hers. "I think that's a good idea. If you started dating her then decided it wasn't working out, you'd still have to work with her. Who knows what she might do? She seemed sneaky to me. Like she'd try to get you fired if you pissed her off. She might be one of those bitter Black feminists who think the world owes them something."

Emmaline flipped over another card. "Donnie, don't let her screw up your job. No woman is worth that."

"Dang, Gram. Let me know how you really feel." He shook his head in amazement, wondering what London had done to rub his grandmother the wrong way. He turned over his next card, thankful his eight of hearts beat her six of diamonds.

"Well, I'm just trying to keep you from making a big mistake. I tried to warn you about Corrine, but you didn't listen. Count 'em out, that's War."

Donovan rubbed his head. Not the lecture about his ex-wife again.

Years ago, when he introduced his new girlfriend, Corrine, to his grandparents, Emmaline watched the girl leave, predicted that Corrine was trouble, and urged him to break things off. Donovan, of course, dismissed her misgivings. To him, Corrine was perfect.

"You're never going to let me live that down. I admitted you were right about Corrine. Can we move on?"

Glancing at the card she played, he counted out four cards, turning over the last one.

*Yes! Ace!* He snatched up his grandmother's pile. He might actually win.

"We have. I'm just saying, I was right about Corrine and I'm right about this one. She reminds me of Corrine. I don't think that woman is worth your time. And she's certainly not worth losing your job over. You have a good job."

As she spoke, Donovan rolled his eyes and got caught.

"Roll your eyes all you want, young man," Emmaline snapped, then her tone softened. "I don't know that picking women is your strength. Which is why I've been working on setting you up with a good woman. If you'd just give one of them a chance, I think you'd be happy."

Donovan raised his head, staring at his grandmother incredulously. "Gram? Are you kidding? First of all, Trina is looking for a professional baller. Do you really see us together? We have literally nothing in common other than we went to high school together. I have nothing against Trina, but she's not my type at all."

He stacked all his cards neatly. "I admit, I haven't had the best track record for relationships, but your picks haven't exactly been matches made in heaven either." Donovan threw a new card down. "Can you leave my love life to me? Please? No more matchmaking."

They continued to play until Emmaline lost the last of her cards in a double war battle.

"You really didn't like anyone I picked out for you? I thought you were just being stubborn." His grandmother looked genuinely surprised.

Donovan's shoulders slumped. "No, I didn't. None of them were interested in getting to know me or accepted who I am. They're just looking for a warm body under eighty years old that they can control."

"Donnie, that's not true! Those are good Christian women who would make any man a good wife." Emmaline scooped up the cards and shuffled them before placing the deck back in its box.

"I think that's the problem, they don't seem to care much about who they marry, so long as they get married. I want more than that."

She looked like she wanted to say something more on the subject but raised a free hand in surrender. "Fine. No more matchmaking."

Donovan smiled at her, confident this wasn't the last time he'd have to tell her to stay out of his love life. "Thank you."

"So, what is it about your coworker that you like? Hopefully, something beyond that big butt of hers." Emmaline rolled her eyes.

"Gram, what did she do to piss you off? You just met the woman. I think she's fun to be around; she's not all obsessed with being on social media all the time and she remembers me winning that gaming competition in South Korea."

Emmaline grunted again. "I see. Basically she's got a big butt and she's a fan of yours." She patted him on the shoulder. "I just think there's something she's hiding. But you're grown and can do what you want." Emmaline stood. "I'm going to make some tea and watch Oprah's network; you want to join me?"

Donovan groaned inwardly. He'd rather sit through a root canal than watch those nighttime dramas his grandmother lived for. He would, however, take this time to scroll through her phone. "I'll take a cup of tea and a slice of cake."

"We'll do the peppermint tea" she said as she strode toward the kitchen. "I'll get the kettle going and you can put the tv on OWN."

Once she was gone, Donovan grabbed the remote, turned the television on and found the right channel. Making sure she was still in the kitchen, Donovan slid her phone closer to him and tapped the home button so that the main screen would be visible.

There was one unread text notification which showed a preview of the message.

**Marine4Life: Call me later tonight...**

He scrolled up, not seeing anything of interest in the messages. Disappointed, Donovan slid the phone back to its original spot.

"Hey Gram, do you have honey?" Normally he liked sugar in his tea but he knew her looking for the honey would delay her return to the family room. She didn't care for it so there was a good chance she didn't have any.

"Um, yep, I think there's some honey. I'll bring it out. Since when do you like honey in your tea?" Emmaline called from the kitchen.

He remembered an article he'd seen in his news feed recently. "Local honey is supposed to help with allergies or something. I thought I'd try it." Donovan willed her not to ask any follow up questions. He'd only skimmed the article.

"Your allergies are acting up? I have some Claritin in my bedroom. You can take some if you need to." He heard the tea kettle being placed on the stove burner with a clink and then the cabinet being closed and pictured his grandmother reaching up slightly on her toes to get two coffee mugs.

Donovan started to decline the allergy medication since his allergies weren't an issue right then but inspiration hit. He could use this as a cover for going to see if there were any clues about this secret relationship his grandmother was having. Not that he expected to find pages of love letters lying about, but he could still take a look. "Ok, maybe I will take some. They aren't bad right now."

"Look on my nightstand. You'll see the bottle," Emmaline called out.

Donovan quickly pushed himself up from the couch and headed into his grandmother's bedroom. The room smelled like his childhood, a mixture of his grandmother's perfume and furniture polish. There was a king-sized bed and matching traditional style furniture. The room had slowly gotten more feminine since his grandfather had passed, going from forest green and cranberry to light blue and white with more ruffles. As always, the bed was made with military precision and nothing was out of order.

Her computer rested on a white writing desk facing the wall opposite the bed. He saw a stack of papers there and hustled over to look through them. One item in particular caught his eye and he took out his phone to snap a picture of it.

"Do you see the Claritin? And how big a slice of cake do you want?"

His grandmother's questions startled Donovan and he fumbled to keep his phone from hitting the ground. He returned the papers to the desk and crossed the room to collect the Claritin. He shook the bottle briskly. "I found them. I'll just take a couple. You don't have much left."

"You can take the rest of that bottle. I have more in the

bathroom. Come in here and let me know how much cake you want."

"Just a small piece." He jogged back to the stack of papers, making sure they were neatly stacked then left the room.

He didn't know if what he found meant anything, but he'd send it to London and see what she could make of it.

## ❧ 6 ❧

## LONDON

Saturday was London's favorite day of the week. Especially Saturdays in fall when the weather in Atlanta was still warm enough to hang out like summer but not so hot that one needed to be positioned in front of air conditioning at all times.

That Saturday, the temperature was supposed to reach about eighty degrees with a bit less humidity, so she might actually be able to tame her disobedient curls into a cute style that wouldn't rise and frizz like it was prone to do.

London sat on the porch swing trying to read the latest Beverly Jenkins historical romance. Thoughts of the last time she was on the swing a couple weeks ago with Donovan, locking lips like they were the last people on earth, kept her from being able to make much progress in the novel.

After that night, she'd vowed to think of Donovan as a client only and forget that night on the swing.

She thought referring to him as *the client* would help reestablish some professional boundaries. In theory, keeping her thoughts about him on a professional level would prevent her from crossing over into thoughts that were full of things happening between them that shouldn't. Like how good his lips felt on hers, or how his smile somehow made her feel like that smile was for her alone. Even the way he said her name made her insides go a little mushy.

*Why was she even thinking so hard about a man she'd just met?*

*Because he checked a lot of her boxes: Tall, down-to-earth, good sense of humor, great kisser, fine as-*

Wait, what boxes? She wasn't looking for a man.

End of story.

She sighed, trying again to concentrate on the love story she knew would end happily. London shifted positions, resting her head on her elbow with her face close to a pillow that *the client* must have leaned on. It still smelled faintly of him. London squashed the urge to take that pillow to her room and try to preserve the scent, as that was some crazy stalker-ish behavior.

She was being ridiculous. London grabbed the pillow and tossed it toward her feet away from her nose.

A few moments passed where London caught herself re-reading the same paragraph for the third time. Giving up, she groaned in frustration and snapped the Kindle cover shut. She tossed it toward the pillow, sitting up and straightening her spine. T day would be more productive if she dedicated it to researching her target: Emmaline Roberson. The more London knew about her, the more she could possibly find out about the woman's new beau, which would be a much better use of her time than trying to figure out her feelings for the woman's grandson.

Since the day was turning out to be beautiful, London wanted to find an outdoor table at a coffee shop near her house. She would get a chai latte and do her digging there while enjoying the mild fall weather. Later on, she was treating herself to a much-needed night out. Now that she had big plans, she checked the time and saw that she needed to get moving as she had a packed Saturday.

After getting dressed in her favorite cropped, slightly ripped boyfriend jeans, a white tee with French phrases and a pair of canvas sneakers, London prepared to leave the house, wondering where her father had gone.

London packed her laptop and a small spiral notebook into a large tote bag, grabbed an apple and some cheddar cheese cubes she had pre-bagged to snack on, and set off for the coffee shop.

Maxie, sensing London's presence, opened her eyes as London strode by, yawned then went right back to sleep.

*Lazy cat,* London dared not speak the words aloud.

WHEN SHE ARRIVED AT THE COFFEE SHOP, THE PARKING lot was fairly empty. Encouraged that there didn't seem to be many people inside, London parked, hoping there would be a vacant table with an umbrella when she picked up her drink. She really wanted to sit outside but only if she could enjoy the bright day from under the protection of the umbrella.

London stepped inside the café and placed her order for an extra spicy, extra hot chai latte. As she stood to the side to wait for her order, she glanced around at the tables in the shop, full of people hunched over laptops or phones with headphones on to drown out the coffee shop's aggressively loud smooth jazz.

She froze, her heart pounding when she saw a familiar head of shoulder length locs with white wired earbuds tapping intently on a small laptop. Her hands immediately reached up to check that her hair was in place.

Donovan must have felt her gaze because he glanced up quickly and met her eyes. He raised his eyebrows in surprise, then a slow grin appeared, weakening her knees. She casually placed a hand on her stomach to settle the powerful flutters running through her.

They gawked at each other for what seemed like a full minute. Donovan removed the earbuds one at a time and motioned at the empty chair across from him where his laptop bag rested. "You want a seat?"

She nodded. Outside could wait. Before she could sit, the barista bellowed her name and drink order. Grateful for the distraction, London turned back toward the counter for her tea and napkins. She couldn't believe Donovan was here, but she supposed it wasn't that far-fetched. They lived near each other and the neighborhood coffee shop was, in her opinion, one of the best in the area with a wide variety of beverages and homemade pastries. She also appreciated the ample seating, good supply of power outlets and strips, why wouldn't he as well?

As she sat down, Donovan leaned toward her. "This is crazy. You were literally just on my mind and then you walked in. What are you doing in here on a Saturday?"

"I'm actually working." She wondered if he thought about her as much as she did about him. *Nope, he's a client,* she gave herself a mental reminder. "I'm behind on documenting my case load so I figured I'd get it done here, then I can spend the rest of the day doing something fun."

He raised an eyebrow. "Oh yeah, what's fun for you? More golf?" Donovan closed his laptop and rested his chin on his hands, giving London his full attention.

"Nah, tonight is date night for me." Determined to make progress on her workload, she pushed her drink to the side to make room on the small table for her laptop. She didn't want to go into detail about her evening plans because some might consider them odd or pathetic or both. "What about you, what are you doing inside on this beautiful Saturday?"

Running a hand over his head, Donovan sighed. "I'm trying to play catch up as well. This is the only time I can get some real work done without constant emails or IMs. I've been in here about an hour and already done more in that time than I did all day yesterday. But enough about work. Where's your date taking you tonight?"

London picked up her drink tipping it toward her mouth. "Fernbank." She sipped the hot spiced tea with milk slowly to avoid burning her tongue, savoring the cinnamon and cardamom fragrance. She should have gotten it iced. The café seemed too warm all of a sudden. Or maybe it was just her.

Donovan cocked his head at her. "Did you say Fernbank? As in the museum?"

She nodded quickly. "Yep, I am taking myself on a date to the museum tonight to watch a 3D dinosaur movie. I loved going as a kid and I haven't been since then. It seemed like a good time to go back as an adult." London shrugged, feeling like she had to explain. "Yes, I like dinosaurs." She raised an eyebrow at him, waiting for him to make fun or call her a geek for loving science as she'd heard all the time growing up.

London watched him consider her words, hesitate for a second. "That's dope."

Then Donovan surprised her by asking, "How would you feel about having some company at the museum?"

London's heart managed to soar for the briefest moment then plummet back to reality. She saw Aja's face, scowling at her for even considering his request.

*What would Aja do?* Aja would have reminded him that office hours were over and politely steered the conversation back to the business of his grandmother. But her cousin wasn't here and London really didn't want to go to the museum by herself if she didn't have to.

"As long as that company doesn't mansplain the exhibits just because he's watched a few NatGeo specials, I'm game."

Donovan sat back, a knowing smirk on his face. "Speaking from experience?" He crossed his heart and gave her his best innocent look. "I promise I'll behave."

She rolled her eyes, stifling a smile. "That wasn't very convincing." Opening her laptop, she motioned at his. "Well, we only get to go to the museum if we get our work done so..."

"In other words, get back to work and leave you alone. Ok. I get it. I do like a take charge woman though." Donovan winked at her as he slipped his ear buds back on.

Having never mastered the fine art of flirting, London was

always a beat behind when men flirted with her, realizing too late what was going on. This time, her reaction was immediate. She felt her cheeks flush along with the rest of her skin. *He's your client*, the thought ran across her brain like foreign movie subtitles, *keep it professional.*

How would she justify going on a *professional* outing that had nothing to do with his grandmother or her secret man?

She sat back, taking another sip of her drink. Maybe she'd ask him some questions about his grandmother and consider this trip a fact finding mission. *Problem solved.* Aja's glaring face appeared again but London willed it away.

There were some administrative tasks London should be doing, such as her weekly status reports for other client research assigned to her, and she had some expense reports to submit. London kept sneaking covert glances over at Donovan. She couldn't explain why she was so engrossed in what he was doing or why she suddenly wished they were at the museum in a quiet dark corner picking up where their last kiss left off.

This time she gulped the tea which was cooler. It didn't help her thoughts stray from Donovan's face. London closed her eyes and tried to focus on her work. She heard faint music coming from his headphones, something with a lot of bass. Every so often, he would tap his fingers to the beat, but he seemed to be in his own world being way more productive than she was.

*What was his story*, she wondered not for the first time. He mentioned he was divorced. London wondered about his ex. Had she managed to gain Emmaline's approval? Had one of them cheated on the other? Although they'd done a perfunctory search of Donovan online to verify he was who he said he was, she hadn't dug into his life as she would normally do for other clients. That felt like cheating to her. They were investigating his grandmother, not him. His life wasn't any of her business, but that hadn't stopped her inner nosy detective from wanting answers.

She pretended to read something on her screen as she watched Donovan out of the corner of her eye. He glanced at his phone then picked it up, typing a quick message. Curiosity about who he was texting ate at her until she realized her phone buzzed in her tote. Donovan eyed her from the side of his laptop, waiting for her to check the phone. Reaching into her bag, London had to dig for the phone. Once she found it, she checked her texts.

**Donovan: Are you getting any work done?**

London raised her eyes to his and shook her head slowly then focused on her laptop again.

She heard Donovan sigh as he banged out another text.

**Donovan: You're jeopardizing my museum time**

**Donovan: Stop distracting me and get back to work!**

**London: You do know these texts would be considered a distraction, right?**

**Donovan: Right! I wouldn't have to text you if you were working instead of peeking over at me every 20 seconds**

She really needed to work on her covert spy skills. And she wouldn't call it 'peeking'. That made her sound like a little girl hiding behind her mother's skirt.

**London: I wasn't peeking at you. I was making sure you were on task.**

Donovan flipped his laptop screen toward him, exposing his whole disbelieving face. Then he grinned, winking at her like he knew he was the reason for her state of nervous anticipation and flipped the screen back up.

London, determined to get something done, silenced all of the inner dialogs and tried to get down to business. She was acting like a young girl crushing on her favorite boy band member. She could deal with a little attraction. And hadn't she just said this morning that *professional* would be the word of the day with her client?

This attraction would fade away soon enough. She could ignore it. London vowed to do her research and take care of her admin tasks, then they would go hang out at the museum together. It could serve as a thank you gesture for his business.

Maybe he would provide a testimonial for Exposé which would help London secure her raise.

With that decision made, London googled Donovan's grandmother, recalling that he'd told them Emmaline had a blog and did cooking videos.

The first results were her blog and cooking channel.

London clicked on the link to see a list of episodes. Emmaline seemed to focus on Southern dishes made from ingredients in her garden. London watched one of the recent links where Emmaline made a shrimp pasta dish with rosemary pan rolls and found herself nodding in appreciation. The video looked like anything found on the major food networks in terms of quality.

Emmaline herself was a natural hostess, London had to admit. Professional, yet the videos had a conversational feel, almost like sitting in her grandmother's kitchen watching her prepare Sunday dinner.

Hard to believe this was the same woman who had so completely dismissed her as being unworthy of her grandson, she huffed. London continued to watch as the camera did a close-up of her sampling the shrimp. As Emmaline's facial features became more prominent, London realized Emmaline and Donovan had the same smile.

Except his reached his eyes when he looked at London and Emmaline's stayed right at her mouth.

Another reason why she needed to keep this relationship strictly business. That woman was trouble and she wanted no part of it. But as much as her brain said that, London didn't want to tell Donovan that it would be best if she went to the museum alone.

Shutting her laptop, London motioned to Donovan. "I'm ready when you are. I'm done for the day."

She was done fighting with her emotions and her conscience.

A good-looking man had offered to accompany her to a museum on a Saturday night. He hadn't asked for her hand in marriage. He hadn't invited himself back to her house. They were *just* going to the museum. She should enjoy the trip and stop overanalyzing everything.

Donovan removed an ear bud and nodded. "Give me five minutes and we can go."

While they packed up their stuff, Donovan offered to drive them to the museum after London dropped her car at home.

At her house, London secured her car, then hopped into Donovan's SUV. The car, a sleek black Jeep that looked freshly washed and fairly new, suited him. She imagined Donovan taking the car off-roading or whatever men did with rugged vehicles. The dark tinted windows and AC meant the car was comfortably cool.

۞

THE DRIVE TO FERNBANK MUSEUM TOOK ABOUT THIRTY minutes. The museum was in the old money part of Atlanta near Emory University. Donovan took I-20 toward downtown, which had less traffic than usual and they sped along at a good pace.

London recalled the last time she was in the car with Donovan. She'd dozed off shortly after they got on the road, which was probably a good thing given her tipsy state and inability to keep her inside thoughts to herself that night.

"What's your grandmother up to tonight?"

Donovan shrugged, taking his eyes off the road for a second to look at her. "You probably know more than I do. Did you check that app today? I haven't heard from her since this morning."

London shook her head. "There wasn't anything earlier today. Last night, Mr. Miami said he was going to call her today, so I'm guessing they talked on the phone instead. For what it's worth, he seems ok so far. He still hasn't asked her for money and he hasn't sent any pictures of his naughty bits so that's a good thing."

"Yeah, hell no. This right here is exactly why I'm not doing this. If I'm spying on my grandmother and some fool sends her a dick pic, I'm gonna want to find him and knock him out."

As soon as Donovan said that, London saw another, more

disturbing thought occur to him. He winced. "She's not sending him any pictures, is she?"

The look of utter horror on his face would have been comical in another situation. London knew better than to make light. "Oh no, I don't think they're into that, based on what I've seen. I think they're still in that early flirting stage," she said quickly, hoping she was reassuring. If his grandmother and her friend did ever exchange adult pictures, she decided she would spare Donovan the details.

Donovan shook his head. "I'll probably regret asking, but what's the early flirting stage?"

"You know, the time in a relationship where everything is new and cute. You've been on a couple dates but you haven't had sex yet, probably haven't had that first major fight."

"Got it. So, you're sure they haven't met in person yet?"

"No, they haven't." London switched subjects. "You using any of the dating apps?"

"Me? Nah, after hearing some of my friend Val's horror stories, I knew it wasn't for me. I need to meet women the old school way."

As they exited the highway at Freedom Parkway, Donovan turned toward her, asking a seemingly out of the blue question. "So, why aren't you married?"

London had no desire to rehash her wedding drama. "Actually, I was supposed to be walking down the aisle next month had things gone according to plan. But, as you can see, I'm here in Atlanta, living with my dad, back in my childhood bedroom, living my best life." She gave him a half smile. "Can't wait for the next class reunion."

She knew she was making light of her current situation but sometimes one had to laugh to keep from crying.

Donovan was clearly taken aback. His eyes got wide. "For real? What happened? That is if you want to talk about it."

"I need a strong drink in my hand for this," she muttered. "You ever been in a relationship that's clearly run its course but you stay because, well, there are a million reasons you can give yourself to stay, and all of them make sense at the time?"

She didn't give Donovan a chance to answer. "Well, that was me. I had been with this man since I was eighteen, hoping that one day he would propose and it would fix all of our problems, prove everyone wrong who said he was toxic, and give me my happily ever after. And when he did, I felt like things were finally falling into place."

London stared out the window as a distraction. Now that they were on Ponce de Leon Road, she admired the stately houses as they neared the museum. "Turns out I was wrong. I ignored all of the warning signs, red flags, and manipulative behavior until I couldn't."

She paused. "Earlier this year, my fiancé wiped out our bank accounts to finance his new career as a professional poker player in Vegas."

This was the first time London revealed the full truth about her broken engagement. She hadn't even told her family about the theft. Her dad would pressure her to take legal action against her ex and she had no desire to deal with any of that.

"Damn...I'm sorry to hear that." He touched her hand briefly. "But it's good you didn't get married. Things would have only gotten worse. Trust me."

She shrugged. London didn't think things could have gotten any worse in her relationship after last year but she changed the subject, not wanting to relive the whole ugly mess. "So how long were you married?"

Donovan turned into the main entrance to the museum and followed the signs for parking. The large open lot was about half full and there were plenty of parking spaces close to the building. As the day faded, she imagined the people with kids were winding down their afternoon visits.

"A little over two years. The honeymoon phase was over pretty quickly." He slid the Jeep into a spot facing the museum.

Before they exited the car, Donovan turned to London,

placing his hand on her arm. "I hope you realize that you're better off without your ex. Doesn't sound like he appreciated what he had."

She needed the reassurance that small gesture provided. The certainty of his words and the warmth of his touch calmed her. "Thanks, I know I'm better off, but that break up really upended my life and I don't know how to put it back together," she finally admitted, as much to him as herself.

"This is a good start. Bet you didn't think you'd have a good-looking chauffeur and tour guide for the evening, did you?" He wiggled his eyebrows and London finally smiled, appreciating Donovan's efforts to lighten the mood.

"No, I can't say that I did. But if that's the case, I need you to put on a chauffeur hat and let me sit in the back seat on the drive back."

"Yeah, you might want to get an Uber back if that's what you want." With that, he exited the car.

As the 3D dinosaur movie didn't start for another hour, they meandered through the exhibits. London enjoyed every minute of it, telling herself it was the exhibits and not her companion. Donovan had random facts about dinosaurs and the history of Georgia that he shared as they strolled from room to room.

She took her phone out to check the time. "We have about twenty minutes before the movie starts. Want to walk through Fernbank Forest for a few minutes?" she asked casually.

She almost bobbed up and down, hoping he'd agree. London was anxious to check out the tree pods she had researched on the museum website.

Donovan nodded then held the door as they exited, stepping onto a cement ramped path that weaved through the forest. Dusk had settled over the city and the forest was naturally lit, seemingly from the inside.

London thought the evening was perfect so far and didn't want to spoil it, but there were questions she needed to ask. They reached the tulip shaped sculpture and London motioned to the seat.

There was one other couple walking their way, holding hands and stealing glances at each other like they were the only people left in the forest. London waited for them to pass. "I told you my sordid tale of a relationship gone bad, care to share yours?"

"Not much to tell." Donovan sat, playing with a leaf he'd picked up. "Corrine and I met in college at Georgia Tech. She was beautiful, super smart and I was young and naive and fell hard for her."

He lifted his shoulders. "I couldn't wait to show her off to Gram." His tone was wistful. "The first time she met my grandmother, she pronounced her name wrong, pronouncing it Emma-leen, and my grandmother never let her forget it. She told me Corrine was not the kind of woman I should marry, but I did anyway after we both graduated.

Donovan sighed. "Fast forward a year into the marriage," he tossed the leaf. "We were fighting all the time and I was having trouble finding a job I liked that paid me enough to live on so I was working part time and she was supporting us. One night, I was coming home from work late and a drunk driver ran a red light, t-boning my car." He looked out past London to the towering trees behind her. "I was rushed to the hospital with a spinal injury and internal bleeding. The doctors didn't know if I was going to make it. I pulled through the surgeries but my prognosis for walking again was bleak. I was in the hospital for about two months."

London raised a hand to her mouth as Donovan told his story.

"When I came home, I found divorce papers waiting for me." His tone was very matter-of-fact but she sensed the hurt still under the surface. "She said she couldn't see herself taking care of me for the rest of my life."

London gasped, "So she left? Just like that?" Her heart broke for him. She wanted to reassure him he was better off as he had told her earlier, but she stayed where she was.

He nodded, shrugged like he'd just mentioned he lost a sock in the dryer "Yep, I got home that first day and her stuff was already gone. So much for 'in sickness and in health'. And every now and then Gram likes to remind me she was right."

Inwardly, London rolled her eyes. His grandmother was a piece of work.

Out of curiosity, she asked, "Have you ever dated anyone who your grandmother liked or approved of?"

Donovan frowned, ran a hand over his head. "Um…it's been a while. Not that I've had that many occasions to introduce someone to her. I'll have to get back to you on that." He checked the time on his smartwatch. "We should go back. Movie starts in a few minutes."

She stopped Donovan as he started to get up, touching his arm. "I'm really sorry that happened to you. I hope that experience hasn't soured you on marriage."

He shot her the gap-toothed grin that did strange things to her insides as he held up his left hand. "You putting a ring on it? I'll need something big enough to blind people when they see my hand."

London rolled her eyes, shooing him away. "Let's go."

❦ 7 ❦

# DONOVAN

A few weeks after visiting the museum outing with London, early one Saturday morning, Donovan practically leapt from his bed, eager to clear his mind. After having another vivid, so real he could feel it, dream about London and waking up rock hard and alone, Donovan gave up on going back to sleep. He needed a good run so he could focus on something other than how much he wanted to call her.

He quickly got dressed, slipped on his running shoes, gathered his locs into a man bun with an elastic band then did some light stretching before he set out.

There was a small park with a three-mile trail about a mile away that he jogged around sometimes when he couldn't make it to the gym or he needed to clear his head. Donovan needed to make some decisions about the source of his confusion and sexual frustration. He shoved his ear buds, keys, and wallet into his pocket and slapped an armband for his phone onto his bicep then set out, locking the door to his townhouse behind him.

Once he was outside, the thick, early morning humid air hit him and he breathed in deeply. Taking in evidence of the previous night's rain, the still wet streets, fallen leaves and sidewalk puddles, Donovan was eager to run. He loved the smell in the air after rain.

Starting out with a brisk walk to warm his muscles, Donovan shifted his thoughts about his predicament as an analytical problem to be solved.

Yes, he was attracted to London. He wanted her in his bed under him, on top of him, beside him, he wasn't picky, as long as she was there. But beyond that, he found her easy to talk to. They could geek out about gaming and their work. He liked hearing her laugh and the way she lit up when she spouted some random fact about dinosaurs.

He liked that she seemed to get him.

Donovan reached the park and jogged to the trail, sticking his ear buds in and cranking up his favorite 90s hip-hop station. There were a few other people out: a pair of moms walking briskly pushing strollers and an older man who Donovan knew would probably lap him at least once.

If he was being totally honest with himself now with the fresh air coursing through his lungs, there might be something else between them. He found himself thinking about something she'd said or done at random times during his day and wanting to text her or call her just to hear her voice.

After their serendipitous Saturday meeting at the coffee shop, he'd asked her if she wanted to meet him there the following Saturday and now it was becoming a routine. They would meet up, share space while getting some work done, and part ways after lunch. Family obligations in the evenings had prevented them from extending their time together, which had Donovan both relieved and frustrated at the same time. Relieved that they weren't blatantly crossing the line, there was still some plausible deniability since they did talk about his grandmother and her mysterious man.

The frustration, he decided as he veered a bit to the right, stemmed from his internal conflict.

He heard rubber shoes hitting pavement on his left. As he predicted, the older man he'd seen when he hit the trail jogged past him easily, his breath in tune with each foot fall. Donovan watched him, thinking the man was maybe around Gram's age and in way better shape than he was.

He reeled his thoughts back in to his conflict. The part of him that desired London was willing to throw caution to the wind and just see where things went, but the more rational part of his brain overrode those base thoughts and kept him safe. If they met in the day and talked about his case, then he didn't consider their meetings dates and he could be himself instead of trying to make sure he didn't do or say anything that was considered off-putting to a potential match.

Like talking about his ex-wife and the buying habits of gamers. Lately, Donovan had been reading up on human behavior in relation to game play and consumer buying habits based on some theories the new senior leadership team at work developed to increase game sales. He'd mentioned some of the things he'd learned to London, who lit up like a kid in a toy store and proceeded to debate with him after insisting they order another round of chai lattes.

Before he met London, he hadn't known what chai was or why anyone would drink it when coffee was so readily available. Now he was a fan. He was even thinking about buying her an Indian tea set. But only because he wanted to see the look of pure delight on her face when she opened the gift.

He shouldn't have been surprised that she had so much industry knowledge; Donovan considered London one of the smartest people he knew and he found himself wanting to continue their debates over dinner and possibly breakfast the next morning. He'd been a breath away from asking London to have dinner with him but stopped short. She would consider the event a breach of their professional arrangement, even though technically they'd already breached it the night of the golf outing.

Working himself up to a faster jogging pace to keep up with the older man, Donovan realized he now looked forward to his Saturdays, which was another problem.

Each meeting gave him a chance to find out more about

London. She had a habit of speaking her thoughts as she worked through a problem, giving Donovan insight on how her mind worked. She would grasp his arm suddenly when she had a new idea, which for her was probably an unconscious act but each time she touched him, thoughts of her hands on him, *all of him*, sent every red blood cell in his body racing toward his groin, making him rock hard and unable to move from the table until he could get things under control.

The first time she did it, the day they met, Donovan hadn't expected the warmth from her hand to spread through him so thoroughly, like he'd just taken a shot of tequila. His face must have reflected the shock of her touch because she quickly dropped her hand, apologizing immediately. She was clearly embarrassed. The awkward moment had passed, but the awareness they both refused to acknowledge hadn't.

They couldn't keep this up. And speaking of keeping up, why was he trying to keep up with Mr. Fitness, who was still several yards ahead of him on the trail? He slowed his pace.

The more he hung out with London, the more he liked hanging out with her, which led to him wanting to spend more of his Saturdays with her.

He needed to stop their Saturday hangouts. Just cut them cold turkey. He grimaced at that thought and two elderly women speed walking in the opposite direction looked at each other and asked if he was ok. He smiled and nodded that he was fine.

Except he wasn't fine. He was jogging half erect thinking about a particular woman touching his arm, of all things.

Donovan sped up for his final lap, his mind made up. He wasn't looking for a relationship and if she was, it was more than likely a rebound thing. London had been engaged to be married only a few months ago.

*What the hell was he thinking?*

Everything about that situation screamed disaster and he was going to steer clear this time, wishing he had a dialogue like this with himself before he'd gotten married.

Stopping at a park bench near the entrance to catch his breath, Donovan wiped sweat from his brow with the sleeve of his warm up jacket. He did some calf stretches and set off for home. As he approached his house, his phone buzzed. Donovan tugged at the armband so he could see who was calling so early.

His grandmother's picture appeared on the display. His stomach clenched as he answered. "Hey, what's wrong? You ok?"

"Donnie, you up? I know it's early." She went on as if he hadn't spoken. "Can you come by and follow me to my mechanic? My car's making a horrible clunking noise." The stress in Emmaline's voice was unusual. He heard her start the engine again, causing the car to knock. "I have a ton of stuff to do today. I don't need this."

"Gram, where are you? Turn off the car."

She huffed and the engine noise stopped. "I'm at home. Can you follow me to Brother Bishop's?"

"I need to shower first; I went for a run this morning."

"All right, just come by when you get done." He heard what might have been a curse word then, "I can't believe this. Thank you, Donnie."

She hung up before he could get in another word. Donovan wondered what the urgency was.

Gram was normally cool headed under pressure, but on that call she'd sounded almost frantic. He considered another thought as he unlocked his front door. She hadn't asked him to look at the problem, which she always did, even though she knew he knew nothing about cars. He dropped his keys, phone and armband on the kitchen counter.

He stripped down and threw the damp clothes in a basket near the closet then headed for the shower.

Now he had a legitimate reason for not meeting London later. Even though he said he was done with their Saturday meetups, his chest tightened at the loss.

❧

Donovan arrived at his grandmother's house thirty minutes later to find her pacing the living room while she sat on the phone, on hold, he assumed since she was muttering.

Emmaline pulled the phone away from her mouth. "There you are. I'm trying to see if they can work on my car this morning and they put me on hold...again."

Grabbing a large tote along with her almost as large purse, Emmaline motioned to the door. "Let's go, I'll see what they say when I get there."

The mechanic wasn't far away, one exit up from her house and the Saturday morning traffic was light. Donovan sat in the car while his grandmother gathered her things and strode into the front office.

As he sat wondering if he should go in and run interference so that no one caught the Emmaline Roberson wrath that day, she hurried out and tugged on the back seat door before Donovan knew what was happening. He unlocked the door and his grandmother immediately opened it, shoving her oversized bag into the back seat.

"Brother Bishop says they can look at it now and call me once they know what the problem is, but they don't have any loaners left." She did a slight leap into the passenger seat and slammed the door with more force than necessary.

"Donnie, I need a big favor. I have a few errands to run today. Would you mind taking your poor grandmother around for a few hours? I'll pay for gas and buy lunch."

Donovan knew this was coming. He'd had no real plans today, beyond figuring out how to fix the London situation. "Sure, anything for my 'poor grandmother' as you put it." He backed the SUV out of the parking spot. "You don't have to buy gas or lunch, you know that, right? Where to first?"

Sighing, Emmaline pulled a small notebook out of her purse. "I know, but I'm sure you had better things to do and I knew you'd come if I called, unlike some of your other relatives." Her reading glasses hung on a chain around her neck and she slipped them on to read off an address. "Oh, I forget you don't have GPS in your car."

"Uh, my car's not as fancy as your Mercedes, so no. But I can use my phone."

"I don't know what good that fancy car is doing me now, seeing as I just dropped it off at the shop and I'm riding with you." She peered over the top of her glasses at his gas gauge. "You need to stop for gas, Donnie! You have less than a half tank."

Donovan glanced at the dash and chuckled. "You act like the tank is almost empty. There's plenty of gas, unless your errands are in Tallahassee. Where am I taking you anyway?"

"I have to drop off my knitting projects at a few senior centers today. Shouldn't take long." Emmaline settled back into the seat. "Now hand me your phone and let me see if I can get that GPS to work. I need to get directions for the first stop, it's my first time delivering to this place."

They hit the highway and ended up at a high-end senior center in Buckhead, home to multi-million-dollar residences for new money and old. Donovan whistled as they pulled into the parking lot.

He teased his grandmother. "I hope you're charging these people extra for your work. They can afford it."

Emmaline gathered her bag from the back seat. "I'm not doing this for the money; I'm doing what needs to be done." She slid out of the car. "I'll be right back, but you can turn the car off. No sense in wasting gas."

*Doing what needs to be done?*

He frowned, wondering what she meant by that. Donovan watched his grandmother practically speed walk into the building. Gram had always been a fast walker and when he was small he'd always had to run to keep up with her. "Donnie, you don't get anywhere in life shuffling along. Pick up your feet and hustle." He had Emmaline to thank for his habit of walking fast, even though as he got older, he was learning to appreciate strolling and taking in his surroundings more.

Deciding that now would be a good time to catch up on a gaming podcast he liked, Donovan picked up his phone from the cup holder and was just settling into the podcast when his grandmother returned, opening the rear door and heaving the tote in. "Whew, I might need a smaller bag."

"Do you want me to carry it in next time?" Donovan glanced back at the quilted tote. "What do you have in there that's so heavy?"

As he went to pull the bag to the front, Emmaline put an arm up to block him. "Donnie, what have I taught you about a woman's purse? You know better. Let's head to our next drop off spot."

"Yeah, but that's not your purse. Your purse is up here." Donovan knew better than to argue with her, but he felt he was right for once.

"No matter. Never go in a woman's purse without permission." Emmaline settled back into her seat and looked at her phone. "The next place is just up Peachtree; I've been there before."

He sighed inwardly. This was going to be a long day.

The routine at the second senior center was the same. Gram jumped out, grabbed the tote, hustled into the building and was back within fifteen minutes.

Donovan wondered why this was going so quickly as they drove to the third stop in Norcross, further northeast of Atlanta.

Usually, his grandmother liked to socialize with her friends. Were these friends she was visiting? The whole thing was odd. It was like she was delivering pizzas.

Donovan knew his grandmother loved to knit and she was making a little money on the side knitting for other people, but he didn't understand why she needed to hand deliver everything. He constantly told her she could start an online store and sell to more customers but she wasn't hearing it. "This is just something I like to do for fun. I don't want to make a business out of knitting." Gram had been firm on that point and changed the subject.

In Norcross, the senior facility was considerably less posh than the Buckhead location, but it was bigger, with a large patio where a couple of residents sat watching the world go by. When she approached the double doors leading into the building, the two residents waved and spoke. He watched his grandmother call out a greeting but she didn't break stride. Gram told him she had a couple of deliveries in this building, so she'd be a little longer and again reminded him to turn off the car.

Tapping his phone on his leg, Donovan debated. He needed to tell London he wouldn't be at the coffee shop. He could just send a text and be done with it. Or he could call and hear her voice.

London picked up on the second ring. "Hey Donovan." She sounded like she was in the car.

"My grandmother's car was making noises this morning and she had me follow her to drop it off so her mechanic could take a look. Just wanted to let you know I've been elected to be her driver today so I can't meet up with you," Donovan said in one breath.

"Oh, that's too bad. You know they're premiering the new autumn drinks today? I was going to treat you to a pumpkin spice chai and a pumpkin muffin." He could hear the laughter in her voice. "You're going to miss out."

Donovan grimaced. He hated all things pumpkin and London knew this. He'd ranted about the pumpkin proliferation that happened as soon as summer started to wind down during one of their meetings. "I feel like I dodged a bullet then. Are you there now?"

"I was going to go, but if you're not coming I'll get my tea to go. I guess I'll have to find something else to do today." She sounded disappointed which made Donovan want to drop his grandmother at home and surprise London.

"You're welcome to take my place. We've stopped at all these senior centers where Gram's making deliveries. It's weird." He sighed, ran a hand over his head. "Is this weird to you?"

"Uh…maybe? What is she delivering? Not pizzas, I'm guessing?"

Donovan chuckled. "That would actually make sense, oddly enough, but no, she likes to knit for people and she's dropping off her orders."

"Ok, what's weird about that? She's not going in with a ski mask and shotgun, is she? Telling you to keep the car running? Like Bonnie and Clyde?"

"You're a mess," he chuckled, "no, actually she's making a point to tell me to turn the car off so that we don't waste gas. But I don't think she'd rob the elderly." He wanted to keep London on the phone as long as possible. "I meant to ask; did she say anything about delivering stuff to her friend? Has she talked to him lately?"

"Well, not really. I checked this morning and all she said was she had a busy day ahead and she'd call him later. He told her he'd miss her and couldn't wait to hear her voice." London's tone changed. "He's actually very sweet to your grandmother." Donovan caught the wistfulness in her voice.

Grunting, Donovan said, "Yeah, I'll bet. I'm sure he's real sweet while he's trying to figure out how to steal her money."

London sighed. "Let's hope that's not what he's trying to do. I'm kinda surprised they haven't done any video chatting or calls, but maybe it's a generational thing. They are probably used to talking without seeing each other. Do you and your grandmother ever do video calls?"

"Nah, I go to her house a lot so no need." Donovan considered what he just said. "Damn, I sound like a grandma's boy, don't I?"

London cleared her throat. "Um, I hate to tell you this, but we came to that conclusion the day you came into the office to hire us. For the record, I also think it's sweet that you look out for her. Not a lot of men do that these days."

Donovan shrugged as if London could see him. He didn't do

it for recognition. "I look out for my loved ones. She taught me that."

Donovan watched his grandmother exit the center. "Look, I'm going to call you back. My grandmother's coming out but I wanted to talk to you about something. You going to be around later?"

"Yeah...um, sure, I'll probably be at home. Let me know how the rest of the day goes."

Donovan hung up as his grandmother jumped into the car and tossed the tote into the back. He recalled London's Bonnie and Clyde comment and stifled a laugh knowing she wouldn't find the comparison funny.

She exhaled and snapped her seatbelt on. "That took longer than I expected. We're a little behind schedule, but I guess it's ok." She turned to look at Donovan. "You look pensive, what were you doing while I was gone?"

"I had to cancel some plans. No biggie." Donovan started up the car and they were off to their next stop. This time they were heading west toward Marietta, another Atlanta suburb. Once they stopped and Emmaline hoisted her tote over her shoulder, it looked to be a lighter load. This complex was larger and again there were multiple deliveries to be made at this location.

Donovan glanced at the time on his phone. It was after 1:00 and he was starting to get hungry. He'd managed to stuff a banana and protein bar in his pockets before he'd left the house, but they were long gone now.

Once his grandmother was done with this stop, he'd suggest they break for lunch. They weren't far from Marietta Pizza, one of his favorite pizza places, and he could go for a huge slice of pepperoni pizza right about now.

Without fail, his thoughts drifted to London again. He should suggest they meet for pizza one day.

Donovan called London again, knowing she'd rave about how tasty her drink was. Her enthusiasm about the little things in life that gave her joy was infectious. Deep down, he realized, he wanted her to talk about him that way.

She picked up quickly, as if she was waiting on the call. The thought that maybe she was waiting on his call drew an uncontrollable silly smile out of him and he was glad to be alone in the car.

"You're still doing the senior center tour, I'm assuming?" she asked as a greeting, her tone playful.

"Yep. We're in Marietta now. You get your pumpkin spice nonsense?"

"Yep. You missed out on good stuff. And, guess what, my drink was on the house. That barista that's always singing hooked me up."

"I told you he likes you," Donovan scowled, annoyed that the man hadn't wasted any time. "He's just trying to get in your pants."

He forced himself to think rationally. He had no claims on her, therefore he shouldn't be sitting here letting the green-eyed monster rule his thoughts. Hadn't he decided earlier that they should remain friends? London was free to entertain as she saw fit.

Not his business.

There was silence on the other end.

"What are you saying?" London asked quietly, her voice flat. "That basically the only reason a man is nice to me is because he's trying to screw me? Like that's all I'm good for?"

Frowning, Donovan wondered how things had gone south so quickly. "No! I didn't say anything like that."

"But that's what you implied." London's tone sounded reasonable, but Donovan had enough dealings with the opposite sex to know a storm was brewing.

"No, that was your interpretation of my words. The reason I said he's just trying to get in your pants is because I've seen the way he looks at you," Donovan said, gritting his teeth and trying to keep his tone neutral. "He watches you walk away from the counter and he's practically panting. Game recognizes game. That's all I'm saying."

"Yeah? Well, we're both adults so I don't see why it's any of your concern," London snapped.

"Of course, it's not my concern. You're free to do what you want, just don't be surprised if he ends up in Vegas with all your money." The moment the words tumbled out, Donovan wished he could take them back but they hung in the air, pungent and painful. "I didn't mean that. I..."

London cut him off, her voice cracking. "Yeah. You did. You meant every word. Have fun with your grandmother."

The call ended.

Donovan felt like the world's worst human.

He banged his head on the steering wheel. *What the hell just happened?* London had shared her painful truth with him and he'd tossed it back in her face like a live grenade. All because he was jealous and frustrated. He glanced up to see his grandmother approaching, looking like she'd just found a twenty dollar bill on the sidewalk.

"That was a good stop. I have five more orders in addition to what I sold today. Yes, indeed, that place is a goldmine." She turned to Donovan. "You look like you have the weight of the world on your shoulders. What's up?"

Donovan shook his head, starting the car. "Nothing. Can we take a lunch break?" He didn't look at his grandmother.

"Sure, I know you're probably starving. Maybe you can tell me what's wrong once you get some food in you. Let's go to that pizza place you love."

## ❧ 8 ❧

# LONDON

ondon's head shot up from her pillow and she gasped for air. She'd woken from a vivid, terrifying dream that she was having trouble piecing together. She frantically scanned her surroundings, realizing she was at home.

In the dream, she and Donovan laid out on towels near water, maybe a beach or a large lake, and London glanced up from her book to see a large wave coming toward them. *Ok, they must have been at the beach*, she concluded.

London pushed her head back into the pillow, willing her racing heart to slow as she played back the scenes she could recall. The huge wave rolled slowly toward them then the next thing she remembered was Donovan rushing into the water.

*What was he doing?*

She took another deep breath, concentrating on the dream. Her mind conjured the image.

*Emmaline.*

Emmaline was out in the water waving frantically and Donovan ran toward her away from London. She had called out, telling him not to go but he ignored her. She then watched in horror as the wave swept over Donovan and his grandmother.

London attempted to run but her limbs refused to move. She woke up right as the wave overtook her.

Frowning at the darkness of the room she checked the time, six a.m. on the LED clock on her nightstand. Her alarm would go off in thirty minutes so no point in trying to go back to sleep. She was too shaken to sleep anyway. Easing back under the sheet and comforter, she attempted to clear her mind, breathing deeply. Though she was still pissed at Donovan for his blunt cautionary words the previous day, watching the wave sweep him away from her had been devastating.

Shifting so she was on her side, London knew one thing was certain. He was burrowing his way under her skin. She'd spent the rest of her precious Saturday fuming at Donovan's words, debating on calling him back to give him what for or keeping her job. He was, after all, still a client.

When she calmed down enough to be rational, London admitted that maybe she'd read more into his initial statement about the barista wanting her than she should have. But his comment about Vegas cut her to the core and he knew it.

He called after he'd finished running Emmaline around, she presumed, but London had turned off her ringer. She watched her phone light up and shimmy with the vibration of each ring but she hadn't answered. The first text arrived and London, refusing to look at it, dropped the phone into her purse.

Another unanswered call came through on Sunday, then the phone had gone silent.

London sat up and stretched, attempting to release the tension in her shoulders while she reminded her brain that she was safe in her own bed and not on a beach.

The nightmare shifted her feelings, she realized. She wasn't as angry now but an irrational fear of losing him settled over her. Not that he was hers to lose. What had she said Saturday? *She was none of his concern.* That went both ways.

Pulling her knees up to her chest, she pushed the covers away, letting the coolness of her room clear the fog of her dream.

Now that she was fully awake and clear headed, she knew what she needed to do. While London had enjoyed their Saturday coffee shop visits, she would tell him that she couldn't do them anymore.

Better to stop this train now and hop off.

Unfortunately, she'd still have to work with him to figure out if his grandmother was being catfished. She could do that. She'd put her game face on and accomplish the mission. All of these feelings he inspired would need to be tucked away so she could do her job and move on.

Resolute, she popped out of bed and started her day.

❦

LONDON WAS SITTING AT HER DESK TRYING TO KEEP Donovan thoughts at bay when Zaria breezed in the main door, looking like she'd just stepped off a Parisian runway in an olive-green military style high necked trench coat. London watched as Zaria took off the coat, trying in vain to wipe off the remnants of the storm outside. The coat was gorgeous; London wondered if Zaria would miss it if she borrowed it.

She snorted softly. She and Zaria didn't have that kind of relationship despite having known each other for years.

Zaria had transferred to their high school during London's sophomore year. At the time, both Zaria and Aja were juniors and they quickly became inseparable, leaving London as a third wheel. Aja got a car that year relegating London literally to the back seat.

Before Zaria, Aja and London would tool around Atlanta in her little Honda until one of their fathers called to see what they were doing. Zaria had been nice enough to London, but she always got the impression that Zaria merely tolerated her because she was Aja's cousin.

Zaria would suggest going to the mall to Aja and Aja would immediately ask London to go too. Sometimes, she would tag along, just to have something to do, but most times, she declined.

They liked to look in all of the trendy teen clothing stores. As London was fully in plus sizes at that point, most had nothing in her size, so rather than get her hopes up on finding a cute outfit, she stayed home.

Zaria strode into London's office, catching her in a full yawn. London covered her mouth as gracefully as she could.

The other woman sighed. "It's one of those days, right? I wanted to stay home and curl up on the couch this morning."

London nodded. She hadn't seen much of Zaria since she started at Exposé. When London did see her, she was either in a meeting or heading to a meeting. London wondered if Zaria was avoiding her, like she still held a grudge after all those years, but London couldn't imagine why. Aja had to have told her about their asshole ex running off to Vegas.

"Yeah, that sounds like heaven right now." London tried to keep her tone upbeat.

"True. Aja said she left you a message about being out today and tomorrow?" Zaria slid her phone from her laptop tote, consulting it before she spoke. "Also, she told me she forgot to let you know she had a check-in meeting scheduled with your client today. It's just a mid-investigation survey that she does. He's coming in," she paused, scrolling, "on his lunch hour, can you do the survey with him? You could order lunch from the café downstairs as an incentive."

*Crap.* London smiled, hoping it didn't come across as a grimace. "Sure, so this was scheduled before Aja left?" She was going to have to put that game face on much sooner than she hoped.

Zaria looked up from her phone. "I would think so. She normally schedules the check-ins right after a client signs up."

"Will you be in the meeting as well?" London braced herself, hoping that Zaria would decline. This meeting would be awkward enough; they didn't need an audience.

Zaria pursed her lips, glancing back at her phone. "I suppose I could if you needed me to, but I was hoping to head out at lunch time. I'm going to a charity dinner tonight in Aja's place and I need to run some errands beforehand."

She looked back up at London. "Do you need me to sit in?"

London almost sighed in relief. From the reluctance in her tone, Zaria didn't want to hang around any longer than London wanted her to. "No, I can handle it."

Zaria stood up. "Ok, he'll be here at noon, and I'll probably head out then if you're sure you've got it covered?"

"Yes, I'll take care of it." London sat up in her chair, wiping her damp palms on her pants. She should have done this a long time ago. "Zaria, before you go, one more thing."

Zaria looked up from her phone, waiting.

London pushed the air out of her lungs, "I wanted to apologize for my behavior when we were kids. I know it was a long time ago and you've probably moved on, but I always felt bad about sneaking around with Derrick behind your back." She forced herself to slow down. "He had me convinced you two broke up, but there were a lot of things that didn't add up and I kind of figured he wasn't being honest with me about you."

Zaria said nothing, but she sat back down.

London rushed on, needing to get all of the thoughts she'd bottled up over the years out. "Back then, I felt like you'd taken Aja from me, so I thought I was justified in taking your boyfriend from you." London paused again, then forced herself to meet Zaria's gaze. "I didn't learn about sloppy seconds until I was a little older."

Zaria smirked at the comment, giving London hope that she wasn't still angry.

"I know Aja is your best friend and I'm not here to get in the middle of that. She was there for me growing up when I needed her and I understand that she basically outgrew me, but if you are willing to forgive me, I'd like for us to start over, maybe be friends?" London dropped her gaze, studying her hands, bracing for Zaria's response.

The silence grew into what seemed like long minutes until finally Zaria spoke.

"Of course, I forgive you, London. We were both young and stupid. I swore that the world as I knew it had ended." She chuckled. "I called home and cried to my mother who said, 'Honestly, Zaria, you will forget that boy in two weeks when another one comes along. Go study something.' That was it. And as always, she was right."

The smile dropped from Zaria's face. "Aja told me the wedding was off and he moved to Vegas, and I'm assuming since you're back home, things didn't end well."

London shrugged, shaking her head. That was putting it lightly. She propped her elbow on her desk and ran a finger over her gold hoop earring, hoping Zaria wouldn't ask for details. London hadn't told anyone in her family the whole story and had no plans to; she couldn't deal with the pity.

"Well, if you ask me, not marrying him was the best decision you ever made. You deserve better. Also, for the record, I told Aja for years that she needed to reach out to you. I had moved on, there was no reason for her to still hold a grudge. But she stood by her decision back then."

Zaria sat back in the chair, relaxing her stance. "I need to apologize for not properly welcoming you to the company; I promise I wasn't avoiding you or angry, we've just been buried trying to get Exposé ready for investors."

Breathing a silent sigh of relief, London wondered why she hadn't spoken up sooner, like when she started the job. Had the conversation occurred months ago, London wouldn't have avoided Zaria and could have approached her with questions instead of working around her, asking anyone else on the team but Zaria.

"Thank you, Zaria. I owe Aja a real apology too, but I wanted to talk to you first."

"London, we're good." Zaria clapped her hands, clearly ready to move on. "Now that we got the drama out of the way, tell me about your first case and how it's going?"

She glanced down at her tote. "Wait, let me drop this stuff in my office and grab coffee first. I could go for something stronger but since it's not even 9:30 yet we'll stick to coffee."

London held up her to go cup. "I'm all set, but I'll run to the restroom while you get yours?"

Zaria gathered her tote and dashed off toward her office. London watched her, wondering if they could ever truly be friends while they were both vying for Aja's attention.

Ten minutes later, London was describing what she'd learned about Donovan and his feisty grandmother.

London stuck to the basics, leaving out all the events that had nothing to do with the case, sharing that Emmaline Roberson was running a lot of odd errands on Saturday that didn't appear to have anything to do with her mystery man.

Zaria took in everything London said and made some notes in a small planner she brought back to London's office along with her coffee. "Client's name is Donovan Willis, right? Aja said he's nice looking?" She stopped scribbling and looked up at London.

London felt her face warm and she fiddled with her earring again. "Yeah, I guess...sure. I mean, I hadn't really thought about him. In those terms I mean." London tried and failed to play it cool.

When had she become so bad at lying? If she added "in the last few minutes", her statements might be true.

Zaria gazed at London thoughtfully, then glanced at her notes. "Ok, so you're not getting much from the app, and Mrs. Roberson hasn't said anything to her grandson. And he told you they went around to a bunch of senior centers on Saturday?"

She didn't wait for an answer. "Why don't you get as much info as Donovan has about the places they went?" She tapped her pen against her planner. "You should visit a couple and ask around among the staff. She may have said something to one of them."

The mention of Saturday brought the painful conversation she'd had with Donovan back to the forefront of her thoughts causing her to miss half of what Zaria said.

"And I would check that dating app and see if you can find any pics of him. We can run his picture through a few databases and see what comes up." She rose from her seat. "Keep me posted. I've got a meeting in a few so I'll let you get back to work. Call me if you need anything."

After Zaria left, London pulled Donovan's weekly report together and printed a copy in case he wanted to review it while he was in the office. She also reviewed the survey she was supposed to conduct, which seemed straightforward enough.

Donovan's appointment was in two hours. Plenty of time, London hoped, to straighten out her jumbled nerves and get her warring emotions under control. She was still smarting from his remark, but she did want to make sure he was all right. And, ok, since she was analyzing things, she could admit that she missed him.

❧

AT TEN MINUTES TO NOON, LONDON BOUNCED FROM foot to foot, trying to decide where to put the food. She had ordered a box lunch containing a sandwich, chips and a pickle for Donovan and a garden salad with grilled chicken for herself.

Should she put the food in the center of the conference table so that he could choose where he wanted to sit?

Or should she put the lunches across from each other?

Was that sending the wrong message?

Should they sit next to each other?

She groaned. She was overthinking again. Slamming both lunches in the middle of the table along with plastic utensils, napkins and bottled water, she huffed out of the small room to take one last trip down the hall to the ladies' room before he arrived.

By the time London returned to the office, Donovan was already there in the waiting area. She had opened the door but stopped, gawking at him.

The man in front of her looked like he'd just finished modeling for the cover of one of the billionaire romances she liked to read. He wore a perfectly tailored stone-grey suit with a French blue shirt and a navy and yellow silk tie. *The way those slim cut suit pants hugged his thighs...*

London ran a hand over her forehead. She felt like a cartoon wolf, drooling at the prospect of devouring little pigs. Yep, she could totally devour this man right now. Hearing Zaria's voice, London blinked, pushing away the images of that silk tie wrapped around a bedpost and his wrists.

"There she is. London, I was just telling Donovan that you would be going over the survey with him since Aja is out. London will take good care of you." Zaria flashed her toothpaste commercial grin at him. Donovan nodded as he caught London's eye.

God help her. The boyish, embarrassed smile he wore would be her undoing. Dark brown eyes she could get lost in searched hers. London's heart pounded furiously as she watched Donovan.

Zaria said something, dragging London back to reality. "Sorry, what was that?"

"I said I was headed out unless you two needed me?" Zaria smirked at London. "Seems like you're ok."

"No, um, I think we'll be fine...lunch is in the conference room," she told Donovan. Then she turned to Zaria. "Have a good time at the...thing you're going to." Why couldn't she think clearly while he was in the room?

Zaria slung her laptop bag over her shoulder and waved at them as she exited. London led Donovan to the conference room, closing the door behind them.

Her back to the door, London turned to face Donovan.

He stood awkwardly, running a hand over his locs slowly. Then he spoke. "London, the last thing I meant to do was hurt you. What I said was mean and uncalled for. I was jealous and frustrated and I didn't think. Please accept my apology?"

"Only if you accept mine for putting words in your mouth." London's words were soft.

"Consider it done," he said, not taking his eyes off London. "So, you forgive me?"

"I think so." London stood still, part of her wanting to be closer to him, wondering if he felt the same urge. "I got you a turkey sandwich."

London groaned inwardly, relieved her job didn't require her to be a brilliant conversationalist.

"Turkey's good." Donovan moved closer, his eyes never leaving her face.

"And regular chips. I didn't know if you liked BBQ flavored..." Her words trailed off as he stepped into her personal space, tugged on one of the loose curls spilling from her high ponytail.

"Yep, BBQ is good," he murmured, his focus on her lips as he reached for her waist, pressing his body to hers. London was sandwiched between the door and Donovan.

"You're not even listening..." London said in mock protest.

On impulse, before she could overthink and talk herself out of it, London met his eyes, grasped his lapels and pulled him in for the kiss she'd longed for since that night on her porch swing.

Her eyes slid closed as their lips met. London let herself enjoy the sensations for a moment. The warm bulk of his body, the slight peppermint scent of Donovan's lip balm, the velvety feel of his tongue against hers.

His hands were everywhere, up and down her back, grazing her hips, then easing lower to cup a cheek. She arched into him, feeling his erection and hoping he knew what to do with it. Not that she wanted to find out here, in the conference room at her cousin's company.

*Right. They were in the conference room, not a hotel.*

Reluctantly, she broke the embrace. With her chest heaving,

she pulled back, using his slightly crumpled suit jacket as an excuse to run her hands over his chest.

"Why are you all dressed up?"

"This is my apology suit."

She cocked an eyebrow at him.

"It worked, didn't it?" He grinned then struck a pose with one hand on his chin.

If her wet panties were any indication, it worked a little too well, but she wouldn't go there while they were in her workplace.

Crossing her arms, she glared up at Donovan.

He stuck his hands in his pockets. "Ok, no, seriously, a huge tech company that shall not be named is looking to buy us and I basically had to interview for my job. It was a dumpster fire and now I'm headed home to work for the rest of the day."

*Can I work on you from home?* "Well, you look very nice." She caught herself leering as she said the words. Was this how dirty old men operated?

"Don't I? You can barely keep your hands off me." He winked at her.

No way she'd admit that she'd been thinking the same thing.

"And modest too, I see." She motioned toward the food on the table. "Do you want to eat? That's the box lunch I ordered for you."

He nodded, pulling out the nearest chair for her. She sat, inhaling his now familiar scent. How was she supposed to switch back into work mode with Donovan so close?

"Oh, that reminds me. I brought a peace offering for you." Donovan took a seat next to her then pulled a small gift bag out of his pocket, placing it in front of London.

"Thank you!" London cheered when she saw the contents. The colorful bag was full of wrapped chocolate kisses and candy corn, two of her favorite cheat day treats. "You found candy corn already?" She looked up at him, incredulous.

"I did, although I still don't understand why you like that

stuff." He made a face. "I hated it even as a kid. It doesn't taste like anything."

London took a candy corn piece out of the bag and popped it in her mouth, chuckling at Donovan's scowl. She held one up to his mouth. Grabbing the candy, he directed it to London's mouth, leaning in to say. "The only way I'd eat those is if they were covering strategic spots on your naked body."

She gaped at him, ignoring the tremors in her midsection from his words. She would never look at the colorful treats the same. Clearing her throat, she muttered, "We should eat."

Donovan removed his suit jacket, then proceeded to attack his lunch while London sat watching him and picking at her salad. She was too unnerved to eat, her body still humming from their interlude. She couldn't believe she'd grabbed him and practically shoved her tongue into his mouth after she had sworn they would remain professional. And, if London was being totally honest with herself, if he pressed her against the door again, she would welcome the opportunity.

"You keep looking at me like that, I may have to throw you over my shoulder and take you to my house," he said casually, finishing the last of his turkey sandwich. "What's going through that pretty head of yours?"

*Now that would be quite an experience,* London mused. She needed to focus on the task at hand. "I was hoping you'd take this survey while we eat. And I wanted to know if you recall any of the names of the senior centers you went to on Saturday? I'll go see what I can find out."

"Yep, they're in my GPS history. I'll send them to you." Donovan used the napkin to wipe his mouth.

London almost fanned herself. He made even that mundane task look sexy. Maybe because she'd had a lesson in what that mouth was capable of.

"So, what's this survey again? Aja told me about it when she set up this appointment. The woman who greeted me said your cousin had to go out of town?"

London nonchalantly grabbed her water bottle, taking a long pull. "It's quick, only five questions. It's just to make sure you're satisfied with our progress so far and that you are getting regular updates. And yes, Aja will be back on Wednesday, I believe. Did you want to wait for her to return?" she asked, grabbing her laptop bag from a chair near the door. She'd update her case notes and check Aja's schedule if Donovan preferred to wait.

Donovan shook his head. "We can do it now. As for the investigation, I have selfish reasons for wanting it to be over quickly."

Nodding, London pulled out her laptop. "Yes, I know you want to make sure your grandmother is not being taken advantage of. I should have it up in a second."

"There's that." He tented his fingers. "I'm also thinking we should go on a real date once my business with you is finished. What do you say?"

# 9

## LONDON

The next morning, instead of heading straight into the office, London found herself in front of the Magnolia Senior Activities Center north of Buckhead in Norcross. The building was four stories and looked like a hip architect's version of a modern antebellum mansion. Her plan was to see if she could chat up the staff and find out more about Emmaline Roberson without anyone getting suspicious.

A burly uniformed security guard, who looked like he would be more at home at the entrance of a strip club, manned the front desk. London saw that he was reading a technical manual on developing phone apps and almost cheered. That intel could come in handy if her cover story didn't work out. She could talk tech with the best of them.

London got into character and smiled. "Hi. How are you? My name is Lisa. I'm a nursing student and I'm trying to figure out what opportunities there might be in the senior care field. Is there a Human Resources person I can speak with for a few minutes?"

The security guard scowled at her. "Do you have an appointment?"

"No." She gave him her best pitiful look. "I don't. I was hoping to pop in. I'll be quick. No more than five minutes of their time. I just need to make sure I have a job when I finish school, you know?"

She motioned to the book he was reading. "You must be smart. App development is a good skill to have."

The scowl dropped by a degree. "This stuff is harder than I thought it would be. I'm in school, too."

London watched as he debated with himself.

Lowering his voice, he said, "Normally they don't let applicants in before ten, but I'll see if Ms. Harris can see you. She's the hiring manager."

He reached for the phone on the other side of the desk and dialed a number. London wondered what she would say to Ms. Harris when he turned back to her after hanging up the phone.

"Got her voicemail," he shrugged. He was settling back into his book when she had an idea.

"So, are you friends with any of the nurses? Maybe I can talk to one of them about nursing jobs here, see what they think?" She flashed another hopeful smile.

He sighed and shut the book then glanced out a side door that led to a courtyard. "There's a woman in scrubs outside in the smoking area named Akasha. She's on a smoke break so you need to hurry. Once she's done with her cigarette, she's got to get back to work. Tell her Curt sent you."

London thanked him and hurried to the side door toward the smoking area. Akasha was the only person outside, cigarette in hand, gazing out at the trees on the property. The woman was slender with long dark hair that had been pulled up into a messy ponytail on the top of her head. She didn't look like she wanted to be bothered but London had a job to do.

Sliding the backpack she'd brought as a prop up over both shoulders, London approached cautiously. "Hey, Akasha? I'm Lisa. Curt said you might be able to help me."

Akasha took a drag on the cigarette and blew the smoke upwards. London wanted to wave it away before she coughed but resisted the urge. "Me? Help you with what?"

"I'm a nursing student and I heard that these senior places are always hiring so I wanted to talk to a nurse to see what the job is like." London hoped that by talking fast, she'd distract the woman from asking questions of her own. "Do you like working here?"

She shrugged a delicate shoulder. "It's all right I guess."

Looking around, London nodded. "It seems secure, is it? I heard sometimes random people will just walk in and take valuables from the seniors. Can people just walk in off the street?" Never mind that she just did.

She smirked as she took another pull on the cigarette. "Well, you managed to get in somehow. But nah, it's pretty quiet."

Akasha glanced at something over London's shoulder then called out, "Hey Ms. LeDonne, you need a sweater if you're coming out. It's chilly today." She used that overly loud voice people use with the elderly and London turned to see a small figure hunched over a walker making determined slow strides toward the small walking track off the courtyard.

The woman raised a hand in greeting and kept going.

Akasha sighed, thrusting the smoldering cigarette into the ash receptacle near London's leg, barely missing her pants. "Sorry. I gotta go grab her a sweater. She's just now getting over the flu. You can come with me if you have more questions."

London turned to watch as the woman continued toward the track. Ms. LeDonne was making pretty good progress for someone with a walker. She was impressed.

The woman hurried toward the side door that led back into the building and London had to practically run to keep up. Akasha stopped at a storage closet near the door and flipped on the light then pulled a jewel toned cardigan out of a box.

The sweater was beautiful. Plum, royal blue and teal was woven throughout a black background. London knew nothing about knitting, but she could tell creating that sweater had taken a great deal of time. The pattern was intricate and she knew that sweater would cost a small fortune in any high-end store.

She couldn't help touching the soft yarn. "This is so pretty. Is it hers?"

Akasha shook her head quickly. "A woman who loves to knit donated a bunch of extra sweaters and scarves for the residents to use. She also sells pieces too but I think she donates more than she sells."

Closing the box, Akasha flipped off the light switch and London followed her out of the storage closet. "Oh, that's nice of her. So, she knit this?"

They speed walked back to the track where Ms. LeDonne was pushing the walker. Akasha smiled and said loudly, "Ms. LeDonne, please put on this sweater. You don't want to get sick again."

Ms. LeDonne gave London a curious glance then sighed and allowed Akasha to help her push frail arms through the sweater.

"I can't believe she donated that one." London said, wanting to keep the conversation flowing. "She could be selling these in some of those fancy Buckhead boutiques."

Akasha shrugged. "I said the same thing. But everybody claims she's not doing it for the money. I think she drives a nice Mercedes so maybe she's rich and bored. She just dropped off the sweaters in that box you saw on Saturday."

That had to be Emmaline Roberson. "How much does she charge? I'd love to get my grandmother a sweater like this for Christmas."

"It's $10 for the sweaters and $5 for scarves, but I don't know if she takes orders for outside people."

London frowned. Emmaline had to be losing money if she only charged $10 per sweater. There was definitely something odd about this situation.

*What was Emmaline's deal?*

"Wow, that's amazing. I bet she spends more than that in materials alone. That sweater was beautiful." Again, Akasha shrugged, looking toward the building, indicating to London her time was short.

She stayed in character, asking Akasha about her hours and benefits. Then she thanked the young woman for her time and made her way back to her car.

On the drive to the office, London considered what she learned. Emmaline was selling high quality hand knitted sweaters for $10. While it was possible Emmaline was that altruistic and did the knitting as a labor of love, London didn't buy it. The Emmaline she'd met wasn't that person.

Something was up.

London felt it in the depths of her soul and vowed to find out what was going on.

❧

THE OFFICE BUZZED WITH ACTIVITY WHEN LONDON arrived the following morning after visiting the senior center. Normally she was one of the first to arrive and she could enjoy the peace and quiet while easing into her day. She could tell that wasn't going to be the case that day. A maintenance worker had a ladder propped up near her office door and glared at her when she attempted to enter. "Paint's wet. Don't touch the trim," he snapped. "It needs a couple of hours to dry."

She scowled. Was this scheduled maintenance?

Deciding that she hadn't the energy to deal with any of that before her first cup of tea, London hiked her laptop bag onto her shoulder and stalked to the break room.

She stopped short, startled to find a raven-haired woman with dark red lips sitting on one of the stools, scribbling furiously in a folder.

The woman looked up when London walked in, cocking her head to one side, taking in London's attire.

Smiling brightly, she stuck out a hand with matching long deep red nails. "Hi, I'm Lavender. Like the color. I love your dress."

London looked down, like she had forgotten what she was

wearing. She scored a cute A-line black dress with white polka dots from a vintage site a few weeks ago and decided to wear it with a low side pony tail and a red scarf around her neck.

"Thanks, I'm London," She shook Lavender's hand and motioned toward the paperwork she was filling out. "You an independent contractor?"

"Yep. If all goes well, I will be here about six months then I'm on to the next gig. You?"

She loved the woman's British accent. Lavender could probably read the dictionary out loud and London would sit still for the entire reading. She realized Lavender was waiting for her to respond. "Nah, nepotism hire. My cousin owns the company and I'm pretty sure she was guilted into hiring me."

Lavender tossed her head back, laughing loudly. London could tell the woman liked to laugh and did it often. "No, seriously. Aja Lewis is my cousin."

Lavender tilted her head again, studying London's face. "You know, now that you mention it, I do see a resemblance. You two have the same nose." London made a face. She didn't think she and Aja looked anything alike. "And that expression. She did that too during my interview."

London chuckled. "What did you say to Aja to get her to make that face?"

"I told her that she was paying the male contract developers too much for the work they produced. I think that's why I got the job. Sometimes my bluntness is helpful, but most of the time it just gets me into trouble. Consider yourself warned. I'm that chick." She clicked the pen in her hand, as if to emphasize her point.

Despite her warning, London liked Lavender immediately. She was warm and personable, not qualities most software developers possessed. "I suppose I could use more people around me who tell the unvarnished truth." London glanced toward Aja's office. "Is Aja here?"

"Nope. She's got some offsite thing she's doing so she won't be in. Zaria? Is that right?" London nodded and Lavender continued. "Yes, Zaria told me to fill this stuff out and she'd get me settled in. So how long have you been here?"

"I haven't even hit the end of the ninety day probation period yet. But with you here, I'm officially not the new girl anymore." Since her office was off limits for the time being, London settled onto a bar stool across from her, setting the laptop bag on the seat next to her.

Zaria strode into the break room, ear buds in, wrapping up a call. She thanked the person on the other end of the line and tapped her phone to disconnect the call. "Looks like you two ladies have met. Lavender, London can offer some insight on the search tools we use. She's one of our Research Analysts." Zaria spoke quickly as they nodded at her.

"Lavender, I have your laptop in my office all ready to go. If you're ready, I'll show you where you'll be sitting."

Lavender gathered her paperwork and stood up. "Nice meeting you, London."

"You too! Normally my office is right there if you need anything." She pointed to her office across the hall. "But since the paint is wet, I will be in the conference room."

Remembering why she was in the break room in the first place, London filled a travel mug with hot water from the dispenser then dropped a tea bag into it. She headed to the small conference room to start her day.

She sipped her tea thoughtfully as she waited for her laptop to update. The first item on her to do list was Donovan's weekly status report. She had no new developments to add; generating and sending the report should have taken all of five minutes.

What she'd learned by visiting the senior center hadn't given her any clues about Emmaline Roberson's Miami man. The only thing she'd learned was that something wasn't adding up, but she had no clue beyond that. On the surface, Emmaline was a retired widow with time on her hands selling hand knit items to seniors for a price they could afford. Maybe things were exactly as they seemed.

But London couldn't shake the feeling that there was more to the story.

She set her tea down and rested her head in her hands, frustrated at her lack of progress. London needed to focus on her actual investigation. Handmade sweaters had nothing to do with Mr. Miami.

Neither did her growing feelings toward her client. She wanted him, there was no denying that. As if on cue, her body warmed thinking about him.

But as much as she tried to fight those feelings, she was also in danger of falling hard for him. London sipped her tea, wondering what Donovan was doing right at that moment. She rolled her eyes toward the ceiling. *Stop thinking about that man like that and get to work. He and his awful grandmother are a package deal you don't need.*

She pulled the container of candy corn out of her bag and bit into a slightly misshapen piece. Her rational brain was right but every time she thought about Donovan's small yet thoughtful gift, her heart melted a little.

London ate another candy corn, saw that almost thirty minutes had passed while she was staring at her laptop pondering her doomed fate, and made a decision.

She found Lavender at her desk, arranging a set of additional monitors and singing off-key to herself.

"I would have never pegged you for a Taylor Swift fan," London mused. Lavender struck her as the type of music fan who was always aware of up and coming artists before they hit the mainstream.

She jumped, turning towards London. "Oh, you startled me!" She gracefully raised a hand to her throat. "Yeah, no, I'd never go see her in concert but a couple of her songs are catchy and that one's stuck in my head."

Lavender turned back to her monitors. "You don't happen to

know where I can get another power strip, do you? I usually have one but I forgot it."

"No, I could bring one from home tomorrow if you want. Or you can run to the office supply store and expense it." London watched as she tilted the monitors, sat down to make sure the angle was comfortable, then shook her head and continued adjusting.

"No worries, I'll make sure I bring mine tomorrow." She sat again, checking the angles and nodding like the setup was perfect, then gave London her full attention. "Welcome to my temporary humble abode. What's up?"

"I wondered if you were free after work, maybe we could go across the street and grab a drink?" She looked at London, eyebrows raised.

London hesitated. Maybe the woman didn't drink. "If you drink, that is. If not, maybe we can get appetizers," she added quickly.

"Not drink? Are you mad? Honestly, I'm always a bit leery of people who don't drink, aren't you? Not that I'm a raging alcoholic or anything but yes, I'd love to. Wait, what kind of food is it? Not that it matters, I will pretty much eat anything set in front of me." All of this came out in one breath.

"Mexican. I've actually never been before but it smells good and it's usually crowded at lunch time. I've been wanting to try the place out for a while."

"London, you have found the key to my heart. Tacos and margaritas it is! What time are we going?"

"Um, let's shoot for 5:00. That will give me time to get caught up. Cool?"

Lavender did a little shoulder shimmy that London found hilarious. "Perfect! Margaritas at 5:05." She turned serious. "Thanks for asking me. Usually at these contract jobs, I'm either ignored because I'm the temp or I'm the only woman on the team and the guys who ask me to lunch are trying to gauge how quickly they can bed me."

"Yeah, gotta love being in a male dominated field. You are safe with me. I have gauged that since you aren't tall, dark and handsome, you aren't my type and thus, not worth trying to bed. No offense." A smirking Donovan came to mind and she forced the image out of her head.

"None taken. I'll come round at 5:00."

London nodded and headed back to her office.

❧

LATER, AS THE WOMEN SAT IN A BOOTH IN THE FRONT of the restaurant near the bar, sipping pomegranate margaritas and deciding what to order, Lavender shared that she'd recently moved to Atlanta, only a month after London had moved back, and she was trying to figure out what to do with her life. Her decision to uproot from New York was due to a breakup as well but she had been the initiator.

"I just looked at him one day and saw this bleak future of me in a minivan with two kids and a dog in the back rushing home to suburbia from soccer practice to make meatloaf and mashed potatoes. My life had become this routine and I couldn't do it any longer."

"But why Atlanta? New York seems to have so much opportunity?" London asked, taking a salty chip from the large basket in front of them and dipping it in the bowl of red salsa on her right.

"I have lived in New York most of my life. We moved from Manchester when I was five and we've been in New York ever since. It's not going anywhere and I can always go back if things don't work out here. I just heard that Atlanta was good for technology careers and it was different from England and New York so here I am."

She shrugged, sipping her drink. "My God, this is like the best margarita I've had in a long time. Anyway, in New York, I had this steady boring job as a software tester, a steady boring accountant boyfriend and we were saving up to buy a house. I looked round at all of it and it was just too much. So I told him I wanted to shake things up, move to another city and he looked at me like I had literally grown another head. He couldn't understand why I would want to move away from family. But between you and me," Lavender leaned in like she was sharing a secret, "I knew he wasn't going to leave the city when I pitched the idea to him. So now I'm here, in a bigger apartment than I've ever had and single and developing catfish catching software."

Lavender took a chip and swirled it into the salsa before popping it into her mouth. "Your turn."

London swallowed more of her drink and shared the highlights of her sordid jilted lover tale. "And now I have come full circle and am living back at home with my dad and his horrible cat, residing in my old bedroom. Except this time, I have a queen-sized bed."

"Well, your ex is an ass, but cheers for dodging that bullet. You would have been miserable in that marriage."

Lavender held up her glass and they toasted. "Adjusting to single life is hard some days and other days, I don't know why I didn't break things off sooner. Like, I don't ever have to worry about the damn toilet seat being up or picking up after a grown man." Lavender tapped her nails on the table. "Right now, no one is wondering where I am or when I'll be home, but I am also going home to a dark apartment where no one will ask how my first day went. At least your dad is there."

"Derrick, my ex, never asked about my day when I got home from work. He would talk about his day and how someone had wronged him then he'd want to know when dinner was ready. We weren't even having sex that often, maybe once a month. I don't know if I miss him anymore. I did at first, but now..."

Normally she wouldn't have been so forthcoming with someone she'd only just met, but the tequila loosened her tongue. Her eyes rolled. Maybe Donovan was right, alcohol was her truth serum.

London leaned in. "Can I ask you a question?"

At that moment, their waiter approached, ready to take food orders. Lavender got her tacos while London ordered a combo plate and promptly forgot what she wanted to ask Lavender so urgently just a few minutes ago.

Lavender asked a question of her own. "So, Aja hired you and what is it you do?"

Eager to share because she found the job fascinating, London explained the research she'd done on her previous investigations and her conversation with Aja and Zaria about her new responsibilities. "But at this point, I'm stuck. I have access to my target's communication in the dating app, but I have no way of figuring out who he is. He's got a generic screen-name. Plus, I think the client's grandmother is up to something else, but I have no idea what it is."

Lavender sipped again, thinking. "You should just access her computer remotely and call it a day."

The food arrived, complete with a cautionary warning that the plates were hot. The server, clearly smitten with Lavender, hovered, asking if she needed anything else. "No, I am quite good. I think my hubby will love these, so I may need a to go order when we're ready to leave. The server's face fell and he hustled away.

"You just broke your admirer's heart, you know."

"Please, I'm old enough to be his mother, or posh older sister." She dug into her food. "Anyway, tell me again why you think the client's grandmother is up to something nefarious?"

Picking at the rice and beans on her plate, London considered the question. "It's a feeling I have. Something is going on there and I bet I could figure it out by accessing her computer. You think I can do that remotely?"

"London, I was joking. You can't do that. You could go to jail." Lavender paused, putting a finger on her chin, "It would be much better if you were able to look at her files on her actual computer."

She sat up suddenly, "You think the client would give you access while the grandmother is away from home?"

Would Donovan let her search his grandmother's computer? "He might." London said, looking toward the ceiling, her thoughts spinning around this new idea. "He did express a desire to help."

Lavender took a bite of her first taco and moaned in appreciation. "These tacos remind me of this hole in the wall spot in Brooklyn." She paused, eyeing London's untouched plate. "Why aren't you eating? Is your food cold?"

"No, I'm getting to it." She'd filled up on the chips and salsa, which she always vowed not to do when she went to Mexican restaurants. Sampling the rice and black beans, London agreed, the food was wonderful.

"Good call on the restaurant. Anyway, back to your client. He can either bring the laptop to you if that's what she uses or get the hard drive and you can search it in no time."

Lavender stirred the ice crystals in her drink. "So, you have access to Grandma's dating app. What are they talking about? Any sexting? Pics? I can't imagine my grandmother taking thirst pics and sending them to my grandfather." Her nose crinkled. "Ugh..."

"Actually, the guy is really sweet. He's always asking about her day and what she's cooking. He's watched all her cooking videos. She has a lifestyle blog and YouTube channel, by the way."

"Really? I can't get my grandmother to use a freakin' cell phone but this woman has a YouTube channel? How old is she?"

"Donovan said she's in her seventies, I think. He films her videos and she's got an assistant who edits and posts them. She looks great for her age though."

Cocking her head again. Lavender narrowed her eyes. "Donovan? Is that the grandson? That sounds informal."

London watched in horror as Lavender continued. "So, if his grandmother is in her seventies, we can assume he's at least in his twenties, but the more reasonable assumption since Exposé's rates are not affordable for an average twenty-something is that he's in his thirties with a decent job or a trust fund?"

"Mid-thirties." London lowered her eyes, focusing on finishing her food. She bit into her taco. "Oh, this is good."

London felt the woman's eyes on her.

"You'd make a horrible poker player." Lavender continued to study her.

London's face got hotter.

She finished up the last of her margarita with a slurp. "Ok, I'm fully aware it's none of my business seeing as we just met this morning but I live for this story."

"There's no story." London stammered, assuming the story was etched all over her face. "Did you want another round? I've got this one."

"You know, I took a course on body language for a client. Long story for another time. Anyway, right now, your body is saying there's all kinds of story to be told. Just tell me this and I swear I will take it to my grave. Have you two..." She made a circle with her thumb and index finger with her left hand and inserted the index finger of her right hand into the circle.

"No, no, of course not!" London tried to inject as much indignation into her voice as she could. "And stop doing that thing with your fingers. It's distracting."

"Hmm...ok." Lavender leaned in, her eyes bright with mischief, "but you do want to? He must be hot."

London hesitated a beat too long. She shouldn't admit that to a coworker, tipsy or not.

Lavender grinned, a triumphant look on her face. "Yep, that's what I thought." She sat back after motioning the waiter for another round of drinks. "I didn't read the employee manual yet; I'm assuming employee client relations don't include the horizontal kind?"

Shrugging, London said, "There's nothing that says dating clients is a no-no, but I'm assuming she felt she didn't need to put that in. She shouldn't have to anyway."

"So, you're keeping your naughty thoughts to yourself until you get the case solved? What are these called anyway? Are they cases? Investigations?" Lavender leaned forward, placing a hand under her chin, giving London her full attention.

"We use investigations. Just because I want something, doesn't mean it's a good idea. I'm trying to keep this strictly professional." *And failing miserably at it,* she thought. In her defense, she also felt that Donovan shouldn't catch her off guard in her workplace looking like male temptation in a well-tailored suit. "I need to be by myself for a while, I think."

Lavender made a face. "No one said you needed to marry the man. He could be a good distraction, a friends with benefits sort of arrangement. Are you planning to move back to DC or are you here to stay?"

London had been thinking about that. Initially, she'd said she would move back home for a little while, get her life together and then return to DC, but being home was starting to feel right. She missed Atlanta and her family more than she thought. "No, I don't think I will go back to DC. There's nothing there for me."

Lavender nodded wistfully. "Too bad we didn't know each other when we first got here. We could have been roommates."

"You wouldn't have wanted me for a roommate. I was in a bad place when I first got here. No money, crying every night, listening to every breakup song ever made. It was bad." London grimaced, thinking about those first weeks home.

"I happen to be an excellent mental cheerleader. I would have had you up and hitting all the pubs and clubs with me. Like the badass single women we are," Lavender said, tapping a red fingernail on the table.

Chuckling, she waved a dismissive hand. "Ok, I'm kidding. I haven't been that woman in a long time. I would have made you tea and forced you to watch bad rom coms with me while we moaned about how all the good men have been taken. Better?" Lavender pushed her plate away.

London noted it was clean enough to skip the dishwasher.

*Where did she put it all?* She wondered with envy as she calculated how hard she'd have to hit the gym later to banish their carb dense meal.

"Much better." London agreed, pulling her phone from her purse. "I'm going to ask Donovan about accessing his grandmother's computer while I'm thinking about it."

**London: Would you get me access to your grandmother's computer? I've kinda hit a wall with the anti-cheating app.**

The response came quickly.

**Donovan: You're in luck. I bought her a new laptop and I'm transferring her files this week, so I have her computer at my house. Let me know when you want to take a look at it.**

London glanced up from the phone. "He's actually got his grandmother's computer. I can check it out without breaking into her house."

"Was that your first option?" Lavender's eyes widened, then she tipped her head to the side. "I might have gone with you though. Somebody needs to be the lookout."

"Well, I guess not." London had to admit, the hacking idea wasn't totally off the table but she drew the line at breaking and entering. "I would probably have asked Donovan to see when she might be gone for a few hours and then he could give me access."

The server swapped out empty glasses with two more margaritas filled to the top then confirmed they were done with their food. He efficiently cleared the table of the plates and silverware.

With more room on the table, Lavender rested her elbows on it and gazed at London. "Again, totally none of my business but it's fascinating. Are you going to be a bad girl when you go over to his house? Assuming he doesn't live like some college frat boy with bean bag furniture that smells like old socks and spilled beer."

London burst out laughing at that image. "Is that personal

experience, Lavender?" Somehow she didn't picture Donovan's place like that at all. "I don't get that impression from him, but in any case, I'll give him time to clean up if that's what he's got going on."

Lavender snorted. "That was the clean version of the house. I must have had some fixation with that type when I was in my twenties. God, so young and dumb." She shook her head.

London's curiosity got the best of her. "So, what are you looking for these days?"

"Nothing for now. I am getting to know the single, thirty-five-year-old me and enjoying my life in a new city where every street has the word 'peach' in it with no rhyme or reason about direction and the train system sucks." Lavender shrugged. "I'll always find something to complain about though. I'm enjoying Atlanta so far. Thanks again for inviting me out. We should make this a regular thing."

"We will." London agreed. "This was fun."

Lavender smiled at her and London got the sense that she wanted to ask something but wasn't sure how it would be interpreted. "Again, I know we just met, but here's my two-step plan for you when you go to his house."

She held up a finger. "Don't shave your legs before you go."

She added another finger. "And wear the worst panties you have. It makes you think twice about taking your clothes off." She tossed her hair over her shoulder. "Unless this is your clever ploy for seducing him. In that case, feel free to ignore everything I just said."

❧ 10 ❧

# DONOVAN

Donovan gave everything a final once over. The steaks he'd grilled earlier were in the oven staying warm along with the grilled pineapple, roasted sweet potatoes and French green beans he'd prepared.

The recipes were courtesy of his grandmother's website. He'd not asked her about any of it; she would have insisted on coming over to "help" and eventually pushed him out of his kitchen so that she could make the food herself.

His townhouse was spotless; the table in the dining area was set with basic elements which meant no flowers and no candles. London maintained this was a professional client meeting.

*Sure, because he held professional meetings with vendors at his home over dinner on Friday nights all the time.* He frowned as he straightened a slightly askew photo on his gallery wall. He couldn't recall the last time he'd gone through this much trouble to make himself and his house presentable for a guest. Hell, he'd even created a little workstation on the island where he'd placed his grandmother's computer so London could access it.

The evening should flow naturally. They would have dinner, then London would get to work and Donovan would be there to answer any questions or he had things he could be doing for work himself. He shook his head, nixing the idea. *Yeah, right.* Work was the last thing he wanted to do on a Friday night.

Donovan remembered he'd gotten a bottle of wine that needed to be opened so it could breathe and rushed to the kitchen to grab a corkscrew.

As he twisted the corkscrew into the bottle, Donovan stared at the computer. He had yet to transfer his grandmother's files to the new laptop he'd purchased for her, but he would do that this weekend after London was finished.

Donovan was pretty sure London wouldn't find anything useful on the ancient computer beyond some church documents and his grandmother's blog posts on the hard drive but if she wanted to spend her Friday evening with him checking it out, he wasn't going to complain.

The doorbell sounded as Donovan pulled the cork out with a small pop. He placed the bottle and corkscrew on the counter and hurried to open the door.

London beamed brightly at him causing the pace of his heart to take off like a runaway train. He lived for that smile. He'd gotten the impression that London hadn't had much to be happy about lately and he intended to give her reasons to smile for the rest of their evening.

She sniffed the air as she stepped into the house. "You cooked? It smells wonderful in here."

"I just threw some stuff together," he said as she entered. "Here, let me take your coat."

She untied then shrugged out of a pewter trench coat revealing an off the shoulder cream colored sweater dress.

He held the coat out. "On second thought, you should keep this on. That dress..."

London's eyes got wide. She glanced down at her dress then back up at him. "What? What's wrong with it?"

He eyed it. "Nothing, it looks good on you, but this is supposed to be a working dinner for you, right?"

"Yep, that was the plan," she said slowly.

He sighed. "I'm gonna be real with you...that dress is begging me to pull it off your other shoulder and down..."

London crossed her arms, giving him a sidelong glance. "So, you're telling me that you, a grown man with a good career who owns his own home, can't control your impulses for a couple of hours while there's a woman with a little skin bared within your line of sight?"

He smirked as he hung her coat in a small closet near the front door. *Was she issuing a challenge?*

"If I remember correctly, *you* kissed *me* the other day at your job, so who can't control their impulses, LL?"

"LL? You can call me that but I can't call you Donnie?" She waved a dismissive hand. "But yeah, that doesn't count. You had on a suit."

"Nope, only Gram can call me Donnie." He rubbed his chin, chuckling. "So, if we were to go walking down Peachtree Street on a weekday at lunch time, I'm supposed to believe you're kissing every man wearing a suit? Is that what I'm hearing?"

"Of course not. Because I have *impulse control*," she said.

"I should go put on a full three-piece suit right now and see just how much impulse control you have."

London covered her mouth with her hand, stifling a giggle. "You're going to sit on your couch in your own house with a three-piece suit on just to prove a point?" She studied him. "Why don't we agree to a no-touch policy?"

Donovan was half convinced London would break first. Then he'd have bragging rights.

Donovan shrugged, "Fine, name your rules."

"No suits," she said immediately, holding up a finger, "that includes business and birthday."

He lifted an eyebrow. "I see you've put some thought into this. But did you think I was gonna resort to dropping trou?"

"No...not sure where that came from. I assume if anyone was in that," she cleared her throat, "state of undress, the rules have already been broken."

Her words hung in the air. Donovan found his thoughts lingering on 'state of undress' in particular. In every image, he was the one breaking the rules. Blinking, he glanced down at London.

She didn't seem to be any better off than he. If she kept throwing those heated looks at him, all bets would be off before they had dinner.

He rubbed his hands together. "So, we're doing this until my grandmother's investigation is done? What does the winner get?"

She glanced away, no longer meeting his eye. "I don't know, what do you want...think, I mean? What do you think?"

He stifled a smug grin. *Yep, she was going to break first.* "Winner gets to choose where he's touched by the loser."

London's head whipped back around, her eyes flashing. "I wouldn't get so cocky over one kiss. You're more touchy feely than I am."

"I guess we'll see who caves first, won't we?" he said, grinning at her. "I need to check on dinner. Make yourself at home."

"Thanks, I will...you have a very nice place." London sounded impressed and from what he could tell, surprised.

"You said that like you thought I lived in a cardboard box," he said, chuckling.

"No, nothing like that. I figured your house would be very stark and man cave-ish. You know, dark colors and leather furniture. This place looks like a professional decorated it."

Donovan said, "Yeah, most of this is my friend Val's vision. When she was describing what she wanted to do, I was worried, but I like it."

"I love your gallery wall. Was that you or Val?" London walked toward the dining room where a wall of black and white images were displayed. All of the prints, save the one in the center, were a combination of abstract images and classic photos in black frames.

"Definitely her. I wanted to put a Samurai sword up there, but she talked me into putting some pictures up." He walked over, pointing to the one in the center. "This is my grandfather and of course, Gram and me. We took this shortly after I came to live with them."

London got closer, studying the picture. "Oh wow...you all look so happy...and you were tall for your age, weren't you? I see where you get it from." She turned back to him. "How tall was your grandfather?"

He placed a hand under his chin, "You're right. Gram told me most of his people were tall. I think he was about six and a half feet tall, give or take an inch."

He didn't know why her conclusions about his family surprised him. She had this fascinating way of pointing out subtle patterns and similarities in people and events that always led to deep discussions between them.

Donovan left her to her thoughts as she continued to study the gallery wall. The level of connection he had with this woman was refreshing.

"So...I set up space for you to check out the computer and I made enough dinner for two in case you wanted to eat while you worked," he said as he walked out of the kitchen after he checked the food.

They stood close and her scent, a floral vanilla mixture, made him want to bury his nose in the soft spot below her earlobe. Suddenly, he wasn't so confident he would win their bet.

"No, I'm fine. I'll just get to work," she insisted, dragging her eyes from the kitchen.

Her stomach wasn't as polite, choosing that moment to stage a protest, growling long and loud.

London glanced up at him, horror and embarrassment evident on her face as she relented. "Ok, maybe a little food wouldn't hurt. But I don't want to eat over the computer. I'll sit at the table, if that's ok?"

Donovan watched her tug at one of the gold hoop earrings she wore and realized she was nervous, causing him to feel more at ease with his own erratic emotions.

"Sure, we can eat at the dining table." Donovan motioned toward the dining table then held out a chair for her.

The table was set for two with a basic white tablecloth and navy placemats. "Have a seat. I just opened a bottle of wine, want a glass?"

"Just a small bit. I'm supposed to be working." London eased into the chair and eyed the table setting. "You were betting I'd want food, weren't you?"

Donovan shrugged. "Well, it *is* dinnertime. I assumed you hadn't eaten since you just left work."

Their gazes met and Donovan saw a flash of something he couldn't name, then her breath caught.

He wondered if she wanted to touch him as much as he wanted to stroke her cheek, caress that soft skin on the nape of her neck then make his way slowly over that one exposed brown shoulder.

*Since when had he become so obsessed over shoulders?* He wasn't going to cave in so easily. "Let me get that wine for you. And the food should be ready in a few minutes."

Filling the wine glass about a fourth of the way, Donovan poured himself a glass with considerably more. A cold shower would be best but he'd have to settle for the cool red wine.

He checked the food warming in the oven. Everything looked like it was ready to go.

Donovan took the two wine glasses to the dining table and placed London's in front of her. "Try that while I get your plate."

"Can I help?" London called out once he was back in the kitchen.

"Nope, just relax, I got this covered."

He returned with two plates filled with food and a dish towel slung over one shoulder.

"My compliments to the chef," London said. "You've got the fancy restaurant server look down pat. And the food looks wonderful."

She picked up her fork. "Thank you for this."

He tipped his head up in acknowledgment, trying to be cool about things. With one alluring smile and a sincere compliment, she made all the effort he'd put into pulling off a 'casual' dinner worth it.

London sliced a piece of steak, slid it into her mouth and moaned slightly. "Wow, that's perfect. Did you make it or is this your grandmother's handiwork?" she teased. She visibly relaxed, possibly due to the wine.

"Nah. I slaved over a hot stove to make all of this. I might have borrowed her recipes, but this is all me."

London took another bite, then put the knife and fork down. "And you just whipped this all up for your normal Friday night meal?" she asked, her head tilted, clearly skeptical.

"Ok maybe not every Friday night. Like I said, I figured you wouldn't get to eat before you came by." He tossed his most charming grin her way.

She quickly grabbed her wine glass, taking a long sip. "Well, I did mean to grab something quick before I got here but I stopped at home instead. I left work late helping Lavender, our newest developer, get set up on our case management software."

"Her real name is Lavender? Like the color? I assume it's a woman?" He cut into his steak, took a bite. Yeah, he had to pat himself on the back; he did a damn good job grilling the steaks.

"Yes, like the color. You know there was a student at Hogwarts named Lavender, remember? And don't act like you aren't a Harry Potter fan."

"Oh yeah, there was. I wasn't going to deny the Harry Potter thing, by the way." He stabbed a sweet potato cube. "So, answer me this: is Lavender attractive?"

London frowned. "Why, you looking to get hooked up?" she asked lightly, but Donovan caught the tone.

"Nope. I have a theory about the women at your company. I haven't really seen any men there so I don't know if the theory will hold up, but maybe I'll test it out one day." He took another sweet potato and gave himself five stars on the meal. The sweet potatoes had a savory spice to them that was a perfect complement to the steak, green beans, and pineapple.

London crossed her arms in front of her chest. "What's this theory of yours? I can't even imagine."

Donovan lifted a shoulder in a shrug. "I think you only hire attractive people. Like I said, I can't speak for the men, I haven't seen any but looking at you and your cousin, then the other woman, what was her name, something with a Z, anyway, you all look like you should be on the cover of Essence."

He raised an eyebrow at London. "So, if the new developer is attractive, my theory is correct."

London stabbed a slice of pineapple. "I feel like I should be insulted on some level because that seems sexist, but then there's a compliment in there I think, so I don't know." She popped the fruit into her mouth then said between bites, "To answer your question, yes, I would consider Lavender attractive, I know that's not why my cousin hired her though."

Donovan raised a hand. "Not saying any of you got hired purely for looks, I'm just saying, I noticed a common theme."

She pointed her fork in his direction. "You should be glad I'm enjoying my meal and not trying to debate with you again tonight, Mr. Willis."

"Thanks, I know when to drag my foot out of my mouth so I'll leave it at that. So, which of the Harry Potter spells did you try?"

"All of them." London laughed. "I loved those stories." They talked comfortably about the popular young adult novels for a few minutes while they ate.

London glanced at her watch. "Ugh, it's getting late, I better get started."

Donovan tried to keep his tone casual. "So, you going out after you leave here?" He imagined her at a club with some other man making moves on her bare shoulder and frowned.

"Probably not. Lavender said she might go out and told me she'd let me know in case I wanted to go. Nothing definitive. You?

Do I need to leave by a certain time?" London asked as she gathered her plate and silverware to take to the kitchen.

Donovan reached for the items and their hands brushed, sending a familiar electric current up his arm.

She glanced at him quickly. "That doesn't count, right?"

He cleared his throat. "Accidents don't count...but take as long as you need on her machine. I'm going to watch the baseball playoffs."

He rinsed both plates and put them in the dishwasher along with the silverware. "More wine?"

She nodded and he retrieved her glass, pouring her another half glass full.

The den where Donovan settled in to watch the game was directly across from the island where London now sat. He'd logged in to the computer for her then turned on the baseball game.

✿

"Oh, how cute!" London gushed suddenly, pulling Donovan's attention away from the game.

"How old were you here?" London was pointing at the screen when he walked over to see what she was looking at.

He peered at the picture. His grandmother had a folder of old pictures on her hard drive and he wondered if she had scanned them and saved them. That was a task she'd normally ask him to do. Focusing his attention on the picture, he frowned. "That's old. I think I was maybe six. That's my mom and we were at this birthday party for this kid I didn't even know."

"Your mom is beautiful. You look a lot like her." She peered at him. "You don't talk about her, is she still in Atlanta?"

His mother was a tough subject, one he didn't like to explore. "No, she lives in Texas with her family. We aren't close. She basically dropped me off on Gram's doorstep when I was ten and hasn't really looked back since."

As much as he tried to make the comment neutral, he knew he sounded bitter. "Now I get cards on my birthday and at Christmas with large checks in them. I guess that's supposed to make everything better."

London had a hand over her mouth. "She doesn't call? Ever?"

"Nope. And it's fine. I've learned to get along without her," he said, dismissively. "I have mourned her like she's no longer living. That probably sounds crazy to you since your mother is gone, but the mother I knew in those pictures doesn't exist anymore. I don't know who she is now and she's made it clear she doesn't want me to be a part of her new life."

"It's good that your grandmother stepped into that role for you. I can't imagine how she could leave you behind and not want to see the man you have become." London turned to him. "You and your grandmother are a lot closer than my grandmother and I are. Maybe if I'd lived with her after my mom died, we'd be closer. I think your grandmother sees you as a friend while mine still sees me as her grandchild. Does that make sense?"

Donovan nodded. He did see London's point. He had always felt like he could talk to his grandmother about anything and she'd listen while not treating him like his feelings and emotions weren't valid just because he was a child.

"That's a good point. I mean, I know my boundaries with her, and there are times, like with this matchmaking she insists on doing, that irritate me, but yeah, we're friends. Which is why this whole thing about this man she's seeing worries me. I don't know why she felt like she couldn't tell me about him."

"Maybe she doesn't want to say anything before she meets him in person? She might feel like he's too good to be true, or that she doesn't know where the relationship is going and she doesn't want her family to meet him until she knows they're serious." She laid her head on her fist, gazing thoughtfully at the screen.

"You think she's waiting to meet him first?" Donovan crossed his arms.

London nodded. "I think so. Your grandmother has a lot of

research about Miami on here." She tapped the screen. "I think she's planning to visit him. But she hasn't said anything like that in the dating app."

She sighed, stretching then yawning. "She might be planning to surprise him with a visit."

"That's crazy. If I hadn't hired you, I'd have no idea if she went to Miami and he meant to do her harm. She could be chained up in his basement and we wouldn't know." He rubbed his head in frustration. There was an urgency and almost panic in his voice.

"She's got a lot of friends, right? I'm sure she's told at least one of her friends about him. And if she goes to Miami to see him, she'll give that friend his info just in case something happens. Your grandmother strikes me as being pretty street smart."

Donovan conceded this point. "Yeah, she is." He studied London. "I see why you're good at your job. You're very calm and reassuring."

She shifted in her seat, clearly uncomfortable with the compliment. "Thanks. I don't know how to describe it, but I get vibes from people and usually they're pretty accurate."

London rose from the chair. "I should go home. I've been sitting in one spot too long, my foot's asleep." She winced, shaking out her legs one at a time.

Donovan noticed she'd ditched her high heeled booties for a pair of fuzzy pink socks at some point after her arrival. The socks looked ridiculous with the sweater dress but Donovan thought they were cute on her.

"Come have a seat. I wouldn't be a good host if I didn't do anything to help you with your foot so this is a time out from our no touching rule, agreed?"

London raised one eyebrow. "Ok, I'll agree for now."

Donovan led her to the couch. Once they were both seated, he had her put her feet in his lap. "Which one?"

London motioned to the left foot. Donovan slipped the sock off and began massaging the problem foot.

They were quiet for a few minutes. Donovan wondered what was on London's mind when she finally spoke. "You know, I can only resist so long."

Moving his hands up to her ankle, he ran a palm over each side of London's foot. "What are you resisting?"

"Seriously?" She gestured in the general direction of his hand and her foot. "You've fed me, loosened me up with wine, given me the best foot massage ever and now you're looking at me like I'm the most desirable woman on the planet and we're supposed to be keeping this," she waved her hands between them, "professional."

London sat up then, pulling her foot away firmly. "I can't do that when I'm thinking about how much I..."

Exhaling, she looked beyond Donovan at the wall behind him. "It would be different if you scratched yourself at the table or burped your name or made a plate for yourself and carried it to the tv while ignoring me. Anything unattractive."

Donovan sat back, studying her, "How much you what?" he asked slowly, focusing on the one thought she hadn't fully voiced.

She finally met his gaze. "Doesn't matter. We aren't crossing that line...again." London crossed her arms, her voice firm. "The No Touching rule stands."

He stroked his chin. "Ok, as long as you remember this was all your idea when you break the rule," he said casually.

She blinked, then her eyes drifted to Donovan's mouth. "I'm not going to break anything."

"Yeah, so you say." He gave her a knowing grin then rose from the couch. "But we'll see. You want dessert? I made chocolate mousse."

"Um, sure." He wasn't a hundred percent sure but he thought he heard relief in her voice. "So, you bake too?"

"Nope. I made this in a blender. My idea of baking is those prepackaged cookies you break off and throw in the oven," he said, heading toward the kitchen.

"Did you want coffee? More wine?" Donovan asked as he set

two ramekins of chocolate mousse dolloped perfectly with whipped cream, plus spoons and napkins on the coffee table.

"Oh no, I'm stuffed. I'm going to try the mousse and ask the chef for a to go container." She scooped out a bit of mousse and dipped it in the whipped cream. "Oh, that's what's up. You made this in the blender?" She closed her eyes, moaning softly as she slid the spoon out of her mouth.

Donovan couldn't watch her any longer. He was rock hard, thoughts of London moaning like that for him as he loved her pushed front and center in his mind. 'I can only resist so long...' she'd just said.

So true. Now he was thinking the exact same thing.

He shook his head at the irony of the situation.

"I know you're probably thinking I act like I haven't eaten in weeks but this mousse is wonderful," she said, scraping the bottom of the dish with her spoon. She gave the spoon a thorough final lick and it was his turn to stifle a moan. Without touching her, he eased the spoon from her fingers, licked it, then slid closer to London.

Donovan's heart thumped in his chest. *Now or never.* "If you want to go home, you should say so now."

# LONDON

She didn't *want* to go home but she *needed* to go home.

Donovan was right there, offering her an out that she needed to take. She should grab her coat and run. Aja would tell her to go home.

She could think of a million reasons to go home but only one for staying. She should go.

London studied his face. There was a small dusting of freckles near the bridge of his nose that she'd never noticed. A strong urge to run her fingers over the contours of his face gripped her. He hadn't known how close he was to the truth when he said she'd break her own rule first. She wanted to know how he felt in her hands, wanted the closeness of touching another human being but she resisted, choosing to stand up instead.

He was her *client*.

Once the investigation was over, he'd be gone.

"I have to go."

Donovan nodded. He stood and got her coat then held it up so she could slide it on.

She left without another word.

*I am a strong woman* was the mantra running through London's head on repeat.

She woke up in her own bed, mostly convinced she'd done the right thing in not listening to her inner bad girl who wanted to stay at Donovan's and succumb to her body's desire to treat him like her personal sex toy. As much as she wanted Donovan, she needed to keep their relationship professional.

No Touching.

Ok, *professional* was a stretch lately. They had danced around that line too much. *Friendly* was a better description. They could remain *friendly* until this investigation was done.

*What then?* While she knew he wanted her in his bed, was that all he wanted?

What did *she* want?

She was less than a year out of a long-term relationship; didn't she need time to reflect, to heal?

London paused the questions swimming around in her head to listen. The house was too quiet. Normally on Saturday mornings, her dad would be up either working out in the home gym he'd put in last year or attempting to fix things around the house.

She checked her phone. Sure enough, her dad left her a text saying he was going to the office.

She wasn't surprised she hadn't heard the text. After coming home so late or so early, depending on one's perspective, she'd quickly changed into her pajamas and climbed into bed, refusing to analyze her warring emotions.

She'd done the right thing in leaving last night, hadn't she?

Since she had the house to herself, she could spend some time alone processing everything that happened in the last twenty-four hours. She needed to sort things out.

A hot shower where she would wash her hair was the first order of business. She'd done nothing with her hair when she came in, and it looked like Maxie had played in it all night with half of it flat from her pillow and the other half shooting in several different directions. The plan was to wash and condition then twist it into submission so she could deal with it later.

London gathered her things and headed to the bathroom.

Once in the shower, enjoying the spray of the hottest water she could stand, London relived the night before. No one, including her ex, especially not her ex, had treated her like she was the most important person in the world. Donovan had taken care of all the details.

From the wonderful meal, including dessert, to creating a mini workstation for her to rubbing her feet, as if he knew exactly what she needed. Donovan had anticipated her every need, and as a result she felt comfortable, cherished, and ready to give him anything he wanted. She had longed for his touch the entire night, even though she insisted they wouldn't cross that line again.

He'd been looking at her all night like a tiger stalking its dinner right before it pounced. He'd made it clear he wanted her and had to know she wanted him.

The depth of her desire for Donovan scared her. She'd tried to convince herself that maybe since he was genuinely a good man, his bedroom skills were probably average at best. She had a feeling he would bring his A game like he did with everything else he endeavored to do and London knew she wasn't ready. What if she gave in, had the kind of epic sex she only read about in romance novels and then Donovan decided his grandmother was right and London wasn't the kind of woman he needed for a serious relationship?

Could she settle for just sex with Donovan?

She contemplated all of this so long that the water cooled. Giving her hair a final rinse, London stepped out of the shower, wrapped her hair in a towel, and put on her coziest terry robe.

After putting her hair in a few sectioned twists, London dressed in lounge pants and a sweatshirt, determined to make progress on Emmaline's case. Last night, London had found some suspicious files on Emmaline's computer and needed to figure out what the files contained.

Her first order of business was a good cup of tea and some breakfast.

She skipped down the stairs, just missing Maxie who slept curled up at the foot of the staircase. The orange furball hissed at her impatiently then threw another reproachful glare her way as she stalked off.

London hissed at the cat's back, causing the cat to stop mid step and glance back at London, as if daring her to hiss again. The sight made London pause on her way to the kitchen, marveling at the cat's human mannerisms.

Cooking wasn't an option, she really wanted to get to work decrypting Emmaline's files. London saw a lone banana on the counter and claimed it. Then she made a piece of toast with peanut butter to eat while she heated water for tea.

She watched the kettle. The electric kettle on the counter had been a Father's Day gift to her dad, and she was surprised to see he used it regularly.

This, London decided, was so much better than those scary whistling kettles which always indicated death in horror or suspense movies. The victim was always in the process of boiling water when the killer struck, and then the kettle would blow and blow.

*No thanks.* She'd take a silent LED light any day.

London trudged back up the stairs with her tea, glad for its warmth that chilly morning, and sat at her laptop. She had saved Emmaline's mysterious files to a jump drive so she could figure out how to open them.

A couple of hours later, London had peeled the sweatshirt off in irritation and opted for a light heather grey t-shirt instead. The sun was streaming in, warming the house quickly and the sweatshirt turned cumbersome and bulky.

She had made little progress. She still didn't know what was on the ledger files after Googling and working her way through solutions that didn't work. Stretching her stiff neck and back muscles, London opted to go for a brisk walk around the subdivision for a few minutes to clear her head.

Grabbing a baseball cap and switching the lounge pants for yoga pants, she set out for her walk.

Maxie, curled up in the sun near the front door, dozing off, glanced up as London left, then immediately went back to her own thoughts.

LONDON TOOK A MOMENT TO ENJOY THE BEAUTIFUL day. The sky was a brilliant light blue with very few clouds. A few neighbors were out raking leaves and putting up Halloween décor. A neighbor three houses down was washing his BMW SUV, as usual. She waved as she walked past and he threw up a hand in greeting then returned to scrubbing his car.

Normally London would have put on some earbuds and listened to music or an audio book, but that day, she didn't want those distractions. She needed to clear her mind and let it work out the problems before her.

Her thoughts meandered as she walked. A few kids in the neighborhood were riding bikes around the col-de-sac and she waved as they whizzed by. London marveled that kids were so tech savvy these days. No one would have considered London a technically advanced child, but in her defense, technology wasn't as accessible back then.

She hadn't really thought about technology beyond her beloved video games, let alone thinking she could make a living from it. Technology had come a long way. She recalled the early search engines and how limited they were compared to Google.

Another thought hit her.

Among Emmaline's files she'd copied was a recovered video file that appeared to be corrupted when she'd attempted to play it. If she could fix that file, she may find something useful.

She had run across a website tool that was supposed to restore video files. Maybe that would allow her to access it, she reasoned, getting excited by the thought and doing an abrupt about face back toward her house, eager to see if she could view the video immediately.

Once she was back at her desk, London found the website in her email and signed up for the free version of the video restoration tool.

She crossed her fingers as she uploaded the corrupted file, wondering what Donovan was doing at that moment. He'd mentioned having work to catch up on so he might be at the coffee shop glaring at the singing barista who had caused so much trouble between them.

Now that she recalled that argument they'd had, she realized he was right about the man's leering eye after she'd caught the barista sizing up the firm round derriere of another woman as she strode out with her coffee.

The file finished processing with a "fix successful" message and London clicked the play icon.

A man who looked to be in his early thirties dressed entirely in black started talking. The video was older, London could tell by the fuzzy edges when she expanded it to full screen. The audio was low and she had to adjust her speakers to hear the man.

After listening for a few minutes, London sat back, thinking. The man was speaking about the origins of a knitting marketplace site that had just launched. He gestured wildly, talking about how the site would change the world, connecting people around the globe committed to the knitting cause.

"Are that many people so passionate about knitting?" she wondered out loud. She had nothing against knitting; it was a hobby she'd added to her "someday when I get my life together" list, but she didn't know there was a whole worldwide *knitting movement* happening.

The earnest speaker emphasized the website again and London paused the video to check it out, curious to see if it was still active.

London was fascinated. Knitbegandborrow.com was very active, with over a million users active at that moment, the site proudly proclaimed. It was a marketplace site where customers could post knitting supplies they wanted to trade.

In order to post or order items, an account was required.

London checked the other files to see if Emmaline had stored her password info in any of the text files she had copied from the woman's computer. No luck there. She drummed her fingers on the desk, thinking.

Picking up her phone, she typed out a quick text to Donovan, following a hunch.

While she waited for Donovan's response, she continued to click around the knitting marketplace. The flurry of activity was like watching the scrolling news ticker at the bottom of the financial networks on tv. One user who needed several skeins of worsted wool yarn had a pristine set of knitting needles that normally sold for $200 new.

There were immediate responses to that request and London watched as knitters offered to throw in bonus items in addition to the yarn the woman was seeking, effectively driving up the value of the needle set.

Donovan's answer came in as London was trying to figure out who the highest bidder would be on the knitting needle set.

Forcing herself away from the rapid-fire bidding, London checked the text, then attempted to enter the network password from Emmaline's computer into the knitting site along with her email address as the user name.

Immediately, Emmaline's account opened and London had access to start offering items to swap.

She clicked a link to access the transaction history. Emmaline was very active on the site; she had exchanged an order within the past week. London reviewed the account for a few minutes longer, not seeing anything of interest.

Deciding to review the other files she'd snagged from Emmaline's old computer, she minimized the site.

One file, named Old Translations, was a password protected spreadsheet that piqued London's interest. What kind of translations would Emmaline have on her personal computer that needed to be password protected? What if it was sensitive financial information?

There were other files without password protection that she could look at. She opened one that was named "Draft 1" and started reading then frowned, not sure what she was reading.

Her phone chimed, dragging her focus from the files.

**Donovan: Since you rejected my charm last night, I figure you owe me a movie tonight.**

London read the text, unable to stop the warmth that flowed through her. While she'd hoped to hear from him at some point, assuming he wasn't pissed that she'd blue balled him by going home last night, she hadn't expected the invitation. She typed out a quick response.

**London: Well, if you're looking for me to pay, we're going to the drive in. And I need you to hide in the trunk until we get thru the ticket line**

**Donovan: You serious? I'm not hiding in the trunk of your car.**

**London: Ok, then one of us needs to pose as a child. Admission fee for kids under 9 is $1**

**Donovan: I will pay for the movie. You can be in charge of snacks. And we're taking my car so no one has to hide in the trunk**

They agreed on a time and a movie as London ignored the little voice telling her she was playing with fire. Friends went to movies together all the time, London reasoned with the voice.

The drive-in part might be tricky since they would be alone in a car together for a few hours, but she could control herself. As long as he didn't throw those heated looks her way, the ones that made her feel like her clothes might melt off from the intensity, the ones that let her know he liked what he saw and wanted more, she'd be ok.

Or so she hoped.

She made herself a quick lunch and returned to the locked files she wanted to access. Closing the draft document, London tried the password Donovan gave her, assuming the same password wouldn't work, but to her surprise she could now view the contents of the file.

London scanned the spreadsheet. None of the dates were recent; the spreadsheet appeared to be a few years old.

She picked a random date tab to review. There were dates and what appeared to be customer names along with prescription drug names. She scrolled through the list, seeing a few popular drugs that she'd heard of because of their television commercials.

There were full names, addresses, phone numbers and prescription info along with distribution dates and dollar amounts.

London sat unmoving, reviewing line after line in the spreadsheet until her back and bladder protested, demanding she get up from her desk chair.

She looked at the clock on the laptop, surprised that so much time had passed. The clock read 3:30.

Where had the time gone?

Reluctantly, she rose and stretched, rubbing her lower back. After a quick stop in the bathroom, she stretched out on her bed, needing to think through what she was seeing. A sense of dread overshadowed her sense of accomplishment.

While she wasn't 100% sure, London's theory was that the spreadsheet was a customer ledger for someone selling prescription drugs.

Was Emmaline the seller? No, there had to be another explanation for this data. London pushed herself up and sat back at the laptop. She scrolled through all the remaining tabs to the last one.

There, the data was different but no less intriguing. London raised one hand to her mouth as she scrolled through the rows of data.

One thing was certain, in looking for more information on Emmaline's online dating activities, London had stumbled upon something far worse than catfishing.

She sat back in her chair. Her head throbbed and she feared the lunch she'd just had would find its way back up.

The question London had before her was did Donovan have a right to know? If she were he, she would want to know. *Maybe he already knew*, her inner critic pointed out.

London wanted to tell Donovan immediately. She didn't know what he was going to do with the information but at least he would know.

Steeling herself and having no idea what she was going to say, she picked up her phone and dialed his number. The phone rang once then went to voicemail. London left him a quick message asking him to call her then she ended the call, tapping the phone against her chin nervously.

The phone vibrated and rang in her hand, startling London.

She answered immediately.

"Hey, sorry I missed your call, I was getting gas. Since I'm out, I can pick up snacks if you know what you want," Donovan said in one breath. He sounded like he was still driving.

"Hey, Donovan, um, no, it's fine. I need to talk to you about something, maybe it's best if you come by so I can tell you in person?"

The line got quiet. Save for the road noise, London would have assumed the call dropped. Finally, Donovan spoke. "Let me pull over." She heard him turn the engine off.

There was a palpable silence now. "What do you need to talk to me about?" The familiar tone was gone.

"Are you sure you don't want to stop by? I just, I think this would be better..." Now she was stalling. She wanted to show him everything she found, see if he would come to the same conclusion she had.

He cut her off. "No, London, just tell me, please."

London exhaled, forcing herself to pause and gather her

thoughts before speaking. When she had to convey bad news, she tended to spit it all out like vomit, spewing words everywhere that no one could follow or make sense of easily.

"Last night, I saw that your grandmother had some encrypted files and a corrupted video file that I wanted to see if I could get into."

"Oh, this is about my grandmother." She heard relief in his voice. "I thought you were going to cancel tonight...what could you have found in those files? I can't imagine she had government secrets or anything. She's been retired for years."

"Donovan, please listen. I have to explain, I need to tell you this." London paused again, getting her words together. She stroked her hoop earring. "I was able to use the password you sent a couple different places."

She heard him grunt. "I've told her a dozen times not to use the same passwords everywhere." Donovan then asked urgently, "Is he stealing her money?"

"No, no, nothing like that." London cut in quickly. "Let me finish. I was able to restore the corrupted video file. The file is like a promo video for a knitting site and..."

Donovan interrupted; frustration clear in his voice. "A knitting video? What does that have to..."

"Please let me finish." London raised her voice, vying for his attention. "The knitting site is kind of like an Ebay for knitting supplies. It requires a password to access it and the network password you gave me allowed me to see your grandmother's account."

This time he waited until she paused before speaking. "Ok?" He drew the word out, clearly wanting to know what this had to do with anything. "What's the problem?"

"I'm getting there. So, your grandmother regularly posts on the site to trade supplies. Here's the thing. I found some old spreadsheets that were password protected and again, I used the network password to access one of them."

"So, what was in the spreadsheets?" Donovan broke in again.

London clenched her jaw to keep from snapping at him. She rubbed her forehead. If he interrupted her one more time, she was going to scream.

Closing her eyes, she willed herself to calm down. The most important thing she needed to do in this moment was get the information out. She took two quick breaths then opened her eyes to deliver her findings. "The spreadsheets appear to contain a customer ledger. And a key to the items posted on the knitting site. That site is a cover for a prescription drug swapping marketplace."

There was silence on the line.

London waited, not sure if she should go on.

"London, what are you saying?" Donovan asked, finally.

She exhaled. "I think your grandmother is using that site to trade then sell prescription drugs."

"What? What do you mean, my grandmother is selling drugs? My grandmother has never even smoked a cigarette, let alone weed. She can't be selling drugs."

"Oh no, I don't think she's selling anything illegal like street drugs, these are all drugs you see advertised on TV." London tried to reassure him, like the fact that she wasn't selling cocaine made the situation better somehow.

"Remember when that big drug company was making the news because they hiked the price of that Epi-Pen like 200%?" She didn't wait for him to answer. "Well, your grandmother can get that pen from the knitting site by swapping it for something else. Then I'm guessing she sells it here, probably at the senior centers you took her to. This is assuming she's still doing it. I don't see any current ledgers."

Donovan was quiet for what seemed like an hour. Finally, he said, "London, there is no way my grandmother is selling drugs. Your info is wrong."

London assumed there would be resistance and probably denial, but she wasn't prepared for the assumption on his part that she was mistaken.

Irritation bubbled to the surface and as much as she wanted to, London refused to let it dictate her response. "I can show you, walk you through everything I found." She sighed. "I wanted the answer to be different and maybe there's a reasonable explanation for all of this."

"There has to be. My grandmother is not selling or trading drugs." His tone was firm.

London decided to let him vent for a few minutes instead of pushing more information on him.

He spoke again, his tone sharp. "Did you even find out anything about the man she's dating? That's what you were supposed to be doing," he snapped and London's mouth dropped open.

*I should have kept my mouth shut*, she fumed.

The silence on the phone was tense. Donovan finally spoke, his tone calmer. "Sorry. I shouldn't have snapped at you. But your info is wrong," he repeated firmly.

Normally in a situation like this, London would say "It's fine. No worries, we all say things we don't mean."

But it wasn't fine.

She wasn't ready to accept the weak apology she got for delivering unpleasant news. "I think you should see what I'm looking at before you just say I'm wrong. Why don't we look at it before we go to the drive in?" London assumed their difference of opinion was something that they could talk through rationally, but she soon found out that was not the case.

"London, you just accused my grandmother of being a drug dealer. A movie tonight is a bad idea. I'll be in touch." With that, Donovan was gone.

Shocked, she sat there holding the silent phone in her hand. She had just been canceled. She hadn't seen that coming. She knew Donovan would be surprised, but she'd naively thought they'd figure things out together.

LONDON'S PHONE RANG AS SHE LIE IN BED, TIRED FROM a sleepless night, dreading the daylight streaming through her bedroom window.

For a moment, she was hopeful, thinking that maybe Donovan had spent the night rethinking what she'd told him and wanting to talk it over with her.

Reaching out to grab the phone from the charging station, dread hit her in the stomach, flowing all the way to her toes.

London knew this was no social call. "Hi Aja."

As was her way, Aja launched right in. "London. I just got a call from Donovan Willis saying he was terminating his contract with us effective immediately."

London's dread turned to cold fear.

She was about to lose her job.

She stopped breathing. She couldn't believe Donovan would do this.

"He said that while the work we'd done up until now was good, we weren't making enough progress on his investigation and your focus seemed to be elsewhere." Aja was furious. "What the hell is going on? I saw he did the courtesy check and survey a few days ago and had good things to say."

London heard fingernails hitting keys aggressively.

*Crap*, she panicked. She hadn't updated the case management software since Monday, which meant Aja had no recent notes or entries showing London's progress when she'd talked to Donovan. He'd surely blindsided Aja with his call.

"Why aren't there any notes in here from this week?" Aja stopped typing as quickly as she'd started. London knew her cousin expected answers immediately.

"Um, I haven't put any notes in just yet. I was going to get that done before I came in Monday morning." London stalled, not quite ready to spill the whole sordid story to her cousin.

"You're supposed to be updating your notes in the system every day so that when I'm called by an unhappy client on a Sunday, I'm aware of what's going on. I can't defend the company or you if I don't have any documentation. What happened? Why did he just fire us?"

London sat up, wishing she had a cup of tea in front of her. Her throat was dry but she had to tell Aja what she knew. "I was able to gain access to his grandmother's computer. I thought that would provide some insight into who she was dating and possibly, if there was a trail of money being passed from the victim to the alleged catfish, I'd see a record of it."

London told her about the data she found and what she thought it meant. "I had called him to let him know I found something he should know about. I wanted to walk through my results and how I got them so he would have a full picture, but he doesn't believe my info is correct and he's apparently fired us because he's in denial."

She heard Aja exhale before she spoke again. "So let me make sure I have this straight. You stumbled upon his grandmother's drug business but you haven't found anything about this man she's seeing? How sure are you about your information?"

"Based on the recent transactions in her account on the knitting site, I'm fairly certain she's still trading drugs. I believe she was making deliveries when she had Donovan drive her around to all those senior centers a few weeks ago."

"Ok, but you didn't find a recent ledger?" London heard Aja start typing again, less aggressively this time.

"No, I didn't." London admitted.

"Did you check her search history? What was there? There has to be something related to this man she's seeing."

"Not much. Her search history was unusually clear. Nothing from the knitting site. There were a few searches related to Miami, so I'm thinking she's planning to visit him there, even though they have only talked about him coming to Atlanta. I guess she's planning to surprise him."

As she said this, something in the back of her mind nagged at her. She hadn't done enough digging into the Miami search history.

"Did she book a plane ticket yet? Or reserve a hotel? That would help."

"No, nothing like that in her banking history." London relaxed a bit. She thought she knew where Aja was going with this. Possibly giving Donovan info about a planned trip to Miami would convince him to keep Exposé on the case.

"When did you search her computer?" Aja asked.

London needed to tread lightly. "Friday."

"Ok, how did you gain access to the computer?"

Taking a shaky breath, London told Aja that Donovan gave her access as he was transferring his grandmother's files from her old computer to the new laptop he'd purchased for her.

"So, you went over after you left work on Friday evening?" The typing stopped and the phone was quiet for a long moment. "Please tell me you aren't romantically involved with a client."

London hesitated, not quite sure how to answer the question. She supposed "romantically involved" might describe her relationship with Donovan, but did a few bone melting kisses really indicate involvement?

Aja, taking London's silence as her answer, huffed, "What the fuck, London? I trust you with your first client and you sleep with him? You better be glad we're family, otherwise you'd be fired. What were you thinking?" Her voice was steel and calm and London knew she wasn't expecting an answer.

Aja's assumptions cut London to her core. She started to protest but what was the point? Even though she technically hadn't, she wanted to.

Slumping her shoulders, she held the phone to her ear, waiting for the reprimand to run its course.

Answering for London, Aja continued. "You weren't thinking, I'm sure. I see your judgment where men are concerned hasn't gotten any better."

London put the phone in speaker mode and threw it onto the bed at that point, anger surging through her as she stared at the wall in front of her. At that moment she wanted to tell Aja screw her and her job and quit but she couldn't.

Aja was right. London had messed up big time.

"Even though I'm not firing you right now, you need to fix this and fast. I have never had a client cancel a contract for incompetency and I'm not breaking my perfect record."

London heard the tap of keys again. "If you don't convince him to come back, you'll be relegated to doing grunt work and getting coffee for the office. And if you do anything like this again, family be damned, you're gone. Are we clear?"

Picking the phone up, London put it back against her ear. She felt like saying "Yes ma'am" like she was back in elementary school which she was sure Aja she would have taken as her being a smartass. "Yes, we're clear."

"Oh, and I want you to stay home tomorrow and focus all your efforts on a plan to fix this mess. I will expect this plan in my email by 4 pm. Not a second later. Good luck."

As soon as Aja said that, the call ended. London stared at the phone, realizing that she'd been hung up on twice now in less than twenty-four hours.

She wasn't going to give anyone else the chance to hang up on her that day. She put the device in silent mode then placed it back on the charger. London wasn't dealing with the day or anyone she decided, crawling back into the warm cocoon of her bed.

# DONOVAN

Donovan and his best friend Val sat contemplating life on Donovan's back deck in patio chairs long ago pilfered from Emmaline's house. Donovan had invited her over after work to help him figure out how to fix the London problem.

After they'd been sitting in silence for a few minutes, Val said, "I'm no detective or anything but I'm gonna go out on a limb based on your moping. I'm thinking Friday night didn't go as we'd planned?"

He was staring out over the small back yard. Thinking about Friday night made him angry about the remainder of the weekend all over again. "I fired Exposé yesterday," he blurted.

"What?" Val, about to take a pull of the bottled beer in her hand stopped abruptly, staring at Donovan. "Why? What happened?"

Donovan ran a hand over his locs and looked at her, hoping she would understand. "Friday night was good. Things went south on Saturday then Sunday they went to hell."

He proceeded to tell her about London's call on Saturday with her findings and their argument.

Val gawked, placing her bottle on the small table between

their chairs. "Wait a minute. Ms. Emma is selling drugs? Dang, I knew she had some ratchet tendencies."

"She's allegedly selling prescription drugs, not street drugs." Not sure why he felt the need to clarify this to Val, Donovan continued. "But, yes, that's what London thinks based on the files she found on Gram's old computer."

"And what's your reasoning for telling her she was wrong?" Val took another pull from the bottle.

"I know my grandmother! That's my reasoning," he said, raising his voice. Val leaned back as if he'd yelled in her face.

"So, did you review what London found? See if there might be any truth to what she was seeing?"

Donovan didn't look at her, stalling by turning his beer bottle up for a long drink. "No," he said finally. "She wanted me to come by but I didn't go."

"Ok, you told her she's wrong, and then what happened yesterday?" Val asked.

"I thought about everything on Saturday night over a couple of beers and early Sunday morning, I called London's cousin and told her to cancel my contract because London seemed to be in over her head." His voice was full of despair. "I did that purely out of anger and spite."

Val stared at him, shock evident on her face. "Shit. Did you get her fired?"

"I don't know...maybe. I wasn't thinking that far ahead. As soon as I hung up, I wanted to call back and say just kidding, but I couldn't. I haven't talked to London since Saturday."

He sighed, pushing the beer away. "Val, what if she's right?"

"D, why wouldn't she be right? I'm pretty sure she wouldn't say anything if her info wasn't solid. You think she's doing this to drive you and Ms. Emma apart?" she asked.

"I guess she could be but that seems like a lot of trouble to go through."

Val nodded. "I hate to break the news to you, but London had no reason to lie to you. And I'm sure she checked and double or even triple checked what she found before she told you," Val said softly. "You haven't known her long, but do you really see her telling you what she found just to be spiteful?"

Shaking his head, he tried to come up with other reasons for London to accuse his grandmother of committing such a crime. He came up empty. And felt sick to his stomach. London was more than likely right and probably unemployed now because of him.

"So, what do I do now?" He met Val's sympathetic gaze. "I need to make things right."

Val scooted her chair forward so she could prop her feet on the deck railing. "Did you talk to your grandmother yet?" Donovan shook his head and she continued. "You should talk to her tonight. See what she says."

"I was planning to do that," Donovan said. "What about London? What should I do about that situation?"

Val sat back, studied Donovan. After a few minutes of silence where Donovan tried to wait for her to speak and failed, he said, "Well?"

Pausing a few seconds more, Val said, "We've been friends for like, ever, so I know you. And you know I say all of this with love, right? She didn't wait for a response. "You are definitely happier these past few weeks which I'm thinking means that you have feelings for her and would like to still see her after all of this is over?"

Donovan nodded. He missed London since she left on Saturday morning.

"So, do you still want to find out about Ms. Emma's new man?" Val asked.

Donovan considered this question. That was the main reason he'd hired London's company, but now, it didn't seem as urgent given the other information he'd received about his grandmother.

Finally, he shrugged. "I guess so."

"I think you should. Because that way, maybe you can protect London's job. Otherwise, I seriously doubt the woman is going to want to have anything to do with you now that she's unemployed, thanks to you." She pointed an accusatory finger at him. "You told her manager she wasn't doing her job well. For her to forgive you, you're going to have to get her job back."

*What a mess*, he thought, rubbing his jaw in frustration. "So, say I'm able to get her job back, you think she can forgive me?"

"D, you need to give her a reason to forgive you. Does she know how you feel about her?"

Donovan's lips flattened in response.

Val nodded. "Right, so yeah, you're going to have to show her as well as tell her. You should plan on making her fancy dinners for a while."

That was a start, but it was going to take more than steak and chocolate mousse to convince London that he was worth her time and affection.

Donovan realized that although he'd only known London for a few weeks, this wasn't the first time he'd had to apologize and atone for his rash behavior. What was it about London that had him all off-kilter? He needed to figure that out and fast.

Looking up, Donovan saw Val waiting for an answer to a question he hadn't heard.

"What did you say?" Before she could respond, his phone rang. He checked the screen. Anticipation and nerves raced through his body. "It's her." He held up the phone.

⚜

AFTER VAL LEFT, DONOVAN STRAIGHTENED UP THE patio area, stacking the chairs and putting the glass beer bottles in the recycling bin.

His mind rewound its recollection of London's call, replaying the short conversation. Her tone had been professional and stiff when she'd asked if he would be willing to meet with her the next day for lunch.

He'd agreed, casually asking what was up, but she hadn't

elaborated, saying only that she felt they needed to talk in person. He was certain she was out of a job because of his actions and probably wanted to tell him to his face to go to hell for ruining her life.

Even though he was dreading that moment, a part of him was eagerly looking forward to seeing London again. And they were meeting at the café in his office building so maybe she wouldn't attempt to strangle or slap him in public.

Donovan stepped back into the house, now almost dark due to the sun's final descent minutes earlier, and turned on a lamp in the living room.

The other problem he refused to deal with was the knowledge of his grandmother's side business. He decided they needed to face this head on. He knew his grandmother would be up for a few more hours watching her favorite shows and he wanted to talk to her tonight instead of letting things continue to fester in his mind.

When Donovan arrived at his grandmother's house, her car was gone. He frowned, wondering where she was. He'd let himself in and wait for her. They needed to talk.

Once he was in the house, he checked the kitchen for snacks, a habit from childhood. Gram was good for homemade treats and after the day he'd had, Donovan felt he could use a comfort snack.

Sure enough, there was a plastic container of blondies on the counter, cut up into perfect squares and stacked four rows high. The treats looked like they were staged for presentation and he hesitated, wondering if she'd already taken the pics for her blog. Then, remembering that they needed to talk about this whole side hustle of hers, he grabbed one anyway. Gram would just have to fuss.

Taking a bite, he closed his eyes in delight. The blondies were worth whatever grief his grandmother wanted to dish out. He set the partially eaten bar on a napkin then grabbed a glass from the cabinet so he could have milk with them.

Emmaline bustled in just as Donovan was wiping crumbs

from his mouth and the counter. "Donnie! I see you found dessert. Did you eat yet? Or was that dinner?" Emmaline asked as she laid two full grocery bags on the counter.

"Are there more bags in the car? I'll get them." Donovan started towards the garage.

"No, this is it. Have a seat. You want me to make you something to eat?" she asked, setting her purse down and reaching for items in the nearest bag.

"Gram, can that wait for a few minutes? I need to talk to you," Donovan said, his stomach clenching.

"I need to talk to you, too. Let's sit at the table," Emmaline said and pulled two chairs out. As soon as Donovan was seated, she said, "I got a text from you the other day that clearly was meant for someone else. Did you let someone look at my computer?"

Donovan sighed inwardly. He'd inadvertently sent his grandmother a text that should have gone to London. "Yes, Gram, London was looking for a basic computer to use for learning to code. I was going to give her your old one."

"How do you know I don't still need it?" she snapped. "What if you missed a file or program I need?" She crossed her arms and sat straight up.

The arm cross was Emmaline's classic annoyed stance and Donovan's hint that his grandmother's mood had taken a turn for the worse, in case he hadn't caught the short tone. This was going to be much harder than he thought.

"Once I wipe it clean, everything is gone so I have to make sure I copy everything over. Don't worry, I got everything copied."

He ran a hand over his locs. "I did see some files that didn't make sense. Gram, are you selling drugs? Is that what you were doing at all those senior centers you had me drive you to?"

"Selling drugs?" Emmaline rose, busying herself with the grocery bags she just brought in. "Where did you get that idea? I knit stuff and sell it or donate it."

"Ok, then what are all those files with the names of prescription drugs in them? And that site you use for so called knitting supplies? I know you don't take all those meds. Especially the ones for erectile dysfunction," Donovan said testily. He put both elbows on the table, "Gram, I thought we were always straight with each other."

He watched her expression darken. "That goes both ways, Donnie."

Emmaline stopped unloading the bag then turned to him, her arms crossed. "Why would you text that woman asking if she was done with my computer? What was she doing on it?"

"I wasn't sure what the files were when I was copying them so I asked her to take a look. She's better at that than me," Donovan countered. "You're changing the subject."

Emmaline's eyes narrowed. "I have a right to know who has access to my personal information. She could be one of those identity thieves for all you know. My personal info could be in Russia by now."

Donovan rubbed his head in frustration. "Gram, she is not stealing your identity. And you still haven't explained those files on your computer. Looks like you're making a good living as a mule."

Now Emmaline pushed the grocery bags to the side, leaving nothing between them, her amber eyes flashing. "You want the truth, fine. First of all, I'm not a mule."

Donovan frowned, then attempted to speak, but Emmaline held up a hand to silence him. "No, you want the truth, here it is. I have found a way to trade legitimate prescription drugs and supplies for people who are on fixed income or just can't afford their prescriptions."

She huffed, stabbing a finger on the table, "These drug companies are only out for the almighty dollar. I go on the site and see what I can trade with. People I work with who can get extras give them to me, and I use those extras to barter for what they need. I add a little for my costs and everybody is happy. Big pharma still makes their billions and gives those fat cat executives their undeserved bonuses and the people that need their meds get them. I'm not selling street drugs or any of those addictive pain killers. That's it."

"Gram, that's still illegal! What if you get caught?" Donovan had no idea she would be so forthcoming after being so secretive all this time. But, he supposed, revealing this information was probably intended to distract him from her other secrets.

"I don't have anything to do with the drugs the feds scrutinize closely. Yes, there's a chance I could get busted but it's slim. I'm not a big fish."

Sighing, she went back to putting the groceries away. "That's the story. And unless you're going to arrest me, I'm done talking about this subject. Now, do you want dinner or not?"

❧ 13 ❧

# LONDON

London glanced again at the time on her phone as she waited in the main lobby of the office building where Donovan worked. He asked her to meet him here at lunch time.

Less than a minute passed since her last time check. She was five minutes early, hoping to get to the building in time to settle her nerves and not appear any more flustered than she already was.

To pass the time, she took a seat on a bench near the elevator and took in her surroundings. The building was one of many high-rise structures in Midtown Atlanta.

London knew Donovan's office was on the top floor based on the suite number listed on the business card he'd given Aja when he'd signed on with Exposé. Each time the elevator dinged and the doors slid open, London's heart pursed, thinking Donovan would step off into the lobby. She needed to stop staring at the elevator.

Out of habit, London raised a hand to her ear ready to rub the silver chandelier earning and found nothing.

Her earring wasn't there. A small wave of panic rolled through her body.

*Where was her earring?*

She'd just purchased the set, a pair of vintage rhinestone earrings shaped like the Eiffel Tower, and was wearing them for the first time. She checked her other earlobe. Luckily, that earring was still intact. She glanced around the tile floor surrounding the small bench on which she sat, hoping her earring had fallen since she'd arrived.

Nothing.

Reluctantly she pulled the other rhinestone piece off, noting how easily the back of the earring slid off when she grasped it. She knew she should have used a different backing to keep the earrings in place. Maybe she'd find it in the car, she reassured herself.

She was already super nervous about this meeting with Donovan. She would have to convince him to reconsider the cancelation. She exhaled slowly, trying to get her jitters under control. She could do this.

What would Donovan say?

She wondered if he was still angry at her for accusing his saintly grandmother of selling drugs. She reached up to rub her earring again then caught herself and forced her hand back into her lap.

It was silly, but she felt a little naked without earrings. She loved them in all sizes and shapes. Earrings were an accessory that didn't care what size the wearer was and she'd always believed you could easily elevate your look with a good pair of hoops. She'd pulled her hair back into a low bun at the back of her neck to emphasize the jewelry in her ears and now they were gone.

Foot traffic in the lobby was starting to increase as the lunch hour hit its peak. London watched the crowds, saw a few men in business suits and rolled her eyes, thinking back to the 'No Touching' conversation. She had no desire to kiss any of those men.

She glanced at the elevator again, looking for Donovan, hoping he wasn't in a suit. She didn't need the distraction.

London checked her watch again as a brown skinned woman with shoulder length locs, one side of her head shaved, exited the elevator and looked around. She then strode toward London's bench. The woman was about London's height, if she had to guess and leaned toward a petite build. The red golf shirt she wore emphasized toned, muscular arms that London envied. Black cargo pants and loafers completed her look.

The woman stopped directly in front of her. "Are you London Lewis by any chance?"

London stared up, taking a few seconds to realize the woman was talking to her. "Yes?" The response came out like a question. "Yes, I'm London," she said with more confidence.

The woman exhaled with relief. "Ok, good. I'm Val. Donovan is running late. He should be here in a few minutes."

This was Val, Donovan's best friend. Somehow she wasn't what London expected. Not that London had any concrete preconceived picture of what Val should look like as Donovan had never described his friend to her, but she would have never picked this woman out of a lineup as his friend. Maybe she expected someone who looked more like his fair skinned grandmother?

She realized Val was sizing her up as well, probably thinking that London wasn't what she expected either. "Thank you, though he could have texted me, he didn't have to send you all the way down here."

Val motioned to the empty space on the bench. "Can I?"

London slid closer to the opposite end to give her room to be seated.

She flopped down like she'd been on her feet for hours. "I volunteered. We were in a team meeting that's turned into a bitching and moaning fest and running way over schedule. I was happy to leave."

Revealing toothpaste commercial teeth, perfect and white, Val grinned. "I wanted to meet the legendary London I've been hearing so much about."

There was a touch of snark in her tone that London decided to ignore. "He talks about you a lot as well. Nice to finally put a face with the name."

Val was still staring, making London want to squirm. She smiled, trying to strike up conversation. "So, are you a game artist too?"

"Nah, I do more of the grunt work for now." Val placed an ankle on her other knee then rested her head on her fisted hand, all while regarding London. "I hear you've had the pleasure of spending quality time with Ms. Emma."

*Well, that was quick.* London started to grimace then quickly fixed her face. Val didn't need to know London's true feelings toward the older woman "Yep, she's not a fan of mine unfortunately."

Val chuckled. "Nice way to put it. You're in good company. She tolerated me when D and I were growing up, but when I got divorced and came out, I was pretty much dead to her."

Donovan hadn't mentioned any of this. London was curious. "Was it the divorce or the coming out part that pissed her off?" she ventured.

Val raised both shoulders. "Probably both, who knows." She gazed at London again. "I figure she's intimidated by you though. You're that lethal combination of pretty and smart. I see why you've captured Donovan's eye and Ms. Emma's ire."

London wasn't sure Val's assessment was meant as a compliment, but she knew it wasn't accurate. "No, she doesn't think I'm Donovan's type since my dark skin won't pass the paper bag test and I'm not a size two." She nearly spat the words.

Val kissed her teeth. "Paper bag test? Where people held a brown paper bag against you to see if you're lighter than the bag? Who is still comparing their skin tones to paper bags? That practice and the theory that having fair skin is an advantage needs to die already." She paused. "But that might explain why she never really liked me," she said thoughtfully. "Anyway, did she tell you that to your face?"

"No, the night I met her, she came into the ladies room with her friends while I was in one of the stalls and I overheard her tell her friends that. She didn't know I was there," London said.

She watched the other woman closely. "I didn't tell him about that."

Val nodded. "Gotcha. He won't hear about it from me."

Relieved, London thanked Val. She didn't want Donovan to feel like he needed to confront his grandmother about her words. The incident brought back painful memories of middle school where the girls in gym class huddled together waiting for London to attempt any of the physical activities assigned so they could laugh and make pig noises. She pushed those memories away; she'd push this one away as well.

Val played with the plastic employee ID badge clipped to her pocket. "Since we're sharing secrets, I wouldn't worry about being D's type. He's been talking about you since he met you."

London wanted badly to ask what Donovan had said about her but managed to restrain herself. They weren't teenagers conducting their romance via gossip and third party representatives. Val wouldn't, she assumed, share details, she'd just decided to throw a glimmer of encouragement London's way.

Even though she was looking at Val, away from the elevator, London knew the moment Donovan stepped into the lobby. She felt him connect with her before she saw him.

She turned to watch him approach, enjoying the view. He wore a baby blue button-down shirt, khakis that looked like they had just been pressed and brown leather boots. He was also carrying a large bag of what looked like lunch in his hand.

London felt her heart beat faster and she willed it to slow down before she had a heart attack. She and Val stood up.

"Thanks for taking care of lunch, Val," he said then focused on her. "London, I'm sorry I'm late." Donovan spoke her name quietly, using the intimate tone he'd used right before he kissed her.

London fought the urge to close her eyes and relish the sound, evoke the memories, but they were in a crowded public space and she needed to focus on getting him back as a client.

London kept her expression neutral. "How are you?"

Turning to Val, Donovan said, "I'll see you upstairs."

Val, getting the hint, bowed slightly. "No problem. Enjoy." She turned to London. "Nice meeting you, London." She waved and rushed to jump on the elevator before the doors closed.

London watched the woman leave. Donovan, she noticed, had at least two women in his life who protected him fiercely.

"You ok with eating at the park?" he asked, holding up the lunch bag. "I asked Val to order takeout for us."

"Sure." She couldn't imagine trying to eat anything with all the stomach flutters she had going on right then, but since Donovan had gone through the effort of buying food to eat at Piedmont Park, which was a quick walk away, maybe he was now willing to talk to her about his grandmother's business dealings.

They exited the office building and set out for the popular Atlanta landmark.

As soon as they were away from the lunch crowds and approaching the park entrance, Donovan turned toward London, his shoulders slumped. "So, did you lose your job?" he asked.

London had spent the previous day rehearsing what she would say when she and Donovan met. She'd made notecards, which were at that moment in the passenger seat of her car and felt reasonably prepared that morning. Now, with him walking at her side so close and looking like brown male perfection, all of her words were gone.

"Aja doesn't want to risk the wrath of the twins. That's what everyone calls our dads," London explained. "So, for now, my job is safe." She hesitated then decided to just spill it. "Will you reconsider your decision to cancel?" London winced at the desperation in her voice but she couldn't help it. The realization that she wanted to see this investigation through hit her at that moment. She needed to figure out the missing pieces of the puzzle.

Donovan continued walking, not saying a word. They entered at the 12$^{th}$ Street gate, walking toward the playground area where there was a covered area with benches. London watched a woman push a small child on the swings near the benches. The little girl giggled with delight then told her mother she wanted to go higher. Her confident tone reminded London of Aja, who had used that same commanding voice since they were that age.

London knew Aja was disappointed in her and that drove her to swallow her pride. She'd beg him if she needed to.

Donovan settled upon a bench near Lake Clara Meer and stared out at the water.

Panicked by his silence, London blurted, "I can see if I can get you a discount. Probably not a big one but something."

London again waited for his response, trying not to fidget. He was probably trying to figure out how to let her down easily. She resisted the urge to touch her naked earlobe again by crossing her hands in her lap.

Donovan placed the bag on the bench between them. "You're not wearing earrings today," he said suddenly like he'd just figured out a complex riddle. "It threw me off for a minute."

Blinking in surprise that he'd noticed, London's hand gravitated toward her ear. "No. I lost one somewhere between my house and here so I took the other one out."

This, she mused, was one of the many reasons she was in danger of falling hard for Donovan if she wasn't careful. He was observant and curious to know more about her, no matter how small the detail.

"Not that you don't look good without them," Donovan said quickly. "I'm just used to seeing you with earrings."

London nodded. "Is it weird that I feel out of kilter or something without them?"

Donovan was unloading the takeout containers and stopped to chuckle at her. "Well, your earrings are usually big enough to be used as weapons."

She rolled her eyes. "No they aren't. They're statement jewelry, that's all. They aren't that big." At least the initial awkwardness between them seemed to be gone. Donovan still hadn't answered her question about hiring Exposé back but she'd figure out how to bring the topic up after they ate.

"Those sparkly earrings you have could put a man's eyes out," he argued, then shot her a half grin. "Anyway, Chicken tenders, potato salad, celery, carrot sticks, apple slices and brownies." He laid the containers out between them. "Plates and plasticware. Dig in."

London made a small plate of chicken, vegetables and apple slices. "Thank you for lunch."

He shrugged. "After that stupid call I made, making sure you had lunch was the least I could do. I know I messed up."

London agreed, but sensed he was working up to whatever was weighing on his mind and decided to let him speak. She bit into an apple slice and waited.

Donovan stared out at the expanse of the park. "Seems like all I'm doing since we met is apologizing to you." He sighed. "But I know I owe you a big one. You were right, of course. I confronted my grandmother about her little business venture and she admitted it."

Not sure how she should respond, London remained silent. Internally, she clenched a fist and raised it to the sky in a Black Power salute to the ancestors. She wasn't one to gloat at her victories, but this one gave her validation on multiple levels. Her instincts could be trusted. Her knowledge was powerful. And Emmaline wasn't so mighty. "Oh?"

"Yeah, she's doing a bad thing for a good cause, she says. She provides affordable prescriptions to people who regularly have to choose between food on the table and their medications."

He absently twisted the smartwatch on his wrist. "I guess I get what she's doing but it's still wrong. She could go to jail and she doesn't seem all that concerned about it."

Donovan raised his gaze to London. "You don't need to give me a discount. I'll call Aja when I get back to my desk and tell her I made a huge mistake."

While London was relieved, she still felt for Donovan's

situation with his grandmother. He was, she could tell, distraught. She watched him as he sat, deep in thought. There was that desire to comfort him again, she noticed, an urge that always seemed to appear when he was talking about his grandmother.

But she couldn't compete with that and wouldn't ask him to choose between her and Emmaline.

They sat in silence for a few minutes while London tried to figure out the best way to say what she needed to say.

He spoke first. "I'm glad you didn't lose your job. I shouldn't have called and told your cousin you were in over your head."

He twisted the watchband, then stopped, looking directly at London. "I really don't know what made me do that. But anything we might have going on shouldn't affect your career. I apologize for that, too. You were right that we shouldn't have crossed the line. I guess I let the fact that I wanted you overrule common sense. It won't happen again."

"It definitely won't." London felt like she'd just been shoved off the edge of a building. Donovan had reduced her to just being something he wanted, like she was the latest tech gadget. Aja was right. Her judgment was worthless.

She wouldn't let him know how deeply he'd cut her.

She rose, grabbing the plate of half-eaten food and shoving it in the trash beside the table. "Well, thank you again for giving Exposé another chance. I've got to get back to the office."

"Wait a minute, let me walk you back..." Donovan scrambled up from the bench.

"No. I'm fine." She cut him off, eager to leave so she could nurse her wounds in the privacy of her car.

"No, you're not. I can tell you're pissed...would you slow down a minute so we can talk?" he said, throwing the leftover food containers back in the paper bag with more force than necessary. The bag finally succumbed to the abuse and tore, causing Donovan to swear under his breath before picking it up and slamming it into the trash. "London..."

"There's nothing to talk about." She refused to let him see her break down. She needed to get out of the park. "I have to go. Goodbye, Donovan." She practically ran to the iron gate entrance, refusing to respond as Donovan called her name.

⚜

"Hey London, Donovan called me to reinstate his contract and he wants to continue working with you. Please find some time on my calendar tomorrow so that we can discuss strategy and get this one wrapped up. Thanks for all your help on this."

London listened to the message from Aja twice before deleting it.

Aja would consider London's visit earlier that day to Donovan's office a success. She'd pled her case and he agreed to rescind the cancellation. But, in that process, he'd also apologized for not believing her about his grandmother, then admitted he wanted her, and dumped her in the same breath.

*What the hell?* This would be twice in one year she'd been tossed aside like a used condom. Except this time, her bank account hadn't been raided. But, unlike before, she would have to interact with Donovan much more. Great, now she would be pining for another man who didn't want her.

London sat cross legged on the floor with her back against the bed, thinking about all the things she'd failed at lately and shoving M&Ms from a family sized bag into her mouth

She tallied up her losses this year as she chewed. She lost her fiancé to an older woman who provided better support, she lost her good, secure job because she was devastated about the ex-fiancé. She lost her savings because she'd put too much trust in that ex-fiancé, which in turn caused her to sell her home that she'd loved for far less than it was worth. She counted that as another loss. Then once she'd moved back home to Atlanta, she nearly lost her job again.

Staring at the empty wall across from her bed, she recalled the posters of hip hop stars she'd put up with such care when she was younger. Her father removed the posters after London moved but kept the room pretty much intact, like he knew she'd be back and need it at some point. *He knows me well*, she thought. She guessed he knew she would eventually fail.

She felt like she should be crying but there were no tears. London considered drinking to numb and forget and went so far as to reach up and open her bedroom door halfway, but she couldn't muster the desire to stand up and go downstairs to raid the liquor cabinet. The candy would have to do.

She slumped back against her bed. Moments later, as if she knew London needed a friend, Maxie strode in silently and positioned herself in London's lap, burying her head under London's forearm.

Shocked, London stared at the cat, not sure how to react. She guessed if Maxie was setting her up to claw her, she'd have done it immediately. Pushing the bag of candy aside, London tentatively scratched the tabby's head and Maxie purred her approval.

As London absently stroked the cat, she wondered what her mother would say if she were still alive. Would she give her a pep talk and tell her things could be worse? The thought caused a flash of anger to hit her, how would her mother know, she took her own life. Were things worse for her? She hadn't lost a house. London's dad had always been the provider, so she couldn't imagine that her mom was depressed over a job loss.

Knowing she would never learn what her mother was going through that made her end her own life always made London sad. London's dad closed himself off after she died. In the past, London tried a few times to ask him about her mother, but he always just says she was gone so they had to move on. London saw that he didn't like talking about her mom so she eventually stopped asking. She saw no point in both of them being miserable.

When London was ten years old, her mother died from an intentional overdose of sleeping pills. Depressed and suffering from frequent migraines, London's mother spent most of her time in bed. London was told she needed to be good and stay quiet so that her mother could rest. London had learned early how to fend for herself. She knew how to use the microwave and could make sandwiches for the two of them while they waited for London's father to come home from work.

The only constant London recalled was that her mother would wash and braid London's thick long hair every Sunday. As she braided, she would tell London to take care of her hair because it was a Black woman's crowning glory.

London begged her mother to let her get a relaxer, a process of applying a curl relaxing chemical onto dry hair and letting it sit for a while, until it burned or thirty minutes, whichever came first, then rinsing the chemical out and washing with a neutralizing shampoo. The finished process resulted in tamer, straighter hair that could be styled easily.

London pursed her lips, recalling her mother refused each time, giving London a million reasons why she wouldn't allow any chemical process on her baby's hair. The main reason, she said, was that London's hair was already growing out of her scalp as it was supposed to and she didn't need to change it. The other reason she gave was that London was too young. London argued unsuccessfully that other girls at school had been getting relaxers forever and she just shook her head. "London, you will thank me one day for showing you how to do your own hair in its natural state. You'll just have to trust me on this." And with that, they continued the process of washing then conditioning, then drying and braiding London's hair.

The process took a few hours but London always loved the braids once she was finished. She would tie them up in a satin scarf before bed and try to sleep as still as possible so that they would stay neat but the scarf always fell off. The next morning, London' s mom would freshen the braids with a little gel and a soft brush and send her off to school.

London had pulled her hair back into a low bun for the visit to Donovan's office and now she undid it, letting her hair fan out from the restrictive hair band. She ran a hand through it, fluffing it out.

Maxie eyed her, clearly not happy that she wasn't being rubbed any longer.

Her mother was right, London thought as she resumed stroking Maxie's soft fur. London loved her chemical free hair now and she was glad her mother didn't allow her to change it. Back when she still had a fiancé, he preferred her hair straight and told her so whenever she dared to wear the curly styles she liked. To avoid conflict, London eventually stopped wearing her hair in its natural state, opting instead to schlep across town to a stylist near Howard University every two weeks to get her hair flat ironed so that it was bone straight. Now that he was gone, the curls were back to stay, at least until London decided differently.

As was her habit lately, she found herself comparing the two men. Her ex had never really commented on her hair unless he didn't like it. Donovan, on the other hand, was always touching London's hair, tugging a loose curl playfully or smoothing any hair that fell toward her face.

She exhaled slowly. She would miss those moments, even though she'd only known Donovan a short time and there weren't a lot of special moments, she would always remember them.

London sat with her eyes closed. Why was her life such a mess and how could she fix it? A little voice inside said, *you're doing a lot better than you were a few months ago. You have a family that loves you and they came through for you when you needed them. Show them their efforts are appreciated.*

That little voice was right. Her dad hadn't hesitated when she told him she needed him to help her get moved back home. Aja had given her a job even though they hadn't spoken in a while. Maybe the family could all get together for a real family vacation, possibly for her dad's and uncle's birthday. A cruise might be nice.

As she thought about cruising, she recalled something she saw on Emmaline's computer.

She frowned. What was it about her search history that London found strange?

She replayed the scene in her head.

Donovan was sitting on his couch, watching the game and she had watched him for a few minutes thinking of how cute he looked all engrossed in the baseball game like a little boy and she was looking at Emmaline's search history and thinking, *this is off.*

*What was it? Think!* London carefully removed Maxie from her lap and stood, trying to word associate. There was stuff about Miami, but not what she expected. *That's it*, she thought.

Initially, when London saw Emmaline's Miami searches, she assumed Emmaline was planning to visit her new boyfriend there, but as she dug in, she noticed there were no typical searches: hotel rates, airfare, things to do. Emmaline had been searching property records and obituaries.

She supposed the possibility of moving to Miami was not unreasonable, but why search for obituaries?

*What exactly was Emmaline planning?*

Her phone chimed indicating a new text message while London paced, analyzing what she knew and she dismissed it.

If she wasn't going to jump up and drown her sorrows in alcohol because it was too far away, she also wasn't going to hop up and see who had sent her a message. She assumed Aja sent some directive for her to remember for tomorrow.

Her cousin didn't seem to ever switch out of work mode. London received texts and emails from her at the oddest times always with a note to ignore until the next work day. Aja had explained that she wanted to make sure she told London before she forgot.

Unable to resist, London sighed. She might as well see what Aja wanted.

The text, it turned out, was not from Aja.

**Donovan: Hey London, I found this in Gram's room a while ago, but forgot to send it to you. I'm not sure who he is, but maybe it's helpful?**

The next text was an image of an obituary notice for a man who had died earlier that year in February. London skimmed the details but one in particular caught her eye.

The man lived in Miami.

**London: You don't know him? Ever heard your grandmother talk about him?**

**Donovan: No on both.**

**London: Hmm, ok I'll check it out. Thanks.**

**Donovan: YW. Let me know what you find.**

**London: Will do.**

## 14

# LONDON

*My wedding was supposed to be this Saturday,* London mused as she stared out the window of her office.

She'd always loved the idea of a wedding in autumn full of vibrant colors and distinctly fall favors. Gathering inspiration from Pinterest boards and bridal magazines, she'd planned on using pinecones, apples, pumpkins, and fall leaves in her table décor, along with an apple cider bar. She had drawn a hard line at having anything with "pumpkin spice" in the name, even though it was a favorite flavor of hers; she had envisioned a very Hallmark movie affair.

London didn't know exactly when she took a wrong turn, but her whole new life wasn't going as planned. Aja was keeping her on a tight leash with Donovan's case, requiring London to check in with her daily and to send the weekly status reports to her before they were sent to Donovan. Resentful of being second guessed and micromanaged like an intern, London wanted to complain but knew she had no one to blame but herself. She was lucky Aja hadn't fired her. She sucked up her irritation and strived to be better at her job.

Reviewing social media posts for another case, the sheer number of red flags London saw was starting to make her head hurt. The young woman who had hired them was clearly being catfished, yet despite the reports from London detailing the misrepresentations she found, the young client still held out hope that her online love was everything he claimed to be. It was all a lie, just as London's relationship was.

Many times over the past few months, London heard from well-meaning relatives that her ex departing before the wedding was a blessing in disguise and that she should be thankful she saw his true colors before they said their vows. She still felt like her judgment should have been better, and deep down she questioned her worthiness. Maybe she didn't deserve to have anyone love her.

London needed a short mental break so she shut the laptop for a few minutes to watch the world outside her window. She concentrated on a tall sugar maple tree with brilliant orange leaves as it swayed in the breeze. Fall had fully settled over Atlanta and London normally loved the season. She enjoyed the crisp chilly mornings that required a sweater or light jacket, and the subsequent afternoon warm up, providing perfect evenings for porch swing sitting.

"Knock, knock!" Lavender, her new coworker said, interrupting her tree watching by rushing into her office and plopping down on the chair opposite London. She turned from the window to look at Lavender.

She was sporting what London dubbed a sexy librarian look that day: long, dark hair pulled up into a neat chignon, tortoise shell round glasses and a beige skirt suit. "London, I need shoes. You're free after work to go shoe shopping, then?" This was all said in one breath.

"Sure, I guess. And do you *need* shoes or do you just want shoes?" Lavender, she'd learned, was extreme about most things. And everything was urgent. But she was smart, quick on her feet, and funny as hell. While Aja didn't get most of her jokes and pop culture references, London could tell that Lavender impressed her cousin. Lavender was making great progress on the software development she'd been contracted to do and she was helping Aja by stepping in to manage the other contractors they worked with.

"Brilliant! Of course I don't *need* them." She mock rolled her eyes at London. "But I have a date this weekend and I'd like to have new shoes for it. So, you should come and keep me from maxing out my cards."

She needed this distraction from her pity party. "A date! Do tell. Where did you meet him?" London asked. "When would you even have time to meet anyone? You're always working."

Lavender had been working crazy hours to design the software Aja wanted. Through the company's internal collaboration tool, London could see when other colleagues were online and Lavender didn't ever seem to be offline.

"Well," she smirked. "he's a client."

London's smile dropped and Lavender quickly added. "Kidding! Too soon, right? Yeah, too soon. Sorry, my idea of a joke that clearly wasn't funny." Wincing, she moved on. "Anyway, I met him at the juice bar by my apartment while I was buying dinner the other night. Apparently, he's a workaholic as well, we were both trying to run in before they closed."

Lavender crossed a leg over, revealing black fishnet stockings. "He asked me where I wanted to go and I have no idea. I haven't really been out since I moved here and I asked him to pick. We're going to Ponce City Market, have you been there?"

London's shoulders slumped. She knew the location. Donovan had suggested going there once but they hadn't had a chance to go. At this point, she doubted they ever would as they weren't speaking outside of the required communication on the case.

She tried to perk up for Lavender's benefit. "That should be fun. There are shops and restaurants plus there's some sort of rooftop bar area that is supposed to be nice. I haven't been since I've been back."

"What's that look? It's not a good serial killer hunting ground, is it?" Lavender asked. Like the rest of the country,

Lavender loved obsessing over true crime podcasts with London and was convinced that most men were undercover serial killers.

Not wanting to unburden herself on her friend right now, London waved a dismissive hand. "Um, I doubt it. There will probably be tons of people there. Just make sure you send me a picture of him and his info so I can alert the authorities if you go missing." She looked down at her closed laptop. "You want me to run his name through our databases?"

Lavender rested her chin on her hand. "No, not yet. If the date goes well, maybe. I feel like looking him up now is cheating in a way since you already know the answers. That's like the best part of meeting someone new, sharing stories with each other, talking for hours, all of that. Until you find out he's a lying piece of shit, of course."

She looked at London over the rims of her glasses. "I've been thinking, your cousin must be so jaded by now, all of the dating gone wrong she's seen over the years since she started the company. I've only been here a couple of weeks and I now have zero desire to meet anyone online for anything. Is she seeing anyone?"

London frowned, thinking. "Not that I know of. I think my grandmother would have said something if she was. My grandmother knows all of the family's business." She was quite sure the woman had spies working for her but London haven't been able to prove it yet.

The phone on London's desk rang and Lavender rose. "I'll stop by on my way out and we can head over to Atlantic Station?"

Nodding, London checked the display on her phone. Lavender waved goodbye and closed the door behind her.

There was this little part of her, holding on to hope there would be a call this week and it would be *that* call.

The call from her ex, acknowledging they were supposed to exchange vows in front of friends and family, acknowledging he made a mistake and wanted to come back, acknowledging that he didn't know what he had until it was gone.

Not that she was planning to take him back, in the unlikely event that he would call, she just wanted the closure of having the last word.

And since she was wishing for things, she wanted the money back that he stole. The display however, let London know she was getting none of that, at least not at that moment. She sighed, getting a notepad and pen ready for the notes she'd need to take during Aja's call.

AFTER WORK AND IN THE MIDST OF TRYING ON SEVERAL pairs of shoes at Dillard's, London found herself telling Lavender the whole wretched Donovan story. As Lavender was the contract software admin, she was privy to the notes added to Donovan's newly reinstated contract and had likely put two and two together regarding the investigation.

London knew her friend probably didn't have all the details so she filled her in.

Lavender listened without judgment, periodically interrupting to ask London if she liked a certain shoe or telling her to try on a shoe she thought would look good on her. London had to admit, the woman had great taste.

"You should just show up at his house in these and that silver trench coat you have," she said, placing a box at London's feet.

They were sitting in a bank of chairs and London was trying on a pair of work appropriate flats which looked horrible on her. Kicking the sensible shoes off, she grasped the large box and took the lid off of a pair of killer over the knee boots.

London lifted a silver and cream snakeskin stiletto boot out of the box. "Ok, these are amazing," She turned the boot. "Yeah, I can hobble into the man's house in these. Look at that heel."

"London, please. Trust me, if all goes well, you'll only be in them long enough for him to pull you inside." Lavender lifted the other boot out of the box, then proceeded to take the tissue and cardboard used to maintain the boot's shape out of it. "Here, try it on."

"Then what? I go over there, seduce him, and he's all into me for the night. Then come Monday morning we're business associates again?"

She grunted as she slid the boot on, barely getting the top over her thigh after much struggle. Like most designer over the knee boots, they weren't big girl friendly.

Giving up, London pulled the boot off, chucking it back into the box. "He dumped me, remember?"

Lavender frowned at her. "Hmm, from what you've told me, I got the impression he's into you." She was next to London on the seat, stacking the shoes she'd tried on and found lacking. "What do you want, London?"

London wanted her happily ever after but didn't see that happening any time soon. "I want someone to love me for me. I thought maybe that could be him."

"Maybe, but if he's not the one, don't settle. You are amazing and deserve someone who realizes how amazing you are. He may come around. If not, we'll find you a replacement. You know, men are like a new pair of shoes, you just have to find a good one and break him in." All of this said while Lavender pulled out a spiked stiletto bootie and stuck her foot into it. "These babies are coming home with me." She put the mate on then did an impressive runway walk for London.

"Those are cute on you." London said, pushing the shoes she didn't want into her discard pile. "Seriously, what do I do? I need to let him go but I'm having a hard time."

"You have to distract yourself with other activities. Maybe get a good vibrator." Lavender took the boots off and put them next to her.

She peered at London over the glasses again, like she would glare at a student in trouble that she needed to lecture. "The grandmother thinks you're not good enough for him...is anyone good enough for him?"

"There was a woman at the singles event that she liked." London wanted to leave it at that. She couldn't bring herself to tell Lavender what Donovan's grandmother thought of her skin tone and weight. She would sympathize, but the tall, slender Lavender couldn't begin to relate. "She teaches Sunday School at their church." London played with a fingernail that was starting to chip, making the damage worse by peeling off more of the nail polish, refusing to look at Lavender

"Oh, so she's looking for some virginal church girl for him? Good luck with that. That is so not you."

She looked up sharply. "What? I can be virginal." Raising an eyebrow at her, Lavender said nothing. "Ok, maybe not," London conceded.

Lavender continued with her analysis. "Let me ask you this. What if his grandmother says it's either her or you and he chooses her? What would you do?"

This exact thought crossed London's mind more than she cared to admit. "What could I do? Nothing. I would have to understand, I guess. She did raise him and they are close. Grandmas before hoes I suppose."

Lavender raised her eyes to the ceiling. "Oh my God. I'm pretty sure that's not a thing. Did you see that on a t-shirt? And since when are you a ho?" She stood up, scooping up the shoes she intended to buy.

"Just remember," she said in a low voice. "There are plenty of things you bring to the table that his grandmother doesn't, and I'm not just talking sex. It's very clear to me you care about him. You and his grandmother have that in common. I think once she sees that, she will warm to you. He can't stay a grandma's boy forever." She patted London's shoulder. "You ready? I want to go to the perfume section, too."

London sat there, considering her words.

"Yep, I'm ready." London gathered up the pair of shoes she wanted and stood at the end of the line waiting to check out.

"Thanks for the distraction," she told Lavender as they approached the cashier. "I really needed one."

Lavender shifted the shoes onto her hip. "Honestly, I think we should head to Miami for the weekend and find ourselves some new talent. Act like we're twenty-five again. That will definitely take your mind off all of this."

*Miami.* A seed of an idea developed. She had never been that far south in Florida, but as London was thinking of the beach and sun and men in tiny swim trunks she had another immediate thought that took her away from the beach. Miami could hold answers to the case. Emmaline's new man was there, and there was apparently some tie to the deceased man's obituary Donovan found at his grandmother's house. The question was would Aja approve a trip to Miami?

✦

THE NEXT MORNING, LONDON WAS IN AJA'S OFFICE bright and early.

Early for her anyway. Aja sat there at her desk, arms crossed, thinking.

After she'd gotten home last night, London tossed her new shoes in the closet and immediately sat down in front of her laptop doing what she did best: research.

She wanted to make a strong case for a trip to Miami and knew Aja would ask her a million questions. She needed to prepare like she was going to try a case in the Supreme Court.

London looked up airfare and flight times, then planned her trip, and put together an itinerary that seemed reasonable.

If Aja approved the trip, London would leave Atlanta via an early flight on Friday, find out what she could all day then fly back on Saturday. She had priced out a few flight options plus hotel and car rental along with her plan for what she would be doing while she was there. She still had no idea who the mystery man, Mr. Miami, was, but Miami could have answers for her getting that much closer to finding out who and if he was catfishing Emmaline.

London was perched on the edge of the horrible chair, her back straight and hands crossed in her lap like she was in the principal's office. She watched Aja review her proposal and waited anxiously for her to say something.

The silence was unnerving.

Finally, Aja looked up. "Why do you think visiting this man will help? What if he won't talk to you?" she asked, her fingers crossed on her desk.

"Emmaline had that funeral program on her desk and she had been searching obituaries around that same date. I'm hoping that man's son will shed some light on the situation."

London crossed her fingers in her lap, mirroring her cousin's stance. She had read somewhere that this was a good negotiation tactic. "Maybe Emmaline contacted him to express condolences or maybe the son knows Emmaline. I do know the deceased man can't be Mr. Miami since he died in February, but there's a connection somewhere."

"Have you ruled out the son being Mr. Miami?" Aja asked. London shook her head slowly, staring at her cousin in disbelief. Aja shrugged. "Stranger things have happened."

The son of this deceased man being Emmaline's new beau hadn't occurred to London until that moment, but it did make sense. Since she had the messages they sent back and forth, it wouldn't be hard to verify. Assuming the man would talk to her.

She made a mental note to ask some qualifying questions when she talked to the subject. "All right. I'll either confirm or rule out the son and see what other info I can get from him, like if he knows Emmaline, and do some digging locally on the deceased man."

Aja sat back, tenting her fingers. London could tell her mind was working every angle, every possible scenario. She reminded London of a high-powered executive, deciding the fate of the family business which rested solely on her capable shoulders. Maybe she did watch too much television.

"If it turns out this man is the one she's been talking to, that will solve your case and you can wrap this one up," Aja said, looking at her screen. "But you don't think that's what you're going to find, do you?"

London shook her head. "No, that doesn't feel right. I think Mr. Miami has a teenaged grandson. This man doesn't seem like he's old enough to have a grandchild that old."

Aja nodded, and London saw that she was back in analytical mode, tuning the world out and running her scenarios.

After another long silence, Aja spoke. "Ok. Go to Miami and see what you can find. But I want you to be safe while you're there. Check in with me regularly and make sure we all know where you're staying. Where are you staying, anyway?" She squinted at the laptop screen.

London's proposed itinerary included a national chain hotel designed for the budget minded traveler.

Aja sighed, "And you don't have to stay at the Murder Inn. I'll get you a room with my reward points."

## ❧ 15 ❧

# DONOVAN

Donovan scanned the email from Exposé again, not believing what he saw. What did this mean? His first impulse was to call London immediately and see what was going on, but he thought maybe a text to gauge her temperature might be better. They hadn't talked in a while and he assumed she was still pissed at him for telling Aja she was in over her head. He was still trying to figure that one out. He typed a quick text and sent it, then decided he should get some work done.

**Donovan: What is this lead in Miami that you're pursuing?**

Before he could get back into the environment he was working on, his phone vibrated.

**London: Hello, Mr. Willis, I'm good, thanks for asking!**

Donovan ran a hand over his head. London was not going to make this easy, he realized. At least she was talking to him. Kind of.

**Donovan: Good afternoon, Ms. Lewis. Glad to hear**

**you're well. Wanna enlighten me on this lead you found in Miami?**

**London: Following up on intel you provided**

Donovan started to respond then threw caution to the wind and hit the phone icon. London picked up after what seemed like a dozen rings. "Mr. Willis, how can I help you?" she said in a perky, efficient office manager voice that shouldn't have been a turn on for him.

"You can send me your itinerary. I'm going to Miami with you," he said in a calm, conversational voice.

"What? Since when?" London sounded panicked.

"Yep. I'm going with you. Better yet, you have my card on file. You can book my travel and just email me the details." Donovan knew she was probably fit to be tied right about now.

"You can't just drop everything and go...what about your job?" London sputtered. "Why would you want to do this?" Her voice was high pitched.

"I told you I wanted to help. This is me helping," Donovan said, enjoying London's discomfort. "Should I clear this with Aja?" This was risky, Donovan knew, but there was a chance her cousin might get the wrong idea and London might suffer the consequences.

"Don't you have to work?" London asked again, calmer now.

"I have plenty of vacation days that I need to take." Which was true. He'd been too busy with his latest project to think about time off, but he would make time for this trip. "What's the issue? Why don't you want me to come?"

"I never said you couldn't come. It's fine. I'll tell Aja that you insisted on coming." She exhaled deeply. "And I'll book you on my flights. We leave early Friday morning and return on Saturday."

"Thanks. So, what are we doing in Miami?" Donovan fantasized for a moment that this was a romantic weekend getaway for the two of them where they'd have a lazy day on the beach, go dancing at one of the clubs, then spend a full day in bed, enjoying each other.

Speaking of bed, they hadn't discussed sleeping arrangements. Donovan assumed she would want separate rooms since they were in this professional *no touching* relationship. "And will you book me a room wherever you're staying?"

"We're following up on that lead you sent me on the obituary." He heard another line ring in the background. "Oh, this is a call I've been waiting on." London sounded a little breathless and the jealous caveman in him wanted to ask who the hell was calling. "Donovan, I'll make the arrangements and send them to you. I've got to go." London ended the call, not waiting for his response.

At least she wasn't calling him Mr. Willis.

Later that afternoon, Donovan got the itinerary email from London. The hotel she'd booked was a higher end chain with a location not far from South Beach. Donovan started to call her and see if she wanted to make a weekend of the trip and fly back on Sunday instead of Saturday but he didn't. Instead, he let his manager know that he would be out Thursday and Friday then started researching things to do in Miami.

*What was London's plan in Miami? Had she found the catfish? And what clue had she gotten from the obituary?* Against his better judgment, he was going to drop by London's office and get some answers. Despite what he said at the park, he wanted to see her.

When he arrived at London's office, she was already gone for the day, but Aja greeted him and led him to her office. Once they were seated, Aja asked if he wanted anything to drink. He declined and she got right to the point.

"I hear you're going to Miami as well?" Her expression revealed nothing of her true feelings on the matter, but Donovan felt he should tread lightly. Even though Aja was several inches shorter than him, he had to admit her intensity scared him just a bit.

"Yes, I'd like to stay in the loop of the investigation. I'm concerned this man has gotten too close to my grandmother," he said, eyeing Aja.

"Of course." Aja sat back in the sleek leather executive chair, her fingers tented. "I looked you up after you initially contacted me. I've learned to take what people tell me with a grain of salt and I am very selective with clients we choose to work with, so I do as much digging as I can before we agree to work with a client."

She paused, now Donovan felt like he was in the principal's office, waiting for his grandmother to come in. His stomach knotted as he waited for Aja to come to her point. "I could tell my cousin was taken by you as soon as you walked in and I understand that you two...connected," she said finally. "She's an adult, I'm aware, but she's family. And she's been through hell this year."

Donovan waited.

"Don't hurt my cousin," she said bluntly.

Donovan tilted his head, studying Aja. He wasn't going to get into details with Aja, especially when she had issues with London to address as well. "Not that it's any of my business, but have you forgiven her? She's been trying to atone for mistakes she made as a teenager and you seem to still be holding her to the past."

Aja's brow raised. "London told you about her ex?" Donovan nodded. "I'm surprised she's shared all the details with you. No one in the family knows the full story."

Donovan wasn't going to elaborate. That was London's story to tell.

"London wants to make you proud and she's trying to earn your love back. She said you two were like sisters up until that asshole came into the picture."

He wondered what he would do if he ever met the ex. For starters, a good punch in the face would work. "She regrets what she did, but she said you won't forgive her." Donovan put a foot on the opposite leg. "So have you forgiven her?"

Aja looked away, sighing. "I want to say this is none of your concern, but I forgave her a long time ago. I just didn't like seeing her with him, knowing she deserved better." She met Donovan's eyes again. "It was easier not to talk to her. I knew she wouldn't let anyone convince her to let him go."

"Well, no better time than now. She misses you." Donovan rose, ready to leave the office. While he appreciated that the Lewis family looked out for their own, he didn't want them to assume he was just like the last guy.

"I miss her too," Aja said softly. "I'm glad you decided to go with London to Miami." She was all business again. "Make sure she checks in with me once you get in. Take care of my cousin, please." Aja stood, walking over to open her office door.

Donovan nodded and strode out of the office.

❧

DONOVAN SAT ON THE PLANE, WATCHING FOR LONDON and eyeing the flight attendants. They were doing their prep for takeoff and London had yet to arrive.

Just as he resigned himself to flying alone and waiting for the next flight in from Atlanta, she appeared.

"I thought I was going to miss this flight for sure," she said, trying to catch her breath. Breathing a sigh of contentment, he got up so she could slide in and take the window seat. Their bodies brushed as she did and they looked at each other, awareness flowing between them. London plopped into the seat and spent considerable concentration on fixing her seat belt, avoiding his gaze.

Donovan took in all of her: the low bun she wore, which he now recognized as her "I mean business" look, the grey blazer over a white tee and dark jeans. The red lips. Those lips he dreamed about constantly. She smelled fresh from the shower, a combination of floral soap and a soft vanilla perfume. He was relieved she'd made the flight, but he was feeling something deeper. Yes, Donovan had missed her and he was also relieved she was there. Relieved that nothing had happened to her. His mind had gone to the worst scenarios thanks to crime shows, local news and horror movies.

"Hey. Glad you could join us this morning." Donovan played it cool, kept his hands to himself.

London turned to him. "You know where I was? Down in the security lines." Frustration radiated from her.

"Hey, it's ok. You're here now. You want a drink?" Eyebrows raised, he pointed to the attendant call button above them.

"What? No, it's not even 8am. I'm not that much of a lush." London eyed him. "You're awfully chill this morning."

"I'm glad you made the flight." He paused, cleared his throat. *What the hell.* "I've missed you."

London met his gaze. "Me too."

"I got the impression the last thing you wanted was to see me," he said, quietly. The safety video started and the flight crew went through their safety routine.

London waited until they were done to respond. "No. Of course not." She let out a short breath. "You, well, we still have to work together, so I'm adjusting to that." She turned to the window as the aircraft pulled away from the gate.

Donovan nodded. Not the time for this conversation. "So, what are we doing in Miami today?" He knew this should have been something he'd learned before jumping on a plane with London, but he figured he'd lived a fairly safe life for thirty-five years, maybe it was time to shake things up a bit.

"I'm going to see a man who works for the feds," London said, pulling the airline magazine from the seat pocket in front of her.

"FBI agent?" Donovan asked, raising his voice in surprise.

"No," London chuckled, "not quite." She flipped through the magazine. "I'm going to visit one of the resident inmates."

Yep, he should have done a little more digging. "Who is this? Not your ex, is it?"

London side eyed him and Donovan knew he'd said the wrong thing. "Really? There is no way in hell Aja would authorize a trip to see my ex."

"Ok, well, who are we going to see?"

"I think I'll get more answers from him if you're not there. Besides, you're not on the visitor's list. I had to get clearance to visit before I left," she said, intent on the article she was reading.

"More answers from who?"

She sighed and put the magazine down on her lap. "That funeral program you found at your grandmother's house, remember that? I googled the deceased man, but I didn't really find anything to tie him to your grandmother. He had one surviving son listed and when I researched him, I found out he's in prison. There's a chance he's the man she's been talking to but..."

Donovan cut her off. "What? Why didn't you say something before now?"

"Because I am 90% sure he's not the guy we're looking for, but he may have info on that man. There's a reason your grandmother kept that obituary."

"Why don't you think it's him? Prisoners get to call people. And he could have smuggled a phone in."

"True, but Mr. Miami has talked about his grandkids with Ms. Emma. Unless this man started having kids at twelve and his kids had kids at twelve, there's no way he's old enough to have a teenaged grandchild. He's maybe forty, give or take a couple of years."

"Ok, so what do you think he knows? And what did you tell him about your visit?"

London avoided eye contact. "I might have led him to believe that Exposé was linked to the TV show."

Donovan was intrigued. "Oh, that show that busts catfish on the air? How did you do that?" Not that he was surprised. London had a voice made for late night party lines. She could put a man under a spell reading a dictionary.

"He asked if I was actually on the show and I told him I worked behind the scenes doing the research. I never said I was doing research for the show. He thinks one of the women who has been writing him might be a catfish."

"Are you taking his case, too?" Donovan asked, his brows furrowed. "Like pro bono work?"

"I don't know yet. I was going to cross that bridge when I got to it. I guess if he gives me some worthwhile info, I could look into his pen pal for him."

"You could create a spinoff! And call it Catfish – Prison Edition. I think your cousin would go for it." He cracked and London gave him another scathing side-eye.

"It's way too early for all these bright ideas you've got. What are you going to do while I'm at the prison?"

"I'll take you over there and wait in the car. I'm supposed to take good care of you." He stopped, realizing he'd revealed too much. "Did you want to stop at the hotel first or go straight there?" Donovan asked quickly, hoping to distract her from probing into his last statement.

London pounced. "Where did that come from? You taking good care of me?" she asked, looking directly at him with her arms crossed. Not that he liked irritating her, but she was sexy when she was annoyed. Her mouth did this pout thing that was a total turn on.

"You don't want to be taken care of?" he asked, deliberately misunderstanding her question.

"Not the point. You said 'supposed to' as if someone told you to do it." London was glaring at him now, waiting for an answer.

Donovan imagined if there was room, she'd be tapping her foot impatiently. Just then, a flight attendant stopped by with the beverage cart and asked what they wanted.

"Are you sure you don't want a drink?" Donovan asked, then told the flight attendant, "I'll take a Coke." The flight attendant nodded at Donovan then looked at London expectantly.

London uncrossed her arms and pulled her tray table down. "Um, no, thanks, I'll just have water with lots of ice."

After they received their drinks, Donovan heard a loud crunch as London attacked the ice in the cup. Once the first piece was gone, she used her tongue to coax another ice chip into her mouth and crunched that one too.

"Crunching ice is supposed to be a sign of sexual frustration." Donovan leaned over and said close to her ear.

"Actually, that's a myth," London said, taking the abandoned magazine from her lap and resuming the story she was reading. She turned the cup up to get another ice cube and crunched it louder.

"You're going to give yourself a brain freeze," Donovan said, wishing they were already in the hotel. They had separate rooms and he wondered briefly if there was an adjoining door.

He fantasized about leaving the adjoining door unlocked and looking up to find London standing there in his room, wearing nothing but the red lip stuff. He pushed the thought away. Maybe he should be the one eating ice.

"Was it my father?" London asked finally, sipping the last of the water in her cup.

"You should let this go. Just be glad you have family looking out for you," Donovan said, pulling his earbuds out of his backpack.

"I take it you're not going to tell me." Donovan could tell she was itching to know.

"Nope." Donovan slouched down in his seat and folded his arms over his chest, hoping to get a quick nap in before the flight landed.

"I'll let you sleep, but the reason I ask is because my family has never really let me grow up. I don't think they trust that I know what's best for me. Then again, maybe they're right and I don't. My decisions thus far haven't been the best." London was staring straight ahead. "I keep waiting for them to say 'we told you so' since I've moved back."

Donovan had the ear buds in but hadn't put on music, so he heard every word of London's confession. He removed the ear buds and turned to her. "Seems to me you were doing fine in DC for years. Was your ex supporting you?"

London snorted softly. "Please. No, it was the other way around. The place we lived in was in my name and I paid most of the bills." Donovan reaffirmed London's ex was a piece of work. He should have been treating her like a queen for putting up with him and supporting him.

"Again, you're better off without him. Since he wasn't supporting you, you managed to buy a property, pay your bills and keep a job, all without your family's help." Donovan continued. "You did all of that once, you can do it again. This is just a minor setback."

"But I couldn't find a job on my own once I got back. I had to have my cousin hire me," London admitted. "I searched for months and didn't get past the first interview."

"Sometimes it takes longer to find a job here. I think Atlanta is a more competitive market for IT than DC. In any case, you are where you're supposed to be, doing what you're supposed to do right now. And we wouldn't have met if your cousin hadn't hired you."

Donovan watched London consider his words. "Thank you for reminding me of that," she said finally. "I just want to show my family that I'm ok. And I want to help Aja succeed like she's helped me. Maybe then she'll be my big sister again."

Donovan heard all the pain London had carried around all this time. His heart broke for her and he vowed to make sure she got what she needed on this trip and beyond.

## 16

# LONDON

couple outside the window of the busy restaurant she'd chosen based on Aja's recommendation caught London's eye. As soon as the low-slung sports car pulled into the parking spot in front of the entrance, a woman dressed in black jumped out of the passenger seat, slamming the door with enough force to shake the car. The driver opened his door and yelled something which made the woman stop dead in her tracks and respond.

The words, even though London couldn't hear them, were like a grenade thrown into the car. Whatever she said made the man decide not to exit the car. He sat in the car, brooding, while the woman stomped into the side entrance of the restaurant. She looked like she was on the brink of tears but she shook off the anger, and prepared to start her shift. London turned back toward the parking lot to see the man start the engine, throw the car in reverse nearly sideswiping an incoming minivan, and speed off.

London wondered how long they had been together, how long before the newness wore off and the messiness began, where words were tossed with full intent to hurt the person you professed to love. Yet another reason to keep her distance from

Donovan. They would probably just end up like that couple after a few months.

Donovan strode back to the table from the men's room. He was smiling at London, ever present gap showing, making London forget her internal declaration made seconds ago. She marveled at him; he looked like he was born in Miami. He wore a short sleeved white button-down shirt and a pair of jeans that were professionally treated to look like they'd been worn for decades. If he were a woman, London would describe the jeans as curve hugging, but that struck her as wrong for a man. He was more angular than curvy, she decided, then wondered why she was having these random thoughts.

Because it kept her from acknowledging how much she missed him. He admitted on the plane that he missed her, which warmed London's entire being, even though she knew he probably missed her like one misses their favorite coworker when they take a week off for vacation.

London, on the other hand, felt like curling up in his lap like a puppy once she saw him.

What was wrong with her? She hadn't really pined over her ex this hard. Yes, there was that bout of desolation she felt right after Derrick left, but in retrospect, London concluded that she missed the routine they'd established in their many years together.

A few months earlier, she'd felt like a limb had been severed when Derrick left, but Donovan's absence had her feeling like her whole world was off center. And now, with one crooked smile thrown her way, London's world was set right again.

"Do you know what you want? I can call the server over."

Right. Back to reality where they were only friends. "I haven't had a chance to look at the menu."

"Aren't you starving? I know I am."

She settled on an egg white omelet with garden veggies and a cup of hot tea. They placed their orders and surrendered the menus.

Donovan focused on London. "Ok, what did you find out?

You were in there so long I thought they'd decided to keep you locked up." He flashed the smile she craved and willed her heart to maintain its composure. Ignoring her, it fluttered shamelessly.

"I don't even know where to start," London said. "First off, he's not your future step grandfather." Donovan pursed his lips at her. She grinned, putting her hands up, palms facing him. "Ok, ok, I'm only kidding."

Their server dropped off a small kettle of hot water and a box of teas for London to choose from along with a glass of orange juice for Donovan. "You're sure he's not the one on SilverandSexy.com?"

She nodded while preparing her tea. "I asked him if he had ever been on the Silver and Sexy site and he thought it was a joke. He also claims he has never heard of your grandmother and I'm leaning toward believing him."

Taking a sip of his orange juice, Donovan asked, "What's he in jail for, anyway? Did he tell you?"

"Oh yeah, the guy couldn't wait to tell me. He was a software developer and he got passed over for a promotion at this Silicon Valley firm so he decided to sell trade secrets to a competitor." London took a tentative sip of the super hot tea. "He got caught. Now he's trying to get a book deal...he asked if I would film a documentary about him."

Donovan smirked. "Maybe you should."

"Um, I already feel like I need a couple of showers to wash off the prison fumes, but he also insisted on calling me Stallion." She held up a hand. "Do not ask why. We shall not speak of it ever again."

He eyed London with a smirk that said he knew why the man had given her the moniker. "What about his dad?"

"Here's what I found out. His dad was a bigamist. The name in the obituary, John Lister, wasn't his real name. When his wife, the mother, found out about the other family, she divorced him and moved to Arizona with Mr. Trade Secret there."

London paused while the server dropped off the plates. She

breathed in the scent of the spiced warm butter and maple syrup drizzled over Donovan's French toast. Suddenly her sensible veggie omelet didn't seem so appetizing now. *God, she missed carbs.*

She concentrated on her food. "I also asked if he or his mother had ever lived in Atlanta or any other part of Georgia. He told me they hadn't but he knew his dad had at some point because he mentioned places in Atlanta that he liked. Now that he's in prison here, his mother has moved back to be closer to him and the rest of her family. He told her we would be calling and she's willing to talk to us."

"I remember you saying that there was very little info on John Lister online when you searched."

London nodded, "Yeah, the little bit I found wasn't useful, but that makes sense now that I know the name is fake."

Initially when he'd bullied his way into coming on this trip, she'd been panicked and annoyed, assuming he decided to tag along just to piss her off by second guessing her plans, but he was turning out to be a good sounding board and traveling companion. She just wished she could stop longing for more from him. "I also got information on the other family. The dad went by Jonathan Werner and the Werners lived in Ft. Lauderdale."

Donovan's eyes got big and he dropped his fork onto his plate. "What? Damn, you're good, you got him to spill all the tea. Does the other family know about him?"

London shrugged, acting like this was all no big deal, but inside she was turning cartwheels. More validation that she was good at what she did.

"No idea. He's one of us, a pro with a keyboard, so you know he found ways to cyber stalk the family once his mom told him everything. I think that's why he moved back to Florida once he was grown; he was trying to be close to his dad."

"Makes sense. You looked up his mother yet? What's her name?" Donovan asked as he shoved pieces of French toast around his plate sopping up the syrup. He glanced up. London couldn't help staring longingly at his plate. "Here, taste a piece... It's amazing." He stabbed a bite sized piece of toast and held the fork out so London could eat it.

London closed her eyes, savoring the small bite of heaven. She caught herself before she moaned, recalling the last time she'd done that in front of Donovan. *Keep things professional.*

"She goes by Gena Dawes now. She dropped Lister when they got divorced. I'm going to do a deep dive in a minute."

Once she was done with her meal, London pulled her makeup bag out of her purse to reapply her lip gloss. She started to say something to Donovan about the family, but when she glanced at him, he was staring at her mouth like she'd been staring at his French toast moments ago.

He slowly dragged his gaze up to hers, the raw desire she saw mirrored her own. They were both still communicating volumes without speaking. This was madness, London realized, but she didn't move. *Damn that no touching rule.* She wanted him to touch her, and she wanted to touch him everywhere.

Finally, Donovan spoke. "I love that color. It's perfect for those perfect lips."

"Thank you." She finished applying the gloss quickly, self-conscious now, assuming he and the world around them could see her feelings for Donovan sketched all over her face.

She tried to compose herself, get her hormones under control. "I should, uh, get my laptop out." London stammered like a politician caught in a lie.

"Did I break your concentration?" Donovan asked, flashing a devilish grin.

London rolled her eyes. He knew full well that he did.

"Because mine has been gone since you brushed against me on the plane this morning." His eyes met hers, heating her insides with the intensity of his gaze. She had no idea such a simple gesture could be so damn sensual.

She cleared her throat, suddenly dry, and struggled to find her voice. "We were having a productive morning and you're sabotaging it."

London couldn't focus. As much as she tried to put thoughts of Donovan out of her mind all of the time, now that he was right in front of her saying things to break her resolve, this was going to be the longest trip of her life.

She had to remember he was off limits. "I'd call your grandmother but I don't think that's a great idea."

"No, don't call her. She thinks I'm here on business." He leaned in, his voice low, "There was a part of me that hoped the dude you went to see was my grandmother's friend. That would mean the case was resolved and I could spend the rest of this trip exploring Miami then later on, I could explore all of your weak spots."

"My weak spots aren't the topic of conversation right now," is what she should have said. Instead, London sat there being seduced by his words.

"What if Mr. Miami is legit? Don't you want your grandmother to find love again?" she asked, trying to focus on something else.

"Of course. If he's the real thing, I wish her all the happiness in the world. I just wonder why she's keeping him under wraps."

"We'll figure it out," she said with more confidence than she felt.

Pulling her laptop out, London began searching for Gena Dawes in Florida. There were several she could eliminate right off the bat because they were too young or deceased. She found a Facebook page for Gena. As she scrolled through Gena's page, she knew she was doing her job but she still felt uneasy, like she was stalking her prey. She had to remind herself that social media users willingly shared details of their lives, but she often wondered if they really understood how easy it was for total strangers to piece together these details and use them for harm.

London and Donovan were at a table that could accommodate four people and Donovan was sitting across from London. "You find anything?" he asked, then switched to the seat beside her so he could see her screen. He leaned close and she silently breathed in his familiar warm scent—the scent evoked all the memories of their time together that she had tried in vain to suppress since he decided they weren't to be.

"Yep," she pointed at the screen. "This is John Lister's ex-wife."

"Did you talk to her already?"

"No, I'm going to call her in a second. I'm not sure what to say. Our visit is probably going to bring up bad memories for her."

Turns out they needn't have worried about bringing up bad memories for Gena Dawes. She was happy to have them stop by. Her son had told her he might make it on the television show and that London would help him find out who was catfishing him. She gave London her address and told her to come by whenever they could.

❦

AN HOUR LATER, THEY WERE SITTING IN THE WOMAN'S living room. Gena Dawes was a tall Bohemian dream. She wore a black tank top paired with a patchwork maxi skirt. Her nose was pierced and her silver hair snaked down her back in a long braid. The house was tidy and small but comfortable and reflected Gena's obvious love of bold colors and patterns. She brought out glasses of iced tea for the three of them, then sat across from London on a chaise with her legs tucked under her. "So, you find people who are catfishing others, my son tells me."

London nodded. "Yes, but we're not affiliated with the TV show. We cater to clients who prefer discretion in these matters."

Gena pursed her lips. "I didn't think he was going to be on TV. He's been trying to get somebody to make a documentary of his story, and I keep telling him he needs to keep his head down and just work on finishing out his sentence. He's only got a couple more years."

London recognized that universal 'I know what's best for you' tone that parents worldwide used. Her father wielded that tone like a sword.

"Actually, I know this may be a sore subject, but I was hoping you could tell us more about your ex-husband. My condolences to your family," she added quickly, not wanting to be an insensitive guest.

"Thank you," Gena said after a slight roll of her eyes. "He's not been my family for a long time. I assume you know that he was married to someone else while we were married?" She eyed them both. As they nodded, she continued. "Yes, so that coupled with that other mess they say he was the mastermind of, I stayed clear."

She sat back and settled into her story. "I was so angry for a while. Years. Here I was thinking he was working hard to take care of me and our son, and I found out he was working hard juggling two families. I was also afraid that something was wrong with me. I had done everything I thought good wives were supposed to do, cooked, cleaned, gave him a son, why wasn't it enough for him? But I learned I needed to let that anger go. And I learned you can give someone you love everything you got and it's never enough if they don't love themselves. John, or whatever his name was, was going to have that other family no matter what I did."

Gena leaned in and spoke to London directly. "Don't let a man, or woman for that matter, love who you want, I say, steal the love you have for yourself away." She turned to Donovan. "And you," she tilted her head toward London, "make sure you show her you love her more than once a year on Valentine's Day."

London's mouth dropped and she quickly jumped in. "Oh, we're not, it's...he's my client," she managed to stutter.

"Huh," she said, clearly not buying it. "You could have fooled me." Gena studied London long enough to make her squirm internally. "Well, I suppose you'll figure things out sooner or later."

London looked over at Donovan, who winked at her but said

nothing. She frowned, distracted by the older woman's words. She needed to get back into interview mode. "Ms. Dawes, you just mentioned some mess that your ex was involved in?"

"Call me Gena, please. Yeah, it was a while ago; we had been divorced for about five years and this big story broke out in the news about this man in Atlanta claiming to be a financial advisor stealing money from this church by running a Ponzi scheme. The man looked just like John but he went by a different name. I couldn't believe it. They were saying John was the mastermind, but the John I knew was bad with numbers. I managed the money for the household, but they said he stole millions." Gena shook her head, like she still couldn't believe the story.

Donovan asked, "Do you know if he was living in Atlanta at that time?"

Gena shook her head. "I don't really know. Once we moved out of the state, John barely called his son. Then he'd call from jail but he was serving time in Florida." Gena seemed to notice the iced tea for the first time and took a long swig from her glass. "He came to Arizona once to see his son before he went to jail."

London had another question. "Does the name Emmaline Roberson ring a bell? She lives in Atlanta."

Gena paused, thinking. "No, sure doesn't. I don't know anybody who lives in Atlanta. Why all the interest in my ex and what does that have to do with Atlanta?" Gena asked London.

Donovan spoke before London could get her thoughts together. "I am looking into this man my grandmother, Emmaline Roberson, is dating to see if he's a catfish. She had a copy of the obituary for your ex on her desk. We thought maybe your son was corresponding with her but he's not. We're trying to figure out the connection between them."

Gena uncurled herself from the chair. "Wait, Roberson? No 'T' right?" Not waiting for a response, she pushed herself up and left the room.

Donovan looked at London, his eyebrows raised, like she had

a clue what was going on. She raised her shoulders indicating his guess was as good as hers.

She took the time to let her eyes wander around the room. She loved Gena's taste. The house, full of things she could tell were placed with thoughtfulness, didn't reflect a designer's touch where no detail was spared, but instead reflected an artist's touch. The art on the walls might have been a local's originals. The room was done in black and white with touches of jewel tones: a black and white rug under a blue leather sofa with rose and magenta throw pillows.

When Gena padded back into the room, she was carrying a pocket-sized leather notebook and she had a pair of reading glasses perched on her head. She slid the glasses on and flipped through the pages. "I told you that John came to see his son once. Well, he left this book with me. Told me to put it somewhere safe and don't let anyone know I had it." She found the page she was looking for. "Of course, I flipped through it after he left and since it didn't make sense to me, I threw it into a drawer and forgot about it. I do recall thinking about the name Roberson and wondering if he'd misspelled it. I'd never heard the name before."

Gena, standing above them, turned the book toward them so they could see it. "There," she said pointing to a name, "See, there's a Roberson in here."

Donovan looked at the book in amazement. "That's my grandfather."

Gena and London both looked at the name and then at Donovan. "Nate Roberson was married to my grandmother. What is this book?" he asked.

The book looked a lot like what London discovered on Emmaline's computer. "Looks like a ledger to me. Each person's name has some numbers by it," she said, feeling like she was stating the obvious.

Donovan ran his finger across the numbers. "I think it is a ledger. These look like payments."

"There are a few pages with names on them. After I saw all

that stuff on the news about him, I expected the police to come knocking on my door looking for this, but no one ever came and I put it back in the drawer," Gena said, then a thought occurred to her. "Were your grandparents victims of his scam?"

"My grandmother told me they lost a lot of money when they first got married, but she never went into much detail," Donovan said thoughtfully.

London continued to look at the names in the ledger. None were familiar to her but she definitely wanted to search each name when she got back in front of her laptop. She also wanted to know more about John Lister.

"Gena," she asked, turning toward the woman, "Do you remember the name John went by when he got caught?"

"Yeah, I do. You all can take that ledger with you, by the way. I remember because it was like a variation of my name and I thought, 'that SOB couldn't even be bothered to come up with an original fake name.' He went by Gerald Dawson. He played everyone."

❧

LATER, AFTER CHECKING INTO THEIR HOTEL AND schlepping down a long hallway, London stopped at her door, fumbling to pull her room key out of its holder while holding her suitcase and tote. She glanced up when Donovan, standing in front of the room next to hers, spoke. "We have plans tonight. Can you be ready by seven o'clock?"

*Plans?* Her tote tumbled off her shoulder and London dropped the key card in her hands. "What kind of plans? I was going to spend the evening verifying the info Gena gave us. Where are we going?"

She let go of her suitcase handle and bent to retrieve the key card. She needed to get her nerves under control.

"Here, let me get that for you." Donovan rushed over to open her door. She passed him the card, careful not to let their hands touch.

He watched her with a look in his eyes that she couldn't read. The door panel lit up green and he pushed the door open then reached around London to take her bag inside the room.

London watched him enter her room and hesitated. They didn't need to be so close to each other in such a romantic setting. She didn't, anyway. She was still trying to convince herself they could maintain a professional relationship, but the temptation was real. And if he kept staring at her like he wanted to slowly strip her bare, she was going to do something foolish. Like let him.

Pushing those thoughts aside, she straightened her back and entered the room.

Aja had booked her a suite with a king-sized bed and a balcony. London took in the spacious room, done in signature Miami Art Deco style. Just inside the door was a kitchenette that she strode past to take in the view from the balcony. They were on a high floor and London could see the expanse of the ocean. She slid the patio door open and walked out, then beckoned to Donovan to join her. "This is amazing!"

She stood at the railing, watching the waves roll in. Donovan walked up beside her, placing his elbows on the railing. "I see why you all charge so much," he said, giving her a sidelong glance. "This would be a nice getaway trip if you weren't working."

Yep, she was thankful their trip was for one night only. Resisting the urge to pull him back inside onto the giant bed would take all of her strength. *Focus, London.* "Where are we going tonight? What do I need to wear?"

She could tell his thoughts mirrored hers by the way Donovan's eyes swept over her body. "Right. It's a surprise. But something for a nice night out. Or," he said casually, "we could stay in...find a way to entertain ourselves."

London backed away from the railing like that would keep her from touching him. Too tempting. "Ok then. That doesn't give me much to work with on what I should wear, but I'll be ready by seven. And I'm kicking you out."

He grinned at her. "Can't resist all this, right?"

She strode to the door, holding it open. "See you at seven."

Seven o'clock found London rushing around to put the final touches on her look. She brought a retro swirled maxi dress that had been tossed into her bag at the last second as a just in case piece which she paired with heeled brown sandals. A matching head scarf, her favorite hoops and frosty eye makeup completed her 70's vibe look.

Donovan rapped twice on the door as she was stuffing essentials into a little purse that could be worn across her body.

London snapped the purse closed and slipped it over her head, wondering again where they were going. Clubbing? Donovan had never mentioned being the nightclub type but this was Miami and the night was young. She didn't care for the club scene. Too loud, too crowded, too much. But if that's what he wanted to do, she'd try to make the best of it.

She opened the door, stepping aside so he could enter.

Reflecting on his comment earlier about a getaway trip, she let herself fantasize for a moment that she wasn't working and they were a couple on vacation. They looked the part. Donovan wore a black button down and khakis with dressy black loafers. Resisting an urge to lick her lips at the sight of him, London was seconds away from suggesting he meet her in the oversized rainfall shower so they could lather each other up.

"You ready?" he said before she could form the words.

She glanced at him and saw the anticipation in his eyes of whatever he'd planned. He reminded her of a kid getting his first gaming system. London sighed. She hoped whatever they did wouldn't cause them to be out until the wee hours of the morning. She was beat from getting up so early to catch the flight.

Gazing longingly at the bed and her fuzzy socks, she nodded. "Let's go check out Miami."

During the drive, Donovan was quiet, which made London nervous.

"So have you been here before?" she blurted, stroking her gold leaf earrings. "I've never been this far south."

"Yeah, we did a family cruise from here once when I was in high school. I didn't get to see much though. We came in the night before the cruise and boarded the ship the next day."

"Oh yeah, how was the cruise?"

"I got seasick and spent most of it in bed watching TV."

"Oh. That sucks." London guessed anything to do with a boat wasn't on the itinerary for the evening.

He nodded and London turned to look out of the window. She didn't understand where the awkwardness between them was coming from. Even though they were keeping things professional, they usually had no problems talking to each other.

Maybe he regretted coming along. She hadn't asked him to come, that was all his idea so he shouldn't take his bad decision out on her. The evening would be long and painful if this car ride was any indication of the future.

Wearing her fuzzy socks and watching bad reality tv, London's initial plan for her Friday evening, seemed like heaven right then.

They pulled into a parking garage, pulling London's attention away from her musings.

She stared, incredulous.

They were at a science museum and judging by the size of the garage and number of cars parked, the place was popular on Friday nights.

She gawked, barely able to contain herself. "This is the surprise? A night at the science museum?"

Donovan maneuvered into a parking spot and killed the engine. "Yeah, unless you'd rather do something else?"

London shook her head, grinning and bouncing in her seat. "Nope. Let's go!"

Donovan held up his phone. "Wait, LL, I need to pull up the tickets."

London scanned the entrance, her eyes landing on a poster advertising a special exhibit. Lord, if she wasn't careful, this man was going to make her believe in love again. She beamed, unable to contain her excitement.

He was taking her to see dinosaurs! She should just toss her panties his way now.

Hopping out of the car, London ran over to the driver's side and taking his hand, practically dragged him out of the car. "Come on!"

He laughed at her but to her surprise, he didn't release her hand once he'd locked the car and they strode toward the entrance. Instead of trying to decipher the meaning, London squashed her inner overthinker so she could enjoy the moment.

Every second of the museum trip amazed her. There was a light and music show in the planetarium and she saw a 3D dinosaur movie that gave her chills and had her clutching Donovan's arm in awe. The evening was perfect and she had Donovan to thank for it.

Later, as they rode in the elevator up toward their rooms, they were silent, each staring forward. London wondered what Donovan was thinking. Her stomach was knotted in anticipation and she wasn't sure why. There were no promises of anything happening tonight. They could part ways at the elevator and that would be that.

Except she wasn't sure she was ready to leave him for the evening. They'd spend most of the day together and it still wasn't enough. Would she be bold tonight? Knock on his door and show him how much she longed for him?

London turned to Donovan. "Thank you so much for the evening. I had a wonderful time."

He smiled, studying her. "You could be a unicorn," he said after a few minutes.

London's eyebrows rose.

"You're probably one of the sexiest, most down to earth women I've ever met, and I'm willing to bet money you would take a night at a museum over an expensive dinner and a VIP club experience, wouldn't you?"

She reluctantly lifted a shoulder, wondering where he was going with his question. "Yeah? I mean, I guess a night like that would have been ok, but come on, you can't tell me the laser show wasn't incredible! They don't usually do those in the VIP section at the club."

He grinned at her. "No, they don't, and yes, I have to admit I enjoyed the museum." He turned serious again. "Mainly because you were so into it. I don't know what it is, but I just wanted to do something to put that smile on your face."

The elevator stopped and an elderly couple shuffled on, nodding at them in greeting before realizing they needed to go down instead of up. Donovan quickly slapped the 'open' button before the elevator started its ascent and held the door as the couple exited.

They were alone again. London watched Donovan as the elevator ascended. He called her sexy. Did he have any idea how much she wanted him? How sexy she found him right now?

She tucked her bottom lip in, refusing to overthink then snaked a hand up his chest around his neck, pulling him toward her. Their lips met and London felt the heat from the embrace surge through her. Donovan pressed her against the back of the elevator, taking possession of her mouth with deliberate slowness. London circled both arms around his neck, pulling him closer, arching against him as if she could merge their bodies into one unit.

Donovan's hands held her waist then cupped her ass. "Too much fabric," he muttered, releasing her mouth and grabbing a handful of her dress.

She chuckled. "It's supposed to have a lot...it's a maxi dress."

"Well, I guess we'll see about that."

The elevator doors slid soundlessly open and they stopped in front of London's door.

Donovan gave her a sidelong glance. "Which room first?"

London scowled. "What do you mean?" She was ready to strip him and he was asking about her room preference?

He shrugged. "I mean, we've got access to two beds and I'm not sleeping without you tonight so which bed first?"

There was no way she was resisting this man's charm this evening. "My room's closer." She held up her room key.

As soon as the door closed behind them, Donovan turned toward London. "You're aware you lost the bet, right? So I get to choose what happens tonight."

"Um, that kiss in the elevator doesn't count," she said, kicking off her sandals and glancing around the softly lit space.

Now that they were alone together with no restrictions, London was unable to stand still. She grabbed her sandals, tossing them back into her suitcase.

He held up his hand, one finger extended. "You grabbed my hand when we parked at the museum. Another finger went up. "You grabbed my arm a few times during the movie, but I'll just count that as one, and," he held up another finger, "during the light show."

*Huh.* London frowned, thinking about their evening. She didn't remember making a conscious effort. Maybe he wasn't the only touchy feely one in the room. Suddenly vulnerable, she tried to deflect. "You tracking that with an app?"

"Nope. I'm thinking there's some hyperawareness where you're concerned," he started toward her, "and you could step into Truist Stadium during the World Series and I'd know you were there."

If the opposite was true, would she know? Her hand hovered over the pajamas in her suitcase. Should she take them out? If all went well, she wouldn't need them.

"What do you want to happen tonight, London?" Donovan asked, as if he knew exactly what she was thinking.

Was it just her or was that a loaded question?

*I want you to cherish and love me like I'm the only woman in the world for you.*

"I want to pretend we met at the museum tonight. Maybe we're both here on business and we decided that what happens in Miami..." London abandoned the suitcase, turning to watch him in the mirrored wall behind the king bed.

Donovan walked up behind her, slid his arms around her waist and met her eyes in the mirror. "So, I just met you and you've already convinced me to come to your room?"

"Yep. We talked for a while, had a lot in common, the vibe was there and we figured, why not, so here we are...hey, I'm trying to set the mood and you're distracting me." She watched him run his hands over her thighs while he nibbled on her neck. Her legs quivered then parted ever so slightly.

"Go on, I'm listening," he said, moving his hands up to her breasts. Her nipples responded shamelessly under his large hands.

"Seems like your halter thing is too tight so I'm just gonna loosen it up." Donovan's voice in her ear made her want to moan.

She felt the tie at the back of her neck holding her dress up unravel.

"Finish your story," Donovan said as he tugged the zipper in the middle of her back down. With nothing holding it up, the maxi dress slid silently to the floor.

"Where was I?" London asked, trying to concentrate while he rubbed his thumbs over her nipples through the strapless, backless bra she wore. London leaned back pushing her body flush against his solid form. The curtains were still open and she glanced at the terrace where the city below glittered in the night sky. She stepped out of his embrace and tugged the curtains closed.

He pulled her back. "The part where I'm fantasizing about your mouth on me as you talk about dinosaurs and you think I'm the smartest, sexiest brother you've ever laid eyes on."

She chuckled. Donovan had to be the only person she knew

who could make her roll her eyes and want to toss her panties at him with one sentence.

"So." London turned around, facing him. "You won the bet. Where...?" Starting at his waist, she ran her palms up his chest intent on unbuttoning his shirt.

"Um hmm...keep going." Once the shirt was open, he tugged it out of his pants and let it fall to the floor.

London ran her hands over the expanse of his broad muscled chest, down the happy trail. His abs tensed under her touch.

"Turn around," he said in her ear. "I want to watch you in the mirror."

Against her better judgment, she turned, her back to him, facing the mirrored wall. London wasn't eager to see her physical flaws, the stretch marks, the loose skin where she'd lost weight, the back roll that wouldn't seem to budge despite her strenuous workouts. She realized Donovan was speaking.

"Damn, you're beautiful..." She felt the clasp of her bra give way, and strong hands cupped her breasts, pressing her against him. She could feel a powerful erection against her back and thanked the heavens for sending him her way.

Donovan nibbled at her neck as he slid his hands down her waist then hooked his fingers through her panties, causing her to throb in anticipation of his touch on her most sensitive spots.

He spread her lips, probing, caressing, stroking and London caught a glimpse of herself. The woman in the mirror was sexy, brazen and desired. She spread her legs, giving him more access and rubbed against his length, wanting to drive him as crazy as he was driving her.

Before dropping his pants, Donovan took a condom from his pocket and slid it on. London rubbed her ass against him, bending so he could enter from the back. She placed her hands on the bed to steady herself, watching as he slid into her. She was slick, ready to receive as he thrust, getting deeper each time.

He felt better than she imagined, she was on the brink of her release, his hands gripping her hips, allowing him to hit her spot...

just right. She couldn't focus on anything but the waves of pleasure flowing through her.

She cried out, her body shuddering as he thrust faster, pushing her over the edge.

Their eyes met in the mirror again.

*What happens in Miami...*

# 17

# LONDON

Acouple of weeks after the fact-finding mission to Miami, London paced nervously around her room, checking the mirror above her dresser for the tenth time, then swearing she wouldn't look again.

Every time she studied her reflection, she found another flaw that stressed her. She didn't think her wig was straight. Maybe the feather was too loud, she should take it off. Then she felt like the costume was too plain without the feather headpiece and plopped it back on over the wig she wore.

She decided to sit at her desk. She was waiting for Donovan to pick her up for his grandmother's Halloween party tonight where London would be meeting his family for the first time.

He told her when he'd asked a week ago that his grandmother encouraged him to invite London, assuring Donovan she wanted to make amends as they had 'gotten off on the wrong foot' as she'd put it. London was trying not to be cynical about the whole thing. If Emmaline was willing to extend the olive branch, she supposed she'd take it.

London's costume was inspired by a trip to the thrift store where she managed to score the dress, once a plain black shift with a fringe hem, for less than the cost of a chai latte from her favorite coffee shop. She then embellished it herself by adding layers and layers of extra fringe. The dress fit perfectly and the fringe made it look expensive.

After the flapper idea took hold, she ran with it, finding the rest of her accessories online or at neighborhood thrift stores. She loved the black bobbed wig she bought and was tossing around ideas of how she might wear it next Halloween as a totally different look.

Even though London had applied it less than thirty minutes ago, she checked her makeup again, paying close attention to her lipstick. She settled on a cherry red lip to top off her flapper costume. Never mind she recalled that Donovan loved this color on her.

She almost convinced herself that she was not doing this for him.

Who was she kidding? She was hoping he'd notice the lipstick and everything else.

The doorbell chimed, causing her stomach to drop. She took a deep breath, trying to calm her nerves and rein in her emotions.

She rubbed her left arm in alarm. Was that a hive forming? She hurried out of her room and down the stairs to open the door before she let fear take hold.

"Word is born!" Donovan stood with his arms crossed like he was posing for the cover of a 90's rap album. Actually, he looked like he'd just stepped off a rap album cover. He wore a classic black Adidas track suit, a red Kangol hat, and a fat faux gold rope chain. A lot of guys his age would have looked ridiculous in the costume but Donovan pulled it off. All he needed was a large boom box to complete his look.

Maxie approached the door, expecting London's dad, then stalked off in the opposite direction.

"Wow, you look straight out of the nineties!" London said after opening the door. The man filled out a track suit nicely. She gawked for a moment then stepped aside so Donovan could enter the house. But he just stood there, staring at her.

London glanced down self-consciously, wondering if she'd spilled something on her dress.

"Damn, LL, I don't want to go to this party anymore." London looked up to find Donovan peeling her costume off slowly with his eyes. Her body heated immediately.

"We have to…" She started to admonish him but found herself pressed against him in her doorway as he stepped into the house. She pulled him fully inside and closed the door. No need to give the nosy neighbors a free show.

Donovan pinned her against the wall firmly. She wanted to melt against him. The kiss he planted on her took her breath away and she wholeheartedly shared his sentiment about ditching the party.

Finally he released her, both of them breathless and needy. He felt so good, London was tempted to press against him again. "I need to keep my eye on you tonight…"

"Don't say that! Your grandmother said no sexy costumes. Is this too much?" London panicked. She had put so much effort into this costume and she thought the final product looked great, but maybe she was revealing too much.

She glared at her chest. Yes, she was busty and the V of her dress was showing a bit of cleavage, but she thought it was tasteful, not over the top vixen cleavage.

London tugged at the dress, pulling it up closer toward her neck, attempting to make it more modest.

Donovan smirked. "I can help you with that." He ran a palm down the side of her dress, causing her body to immediately respond by stepping closer to him. "I feel like a horny teenager asking this but is your dad here?"

"No." London's voice was too breathy, too needy. She exhaled, trying to be firm. "He's in New York but that's not relevant because we aren't staying."

Donovan kissed her jawline. She swore she saw stars. She threw her head to the side to give him more access, marveling again at how the man seemed to zero in on her *right there* spots.

She was beginning to think her whole body was a weak spot for him. "We need to get to your grandmother's party." There was that breathy voice again.

"Yep, we're getting there." But instead of moving, he hit another spot on London's neck that turned her knees into pudding. "When is your dad coming back?" His breath teased and tickled her ear.

She gasped. "Tomorrow. You're going to mess up my costume." Her words fell on deaf ears. Not that she wanted him to stop.

Donovan groaned. "We have the house to ourselves until tomorrow? London…"

The way he said her name melted her insides. Part plea and part promise spoken close to her ear, that one word conveyed all of the things she was feeling. Her desire to be skin to skin with him, her need to talk to him about everything or nothing, from why he hated pumpkin spice to how he dealt with not having his mother present.

That was a common thread between them; they'd both spent only part of their childhood around their mothers and had their grandmothers stand in as surrogates. London had learned a lot about Donovan over the course of their meetings in the coffee shop but there was more she wanted to know. She realized meeting his family would give her more insight. So far, she'd only met Emmaline. Hopefully, his other family members would be more accepting.

"We have to go to the party, don't we?" They both knew the answer, but she hoped he might say no.

Donovan sighed in defeat, releasing her. "Yeah, I'm in charge of music." He straightened up, then smoothed her dress downward, causing more cleavage to show. "There. That's better. I will never hear the end of it if I skip the party. That also means we can't slip out early."

London readjusted her dress back to its more conservative position.

His face held a gap toothed, unapologetic smile. "Good news though. It will be over by ten."

"So maybe at 10:30, we meet right here and pick up where we left off?"

"I like where your head is, LL. Let's go."

DONOVAN KEPT HER MIND OFF HER NERVES BY TELLING her hilarious stories about his relatives. Most had lived in Atlanta all of their lives so he was able to grow up surrounded by aunts, uncles and cousins on his mother's side.

Far too soon for comfort, they pulled up at Emmaline's house. The driveway was full of cars and there were cars lined up on both sides of her street.

London tensed, unable to shake a feeling of dread. Was it seeing Emmaline up close and personal again? She acknowledged that was indeed part of her reticence but not all of it. Was she concerned the family wouldn't like her? Maybe that was it. Donovan had described everyone as down to earth, going so far as to call some of them 'country.' London had some relatives like that in her own family; she could relate. She straightened her spine, putting on her game face. Donovan gave her hand a reassuring squeeze and they exited the car.

There were two older teens standing outside who looked up as they approached. They were both wearing Black Panther t-shirts, which London guessed was their version of dressing up for Halloween.

"Hey, Uncle D, nice costume. Yo, is that your girl?" one said, walking over to inspect London like she was a model car on a dealership floor. London frowned at him, thinking this was one of the country relatives Donovan described.

"Tae, act like you been somewhere. Introduce yourself. And this is a grown woman, not a girl."

His eyes traveled down her. "You right, Unc, that booty on her is all woman."

Donovan shot Tae an evil eye London was positive he'd gotten from his grandmother. "Tae, say one more word."

Tae straightened up immediately. "Dang, Unc, I was joking."

He turned to London then stuck out a hand. "I'm just kidding. I'm Taevon, that's my boy Jaden." Jaden threw up a hand in greeting but stayed where he was. Tae eyed London's headpiece and wig. "What's your costume supposed to be? Old school teacher or something?"

Raising a dubious eyebrow, London shook Tae's hand. "I'm London and no, I'm a flapper, from the 1920s."

Nodding, like an adult would at a child who just said something serious to them but hilarious to anyone else, Tae said, "Gotcha," then added, "you're kinda dressed like that dude inside." With that cryptic statement, he turned and joined his friend.

Donovan said in a low voice, "Those are not my nephews. Tae is my cousin's girlfriend's son. Damn kids have no home training these days."

London stifled a smile. Donovan sounded just like her father when he was ranting about the young interns at his firm.

They continued toward the house, entering the front door. The house was packed with bodies of all ages and London saw Emmaline as soon as she walked in. Emmaline hustled over to help Donovan get the music setup, then smiled sweetly at London who responded with a fake smile of her own.

"Make yourself at home," Emmaline said, glancing at a table where four people were in the midst of a card game.

London took in the house, finding it to be much like her own grandmother's house: Lots of traditional style furniture, mirrors, and family photos everywhere. Emmaline liked red and black, she noted.

There was one red accent wall with a large portrait of Emmaline and she assumed, Donovan's grandfather, Nate when they were younger. She noticed young children playing a board game on the floor in a corner, supervised by a young woman dressed as a witch. The house was bigger than it looked on the outside but smaller than London's house.

London then glanced over at a card table where four men sat, a deck of playing cards spread out on the table.

She blinked as one of the men stood up, looking directly at her. She frowned, confused.

*What was going on here? That can't be.*

The man smiled, spoke. "Hey London." He held his arms out like he expected her to run into them.

London's heart thudded in her chest and she felt her face heating up. "Derrick?"

She mouthed the name, not certain if he was really standing in the middle of Emmaline's house. She wanted to grab her own arm to ensure she wasn't in the midst of a horrible dream.

She could feel the curious eyes on her but she didn't acknowledge them. Embarrassment and confusion flowed through her making the costume she was wearing feel silly. All the care and detail she'd put into creating her 1920s fantasy to impress Donovan's family was wasted. She wanted to throw the wig and headpiece into the nearest dumpster and trash the stupid dress on which she'd spent so much time. Aside from the costume she now knew she would never wear again, one question ran through her mind.

*Why was her ex-fiancé here?*

Switching into analytical mode, London looked at the facts. He'd clearly been at the party for a while, playing cards with the rest of the men at the table. He was wearing a costume, she noted, so he'd been briefed that it was a costume party. Since he was supposedly living in Vegas now, the chances that he'd just casually crashed the party were practically nonexistent.

*Why the hell was he here?*

There was a touch on her arm and she flinched, thinking it was Derrick but he hadn't moved from the table. London snapped out of her head for a second and heard Donovan speaking quietly to her. "Is that your ex-fiancé?"

Not taking her eyes off Derrick, London nodded once.

Derrick, dressed as a throwback gangster pimp, stepped toward her.

The world sped up. Everything had been in slow motion for her but as soon as Derrick moved toward London, his arms still open, Donovan lunged at him, his fist connecting with Derrick's smooth jaw before anyone could react.

Derrick, stunned for a second, quickly recovered, smashing his fist into Donovan's gut, sending the Kangol Donovan wore flying off. Another fist flew, catching Donovan's cheek and London stood there stunned for what seemed like hours.

She shook her head then screamed at them to stop.

Everyone in the room stood still, processing the fight.

Emmaline rushed from the kitchen, screaming at a tall man who looked just like her to break them up, but he seemed hesitant to throw himself in the middle of the melee.

He stood still, staring at Donovan and Derrick.

Another older man who had been sitting at the card table jumped in and pulled the two apart. Everyone stood, gawking at the two men, then at London.

London stared at Emmaline, in her ridiculous 70's costume, her Afro wig twisted. She was bending over Donovan, her hand on his face. There was blood on Emmaline's dress which had to be Donovan's.

Willing the older woman to face her, London continued to glare, seething.

Now Emmaline's insistence that she attend the party made sense.

Emmaline had set all of this in motion and for what? Because she had deemed London unworthy of her precious grandson? London had never had a reason to hate anyone as much as she hated Emmaline at that moment. Since this was turning out to be a fight party, London wanted to take a shot at the woman but she knew that wouldn't solve anything.

Emmaline rose and hurried to the refrigerator in the kitchen, returning with a bag of frozen peas that she placed on Donovan's cheek.

London bent down beside Donovan, who was sitting on the floor, holding the peas against his swollen, bloody face. "You need to tell your grandmother what's going on before someone else gets hurt," she hissed, her teeth clenched in anger.

Derrick, sitting back in his original chair with the older man sitting in front of him, looked at London warily as he rubbed his swollen knuckles. London approached him, her arms crossed. She wanted to punch him, too. This had to be something he and Emmaline cooked up.

"We don't belong here. Let's go." She motioned to the front door. Derrick rose slowly then limped toward the door. He looked like he wanted to say something as he got closer to London then thought better when she glared at him. He followed her out the door.

London heard Donovan call her name as they exited the house, but she kept walking toward the street.

She stopped, turning toward Derrick. "How did you get here?" she snapped.

In response, she watched as he patted his pocket and pulled out a key fob, pointing it toward a mid-sized white sedan parked at the house next door to Emmaline's. The car's lights flashed once and she heard the doors unlock.

"Good. I need a ride home." London put her hand out for the key. "I'll drive."

Once they were settled in the car, Derrick turned to her. "So, I guess that's my replacement?"

Silently, London took her time adjusting the seat and the mirrors, trying to calm down. She wanted to scream, let out all the rage rolling through her.

She glanced at Derrick. He had some nerve. She started the

car, trying to recall the route back to the main road. "What are you even doing here in Atlanta?"

Derrick brooded in the passenger seat. "That woman, Emma, contacted me on Facebook and said that she knew you. She told me you wanted me back and that I should surprise you at that party." He rubbed his jaw where Donovan had hit him. "Your man's got a decent right hook."

London rolled her eyes. "*Really?* So, you just dropped everything and flew to Atlanta?" She couldn't believe this. "What happened to your sugar mama in Vegas?"

"That didn't work out." He looked away. "This is a nice neighborhood."

"Forget the fucking neighborhood!" Which, she realized, she should have paid more attention while Donovan was driving. Nothing they passed looked familiar. "When was all of this arranged? And who's paying for this trip? I know you aren't."

At this point London wouldn't be the least bit surprised to find out that somehow she had sponsored this trip. She seemed to always be paying for Derrick's grand ideas. She miscalculated a turn and ended up in a cul-de-sac. Cursing, she whipped the car around.

"I bought my own ticket," he said peevishly. *Like he had a right to be offended,* London fumed.

"And I paid for the car. I'm staying at my mom's." He crossed his arms, which London recognized as his classic 'I've been wronged' stance. "And I don't know why you're snapping at me. He hit me first."

What the hell had she ever seen in this man child sitting beside her? He sounded like a whiny five-year-old.

"If you had called or texted me before you flew out here, I would have told you not to bother."

London was driving aggressively now, taking her frustrations out on the gas petal of the rental. "You thought you'd invest in a plane ticket so you could get your main meal ticket back. Good ol' London would be more than happy to take you back, right?"

Seeing the main entrance and exit to the subdivision on her right, she slung the sedan toward it on two wheels, causing them both to lean to the right.

"London, Baby, could you slow down?" Derrick had a death grip on the handle above the passenger side window. "No, it wasn't my idea, I swear. The lady, Emma, she told me you talked about me all the time, how you missed me and all."

"Don't call me that. I'm not your 'Baby' anymore." On the main street, London eased off the gas petal. Maybe she did need to slow down. "Why didn't you contact me? My number hasn't changed since you blocked me."

She was feeling all of the anger and resentment toward Derrick and their broken engagement bubble to the surface and she wanted to punch something.

"I mean, I don't know. She made the surprise sound so good. I'm thinking, 'Ok, yeah, I screwed up but if London is willing to take me back, maybe we can make this work in Atlanta' but I guess not." Derrick was doing his best wounded voice trying to appeal to her sensitive side.

London jerked her foot on the brake, stopping abruptly at a traffic light. *Was this man serious right now?* "Derrick, you stole my wedding money and moved out! How would we possibly 'make this work'?" She took her hands off the wheel and made air quotes.

"Yeah, I mean, I know, but I thought we could get past that. I was gonna pay you back once I won a few poker tournaments." He glanced at her slyly. "I missed you."

"They should have let Donovan finish beating your ass," she muttered.

He frowned at her, which pissed her off even more.

"Do you know how many nights I cried in that townhouse alone over you?" she screeched. "And for what? You're not even remotely remorseful. You don't give a damn about me or anyone else. You missed me. *Please.*"

The light turned green and she hit the accelerator. Hard.

"Jesus, can you slow down?" Derrick huffed. "Let's get one thing straight. He wasn't beating my ass. He got that first sucker punch in but that was it."

London shot him a dirty look. "Is that really the point you want to make right now?"

"I'm just making sure you understand who was winning." Derrick shook his hand, flexing his fingers. "My hand is swollen and I got blood on my costume. You haven't even asked if I'm ok."

Yep, same old Derrick. Everything was about him. "You no longer have a place in my life where I need to be concerned with your well-being. You forfeited that when you walked out," she reminded him.

"Yeah, I know. That was kinda wrong." Derrick was contrite. "But London, I wasn't ready to get married. I wanted to tell you that but you just kept on with the wedding plans and it was too much. You couldn't tell I wasn't happy?"

The confession from Derrick confirmed everything she'd just come to realize. "Why did you propose in the first place then?"

"I thought that's what I wanted. I figured it was time to settle down and I wanted you to help me with the poker tournament sponsorship. I knew you'd be more willing to do it if we were getting married. It would have been a good investment."

*Why the hell had she wasted so many years of her life with this selfish asshole?*

London guessed sometimes you needed to do something new in order to understand how far you'd come. Even though she hadn't known Donovan nearly as long, she knew he'd never say anything like this. He'd never commit to her just so she would help him with his career.

They drove in silence for a while. There was a time when London would obsess over what she thought Derrick was thinking or feeling when he was silent. Now she no longer cared.

When they reached her house, she pulled the car into the

driveway and cut the engine. "Derrick, we're done. I wish you the best, but I don't need to ever see you again."

He ignored her parting statement. "So, what was that all about? Why did that woman have me come here and crash her party?"

London sighed. "She doesn't want me to be with her grandson, the one who hit you." Emmaline had gone to great lengths to make sure London knew she didn't want her anywhere near Donovan.

Derrick snorted. "Well, seems to me you got his nose open so I don't know what she thinks she's gonna do. That man has made his choice."

London frowned at him. "I didn't open his nose or whatever you're talking about. And I'm sure that anything we could have had is now over, thanks to you."

Derrick waved his good hand dismissively. "Hell, he didn't hesitate to stake his claim once he saw me." He gave her a sidelong glance. "You look good, by the way."

She blinked, not sure how to take Derrick's words. She hadn't gotten a compliment from him in years. "Thank you." London rested her hand on the door handle. "I should go."

"Yeah, tell him I said he's a lucky man."

London nodded, not sure where this side of Derrick was coming from. Not her concern anymore, she decided and got out of the car.

Derrick got out too so that he could take her seat behind the wheel. "Take care, London."

⁂ 18 ⁂

# DONOVAN

onovan's stomach constricted as he watched London leave with her ex. With whats-his-name's throwback gangster outfit and London's flapper costume, they looked like Bonnie and Clyde. She didn't even appear to be concerned that he was hurt. Technically, he started it but still.

They looked like they belonged together.

He willed himself not to continue that painful train of thought. Her ex had blown his chance with her. Or so Donovan thought.

Dammit, his face and hand already hurt. Now he'd added his pride and his feelings to the list.

His grandmother's cousin Terrie Lynne, dressed as a faux fur wearing pimp, stared down at him. "Donnie! You ok? You should have said something, I would have stomped his ass for you." She stamped a platform shoe for emphasis.

Donovan blinked, realizing everyone was surrounding him, staring at him like he was drawing his last breath.

"Yeah Unc! I had your back, too. I didn't like the look of that fool when he walked in," Tae said.

Everyone parted as his grandmother came to stand over him. "Terrie Lynne, go sit down somewhere." She had her hands on

233

her hips. "You're too old to be fighting like a hoodrat. Tae, you are not to be fighting anybody anywhere, you hear me?"

As she said this, she kneeled, removing the pack of frozen peas on Donovan's throbbing cheek so that she could examine his face. "Can you see ok?"

He ran a hand over his locs and realized his hat was missing. He closed his eyes. Maybe if he thought hard enough, he could will himself home and in his bed. His rash actions would be the talk of every family gathering for the next hundred years. "I can see fine, Gram."

Nate Jr. sat back down at the Spades table, peering at Donovan. "Ma, he's all right. You messed up a good game, D! I was on fire."

Emmaline glared at her son. "He's not all right. Can't you see he's hurt?"

She turned to Donovan. "What was she talking about, you needed to tell me something?" she asked, touching his face, looking for injuries. "Don't tell me she's pregnant."

Terrie Lynne bent over him again. "She's pregnant? Is that why you hit that man, Donnie? Is it his?"

"Make sure you get a paternity test," Nate Jr. added.

Rolling his eyes at all the unsolicited advice, Donovan watched his grandmother bark orders. "Go get another drink, Terrie Lynne. I need to talk to Donnie and you all aren't helping."

He sat up, searching his grandmother's face. "Gram, why did you bring her ex here? How did you even find him?"

"Donnie, we'll talk about that later." Her dismissive tone indicated she wasn't discussing any of that. "What did you need to tell me?"

Donovan paused.

As much as he hated to admit it, he knew London was right, he needed to come clean before anything else happened. He exhaled. "Let's go in the other room, Gram. It's a long story."

The rest of the family looked expectantly at Donovan.

Terrie Lynne stated the obvious. "Looks like the party is over, Donnie, you might as well tell her now."

Emmaline shot Terrie Lynne a look. "What, Em? He might as well spill the liquor."

"Gramma, how many times do we have to tell you? It's tea, not liquor. You spill the tea." Terrie Lynne's granddaughter, Mikayla said, hands on her hips.

"I don't drink tea, so why would I say tea?" Terrie Lynne wondered.

"You all can start cleaning up since you look like you have nothing better to do." She directed her gaze at all of the family members. "Donnie, in my room. Now."

Emmaline led Donovan to her bedroom where they could talk privately.

Donovan, still holding the peas in place on his jaw, told her how he had hired Exposé to check out her new boyfriend. Once he was done, he waited for his grandmother to speak. They sat on a bench at the foot of her bed. Donovan glanced over at her, wondering exactly how pissed she was. Normally she yelled first and asked questions later but she sat silently now.

Finally, Emmaline rose, fists on her hips. "Donovan, you should go home and take care of your wounds," she said in a quiet voice. "My love life is none of your concern, which is why I didn't share any of it with you. I'm still your grandmother, and I'm perfectly capable of conducting my life without your permission."

"Gram, I know, I just..."

Emmaline cut Donovan off, pointing to the door. "I don't want to hear it. Shut my door on your way out."

Donovan knew better than to argue with her.

Once, when Donovan was about twelve, he and some friends from school skipped their last afternoon class and walked to a nearby convenience store where they pocketed a few candy bars. Of course, being better at committing crime via video game rather than real life, they were caught and Emmaline, as Donovan's official guardian at the time, was contacted and told what happened.

Donovan waited in the store for his grandmother to arrive, all the while wishing and praying that the ground would swallow him whole so he wouldn't have to face her. He knew she was going to be furious and it wouldn't matter if he told her he hadn't actually stole any candy.

Gram expected him to not only know the difference between right and wrong but also discourage anyone he associated with from doing anything that might land them all in trouble. As he'd done the exact opposite of that, he knew any attempt to convince his grandmother of his slight innocence would be futile. He sighed and continued to pray for a miracle.

Emmaline had burst into the convenience store, still wearing her work clothes, heels tapping purposefully on the tile. The owner greeted her and they stepped out of earshot to talk. Emmaline spent what had seemed like an hour talking to the owner, then she shook the owner's hand and strode back over to the boys.

"Donovan, get your things and let's go," said Emmaline. She had used that same tone of voice that she used today, calling him by his full first name. Once they were in the car, she informed him that not only was he grounded from all video games and television for the next month, he was also expected to spend his entire Saturday stocking shelves at the scene of the crime.

That tone he knew so well meant there was no room for argument or negotiation or compromise. Emmaline Roberson had spoken and that was that. Pushing that memory from his thoughts, Donovan slunk out of his grandmother's bedroom, feeling all of twelve years old again.

Cousin Terri Lynne was the first to speak up. "Donnie, what's going on? Where's Em?"

Nate Jr. added his two cents. "The golden boy messed up? What'd you do?"

Donovan glared at his uncle as he gathered his equipment

awkwardly with one hand. No one offered to help. "I was told to leave so you all need to make sure everything gets cleaned up and put away."

Everyone watched Donovan sling his backpack over his shoulder. He spotted his hat on the card table and stuck it on his head, then left without another word.

Pulling up at his house, Donovan sat in the driveway, in no rush to go inside.

The wind was blowing and random lightning strikes lit the quiet darkness. All of the kids who might have gone trick-or-treating were home now, safely tucked away in well-lit houses.

The weather had held for as long as it could but he could tell the rain was coming.

Donovan watched the lightning strike then did a silent one Mississippi count of the seconds that passed before he heard the rumble of thunder. His grandfather had taught him to count the seconds then divide his count by five to get the distance in miles of the lightning. Growing up, counting and calculating the distance distracted him from being scared of the storms.

The thunder took fifteen seconds, meaning the lightning struck about three miles away.

Normally Donovan didn't mind rainy nights. He found the repetitive sound of rain on the window comforting, especially if he was designing or drawing.

Tonight, the rain matched his mood. After his fight with London's ex, he'd been pumped, adrenaline coursing, but watching London leave with the victor, the man had gotten at least one good punch in before Donovan had been pulled away, his confession to his grandmother, and her shutting him out, he was drained.

London had said, "We don't belong here."

The "we" part dropped his heart to his knees.

*What the hell did that mean exactly?*

Were they reconciling now, huddled together in her house, with her father gone? Were they on the porch swing, her favorite spot, cuddling and...he didn't want to think about all the things they could be doing right then.

He sat up, turning the engine on. He could be at her house in a few minutes.

The rational part of him took over. To do what? Torture himself? The thought of London appearing at the door in a robe looking freshly sexed and telling him to get lost made his head throb in pain.

*No thanks.*

He sighed, turned the car off and started for his house.

Once inside, Donovan stripped off his costume, feeling ridiculous in it, and shoved it in a closet he never used. His face and knuckles still ached from the fight. He examined himself in the mirror. No more bleeding, but everything, including his heart, hurt. While he didn't consider himself a violent person, he wasn't sure what had come over him when he punched London's ex.

*What a mess.* Ironically, his grandmother was pissed at him for interfering in her love life even though she was doing the exact same thing in his. And because of her machinations, London had taken off with her ex-fiancé.

He wanted to pound the man all over again.

Donovan liked to analyze his options before acting. He figured instead of rushing over to London's and potentially making a fool of himself if she was there with Mr. Vegas, he could drown his sorrows in whatever alcohol he had in the house.

Dismissing the idea, Donovan swallowed a couple of painkillers that contained a sleep aid and stretched out on the couch to watch tv until he got sleepy. Maybe things would look better in the morning.

As he was sitting on the couch watching sports highlights, the rain started, softly at first then nature released full fury and the rain pounded the roof. Donovan yawned and rested his head on the arm of the sofa letting the rain lull him to sleep.

The chime of the doorbell followed by two urgent knocks woke him and Donovan jerked up, unsure of where he was for a brief moment. He looked for his phone, thinking it was ringing but the doorbell rang again.

He realized he'd never taken his phone out of the holder in his car. Maybe the noise was coming from the doorbell? He shook his head, trying to clear the sleeping pill induced fog and stumbled to the front door, wondering who would be venturing out in the cold heavy rain. Donovan checked the peephole and opened the door quickly.

London stood there, looking a bit like a drowned cat.

Not sure if he was still dreaming, Donovan blinked at her then stepped aside so she could enter. She struggled a few minutes with her mini umbrella, a colorful useless accessory meant for light rain only, before giving up and leaving it dangling on the porch.

Donovan stood there, watching London shrug out of her wet coat, trying to make sense of what he saw. London was really standing there in his living room. He looked at the water dripping off of her coat onto the carpet. Taking the coat, he hung it in the bathroom where it could drip into the tub.

They stood facing each other.

He wondered what was running through her mind as she stood there in his space. As much as he wanted to, Donovan resisted the overwhelming urge to touch her, make sure he wasn't still dreaming, but he stayed where he was trying to will her near.

London made the first move. She got close enough for him to see a pulse at her neck. He could, if he concentrated hard enough, taste the skin there.

Dragging his gaze from her neck, he reminded himself he was angry at her.

London studied the damage to his face, then ran a cool thumb over his cheek. "Are you ok?" Her voice was soft, concerned.

Her touch coupled with the worry in her eyes almost made the anger dissolve. *Almost.* "I'm fine. How's your man?" His tone was cold and he knew he sounded like a petty teen.

Snorting, London withdrew her hand. Donovan immediately missed the touch.

"Are you serious with this? *You* are mad at *me*? Do I need to remind you that this was all your grandmother's doing? I came to make sure you were ok. You didn't answer your phone and I thought..." she crossed her arms; he knew now that this was her protective stance. "Clearly you're fine so I can go." London glanced around for her coat.

"Why did you leave with him?" The question came out as more of a plea and he hated it but his need to know overrode his pride.

Rolling her eyes, London said sharply, "I left with him because neither of us should have been there in the first place. I didn't know your grandmother hated me that much, but I wasn't raised to disrespect my elders in their own home. I was trying to diffuse a bad situation before anyone went to jail."

London played with the hoop in one ear. "Why'd you hit him like that?"

"He deserved it for what he put you through! Don't tell me you're getting back together with him." He was pouting now and thinking of them together, London tending to his wounds, caressing his face with her hands. He clenched his fist reflexively and winced at the pain.

London relaxed her stance. "Please. Why would I do that?" She eyed him. "I had him drop me off at home so that I could change and get my car." She looked past Donovan. "I was worried about you," London admitted.

"I had all these visions of you curled up with him on that damn porch swing." Donovan looked sheepish.

"The old me of a few months ago would have gladly taken him back," she said. "When I looked at him today, after the shock of seeing him, I just felt sorry for him." London smirked. "I think I might have scared him. I drove home like some road raged soccer mom and ranted about how this all happened. I also asked him why he didn't call me to verify anything before he just flew in on the word of some woman he didn't know. Besides," she said, moving closer and taking his hand, "that porch swing is our spot."

A table lamp, the only source of light in the room, flickered.

Donovan dropped London's hand to grasp her waist, pulling her toward him. He wanted her close. "Good. Tell him to go back to Vegas or wherever he was living." He murmured near her ear before catching the lobe in his lips. London's breath caught and she turned to give Donovan full access.

"Now, I think we have some unfinished business from earlier today before the party." He bent, capturing her lips in a slow, deliberate dance. He felt more than heard London's moan. He pulled her lower lip into his mouth, teasing it with his teeth, wanting to savor all the sensations.

When they were both breathless, London spoke. "I should probably go home while I still can."

"Later." Taking her hand, Donovan headed toward the staircase then up the stairs to his bedroom.

"Donovan..." London stepped inside his room and stopped, her voice full of uncertainty. She paused, as if working through what she wanted to say, then said, "This isn't Miami. What are we doing?" Breaking eye contact, she crossed her arms over her chest. "I just want to know beforehand so there's no confusion."

Donovan's heart raced.

When he didn't respond, she continued, "We're just enjoying each other's company, right?"

As soon as he'd decided to stop denying his feelings for London, she sucker punched him into the situation zone.

*Hell no.* "Is that what you want? Casual?" He held his breath then held up a hand. "Before you answer, I'm just going to say this. If that's what you want, it's fine."

Even as he said the words, he knew they weren't true. He was tied in knots just few minutes ago thinking about London and her ex.

He ran a hand over his face. "No, fuck that. It's not fine. I literally fought for you earlier. And would gladly do it again if you wanted me to. That's more than enjoying each other's company when the mood hits. If you want casual, then you should probably go. I think we're well past casual...what?"

All of the steam went out of his argument as he realized that London was staring at him, full lips pursed.

"You know, I'm finding your indignation and filthy mouth really sexy right now," she said, slowly running a finger down his abs. "Glad we're on the same page."

"Nope. It's not going to work. I'm still angry." Donovan wanted to cross his arms in protest, but London was caressing his belt buckle which had him confused and aroused in equal parts. He wanted to grab her hand but didn't as the aroused part wanted to see where she was going with this.

He stood motionless.

Soon enough, she slid the belt from the loop on the side near his hip. A sudden flash of lightning illuminated the room as the rain hit the windows.

London removed the belt from the loop closest to the buckle.

Donovan held his breath. She hadn't touched his hard length yet but she was close, so damn close and it was pushing him to the edge. He was ready to snatch the belt from his jeans like his grandfather used to do when Donovan was in trouble, but he willed himself to stay still.

Pulling the leather end, London eased the prong from the hole of the belt.

"What were you saying? You want me to go?" She stopped working on the belt to meet his gaze from hooded eyes.

"You know I don't," he growled. He might sink to his knees and beg her to stay at this point.

Acknowledging his answer, London freed the silver buckle from the tip of the belt and tugged until it slid easily from Donovan's pants. The belt was tossed into the closest chair. Donovan forgot to breathe wondering what she would do next.

Normally, the removal of pants right before sex was rushed,

frantic, and without regard for the subtleties. London had him reconsidering his stance. She was taking her time, tormenting him.

He felt her finger glide along the skin covered by the waistband of his jeans and in one motion, the button was undone. His erection twitched in response. *So close.*

Thunder rumbled outside, loud and threatening, followed by another flash of lightning that lit the house for a brief moment. The rain continued a steady rhythm against the roof as Donovan watched London slide his zipper down. As soon as the palm of her hand made contact with his penis, his eyes rolled back in his head.

Donovan grabbed her hand, tugging her toward the bed, but she stopped him, motioning toward his jeans. She pushed them lower so that Donovan could step out of them. He kicked them to the side once they were off. He forced himself to go with the flow as much as he wanted to finish shoving his and London's clothes off, he'd let her be in charge.

London pushed the well-worn Morehouse sweatshirt he wore up and over Donovan's head, then ran her nails up and down his chest. Her warm fingers on his bare skin were pushing him precariously close to the edge and that wasn't the plan for tonight. He meant to savor every inch of London's body while she was in his bed. He just needed to get her there. London stood between Donovan and the door to the hallway. Grasping her waist, Donovan spun London around so that her back was to the massive bed.

Before he knew what was happening, London leaned back, pulling him with her as they fell onto the bed.

How many nights had he lay in bed, replaying their passionate night in Miami?

Too many to count. Now she was here, beneath him, soft and willing. He kissed her, biting her lower lip, causing her to arch against him.

He needed to slow down.

"You got to strip me, now it's my turn," he said, tugging her sweater over her head. London was wearing a chocolate lace bra and panty set that blended with her skin giving her the illusion of being nude. Donovan could swear his mouth watered at the thought.

She unhooked her bra while he slid the lacy panties down and off. Donovan paused to relish the vision of her: lush, thick, brown, beautiful.

He placed a trail of kisses down her stomach then got down to business even lower. London arched, gasped, his name on her lips as she came.

The rain slowed. The house was quiet as Donovan made his way back up London's body, stopping to savor the dark nipples he loved.

He couldn't stop touching her, exploring her dark curves, enjoying the softness, feeling her skin on his. London ran lazy hands down his chest and abs, pausing to free him from the boxer briefs he wore.

London rose as she stroked him, then pushed him back against the bed, reversing their positions. Running her fingertips down his chest, London took her time exploring his chest. His abs tightened with pleasure as she took him in her mouth.

He made the mistake of opening his eyes to watch her, the sight of her red lips pleasuring him was almost his undoing.

"London, I'm going to, I don't want..." he couldn't even form words, but he knew he needed more, wanted to be inside her, loving her as she should be loved.

She licked her lips, a self-satisfied, lusty gaze in her eyes as she crawled up beside him.

Damn, she was everything he ever wanted.

"Don't move," he commanded, grabbing a packet of condoms from a drawer in his nightstand, he tore one open as if it might leap from his hands then slid it on.

Pinning London down on her back, he positioned himself

between her thighs. London arched against him, grabbing his hips, guiding him into her.

He sank in slowly, felt every nerve-ending in his body respond with a jolt, so she could adjust to him. He watched her eyes slide shut and the moan he knew well escaped from her throat.

As the rain pelted the windows, they moved as one being toward the final release. This time, when his release came, Donovan gritted out London's name before collapsing onto her.

Later, as they lay tangled in the sheets, their bodies huddled close, Donovan pulled his comforter over them, knowing there was no other place on Earth he wanted to be at that moment.

## ❧ 19 ❧

# LONDON

"That was quick. What did you...?" The next morning, London, feeling like everything was right in her world, bounced down the stairs. She stopped abruptly halfway down when she saw Emmaline. Her face fell. "Oh, Ms. Roberson."

When she heard a key in the lock, London assumed Donovan, who insisted they needed chai lattes to replenish their energy, forgot something and had to come back home. Climbing out of the warm bed, she threw on the closest thing she could find in his dresser drawer, a well-worn t-shirt from some game she wasn't familiar with, and hurried down to see him, maybe get in one quickie before he left for the coffee shop.

Now she wanted to run back upstairs and put her own clothes on, her panties at the very least, but curiosity kept her still.

Emmaline had her hands on her hips, looking around the space. "Where is Donovan? And what are you doing in his house while he's not here?"

London could tell by Emmaline's aggressive stance that this wasn't going to be a friendly visit. "He should be back in a few minutes." She crossed her arms to cover herself, wishing the t-shirt was longer, as Emmaline's disapproving gaze roamed over her. "I can tell him you came by or you're welcome to wait."

"I know I'm welcome to wait. I don't know why you're still here though. Usually women like you take their money and leave before the sun comes up." Emmaline crossed her arms, mirroring London's stance. "I'm sure his leaving was your cue to get dressed and go."

London's lips parted in surprise. She didn't expect such venom so early in the morning from a self-proclaimed God fearing woman.

Emmaline struck again. "You young women are always so willing to show a man what's between your legs thinking it will make him love you." The older woman took a seat on the sofa, acting like she owned it. "He only wants one thing from you and now that he's gotten it, he'll move on, like he always does."

London was done. "I was taught to respect my elders and I've tried to do that from day one, but you know what, respect is earned and you shouldn't just get a pass to be a jerk because you've reached a certain age."

She stomped down the stairs as she spoke. "Yes, I am digging into your love life. It's my job. Your grandson hired me. But I'm pretty sure you didn't know that when you brought my ex-fiancé here."

London stopped walking a few feet away from Emmaline, maintaining her distance. She could slap this woman but she wouldn't choose violence. Someone needed to be the bigger person.

Staring at Emmaline, she crossed her arms. "So why did you do that? I was trying to close that chapter of my life and move on, but it's like you ripped a bandage off of a wound that's started to heal and stuck a dirty fork into it."

"Word of advice from an old jerk. Only commit to men who love you more than you love them. Sounds like you did the opposite." Emmaline smirked. "Clayton is wrapped around my finger, and once I'm done with him, he won't know what hit him.

Here's the thing, you aren't the only one who can dig into people's lives."

She rose then, stepping closer to London. "You need to back off. Tell my grandson whatever you need to tell him to get him to leave all of this alone and stay out of my business. Maybe you go back to DC, whatever. Otherwise, I'll make sure he hates you before all is said and done."

London could only stare. *Were they in high school fighting over the star quarterback? Or competing on some stupid reality show? Was this woman for real?*

"Think I won't? Try me. And if I were you, I'd get dressed now." She peered at London over the rims of her glasses. "You should be gone before Donnie gets back. Don't worry. I'll make up an appropriate excuse for your absence."

*I will not engage this unhinged woman in Donovan's house,* London decided. The woman was right about one thing, London needed to get dressed.

Emmaline was seated in the middle of the couch when London came down the stairs a few minutes later.

Ignoring her, London took a seat at the dining room table and pulled out her phone. She debated on texting Donovan to forewarn him when she heard his car pull up.

Donovan entered, his hands full, struggling to get the grocery bags and their drinks into the house. London stood quickly and took the to go beverage holder from him.

London watched him, her heart pounding with dread. What lengths would Emmaline go to in order to keep them apart? How could such an evil woman raise such a good, loving man?

"Gram, what are you doing here?" he asked, placing the grocery bags on the kitchen counter. "One of those is a chai latte for you." He stopped, staring at London. "What's wrong?" His eyes swung toward Emmaline. "Gram, what did you do?"

London made a decision.

"Donovan," London said suddenly, "did your ex-wife's

departure seem abrupt? Did she give you any indication she was going to leave while you were in the hospital?"

Donovan frowned, glancing at Emmaline then at London before he spoke. "Not that I recall," he said slowly. "Why?"

London held Emmaline's gaze as she spoke. "I'm pretty sure she left because your grandmother paid her to."

Emmaline jumped up from the couch. "That's ridiculous. Corrine couldn't leave fast enough when the doctors told us Donnie might not ever be able to walk again."

Donovan stared at London in disbelief. "Why would you say something like that?"

London turned to him. "I saw a draft of an email she sent to your ex in those files I pulled from her computer."

"That's just a draft. Doesn't mean she sent it or paid Corrine." Donovan sounded desperate to believe his own words.

Emmaline sidled closer to Donovan. "Of course, I didn't pay her." She touched his arm and London thought she might be sick. His grandmother was laying it on thick. "I talked to her about your recovery and told her we had a long road to recovery ahead, but I had faith that you would walk again. She wasn't willing to stick around. Sure, I told her it would be hard adjusting but that was the truth. I didn't want to sugar coat it. Maybe that was on me. I thought she was stronger than that."

London shook her head in defeat. Donovan wasn't taking London's side on this, email or not, but she had to make him see reason. "There's a reason she kept that draft and stored it with her other secret files." She turned back to Donovan. "You think about that. I have no reason to lie."

With that, London quickly gathered her things, grabbed her keys from the table and closed the front door behind her.

Leaving Donovan's house was London's only option. She was tired. Tired of fighting her feelings for him, tired of battling with his grandmother to find out the truth, tired of justifying herself to both of them.

She promised herself she wouldn't reveal her knowledge of

that email Emmaline had drafted to Donovan's ex but she refused to let Emmaline bully her. She shouldn't have said anything. She also shouldn't have expected Donovan to believe her.

Well, she concluded, she was done. She didn't need any of this.

She realized suddenly that was the second time in as many days that she had walked out on Donovan. But that was what she did, she knew.

Since the beginning of time, humans have been facing the fight or flight response intrinsically within them and she had always chosen flight. She wondered why, not for the first time. Why didn't she ever stay and fight? "Because I'm not a fighter," she said out loud, resigned.

But London had to consider a new question.

What had fleeing ever gotten her?

Thinking about the major events in her thirty-two years, London recognized a consistent pattern. She had run from Atlanta when she got out of college. She had run from DC when Derrick left. The same question ran through her mind on a loop. What if she chose to fight instead?

When she reached her car, London unlocked the driver's door and got in. She wanted to sit in the car and fully embrace her pity party as she rehashed a new thought. Donovan had yet to come after her either time she had walked away. Granted, at the party, he might have been indisposed and not able but there was nothing wrong with him today.

Perhaps Emmaline was right. He wasn't serious about her and now he was free to keep looking for that perfect, baggage free, petite, lighter skinned woman his grandmother wanted for him.

*Oh God.* The thought of Donovan playing with another woman's hair like he did hers right before he kissed her, cherishing her, loving her, shredded her already battered heart into a pulp. She was on the verge of tears but she wouldn't sit out in front of the man's house crying. This was an upscale, quiet neighborhood.

There were probably rules against this sort of drama in the homeowner's association handbook.

London sat up, squaring her shoulders, thinking she just needed to get home and she'd be ok.

❧

THE FOLLOWING WEEK, LONDON WAS SWAMPED AT work with another client who needed results fast tracked leaving her unable to follow up on Donovan's case until that Friday.

She was happy to be busy. Being busy meant she didn't have time to think about Donovan and what could have been. There were some loose ends on his case she wanted to tie up.

London figured at some point Donovan would tell them to stop working on finding Emmaline's suitor since she now knew what they were up to. She was both dreading the call and wanting to get it over with so she could move on with her life. Once that case was closed, London would have no official reason to interact with him. He hadn't called since she'd walked out and London was trying to break herself from wishing that he'd reach out.

She sighed, needing to get back to work. Looking at her email, she saw that her next appointment had been rescheduled, which freed her up for a couple of hours. She'd torture herself by digging into Donovan's case again.

Emmaline said Mr. Miami's name was Clayton. Even though the name was fairly common, London thought she might be able to make some headway and get the number of results low enough that she could check them out and get to the right one.

Aja stuck her head in London's office right as she was writing the name Clayton in her notebook. She kept one handy in case she wanted to jot notes or her thoughts down quickly. "Hey London, can we talk for a second?"

*Uh oh. This can't be good.* "Of course. Come in." London gestured towards the extra chair by her desk.

Her cousin, ever the professional, closed the door to London's office and posed herself in the chair like she was ready for a magazine cover shoot.

London glanced at Aja before she sat and did a double take. Aja was dressed casually, in a black and white tunic, a pair of bootcut jeans and stiletto heeled boots. Aja never wore jeans in the office. London wondered what the deal was.

Before she could inquire, Aja spoke. "I'm going to meet with some investors today. They insist this is a casual thing, no suits, just jeans." She rolled her eyes, muttering. "This all better be worth it."

Aja focused on London. "Anyway...I saw the report you did for the Andrew investigation. That was great work. They loved working with you, by the way."

Aja beamed at London, making her uncomfortable. She wasn't used to praise from Aja, especially lately.

"Thanks, that case was pretty straightforward." London said, fidgeting with the pen in her hand.

"Figures." She crossed one leg over the other. "So, Donovan sent me an email asking for a final bill and investigation summary report." She paused. "How is all of that going?" London had given Aja a rundown of the Emmaline drama.

She nodded, trying to keep her face neutral.

Donovan had already requested his last bill without saying anything to her. She knew this day would come, but she didn't feel any less heartbroken. "I have a few loose ends to research. Emmaline mentioned a name and I want to see what I can find."

Aja leaned in. "A name? Her online friend?"

"Yes, she told me she had Clayton wrapped around her finger. No last name though. I think she thought I already knew his name."

"Hmm, if you don't find anyone directly connected to her social media, also look at people posting comments on her videos. Do we still think he's a catfish?"

London dropped the pen on her desk and thought about that question for a minute. "No. I think Emmaline has some end game she's running. Honestly, I wouldn't be surprised to find out Emmaline is the catfish."

Aja sat back, crossing her arms across her chest. "Wow, just when I think I've seen everything. How long will it take you to put together a final summary and conclusion?"

"Well, let me see," London looked at her calendar. She didn't have a ton of meetings scheduled for the upcoming week. "Is a week from today ok?"

"That's fine with me." She raised an eyebrow. "I guess you would know better than I about any objections your client may have for waiting another week. With the case over, I assume you'll be seeing more of each other?"

London shook her head quickly, not trusting her voice to stay steady.

Aja looked surprised. "No? What happened?"

London broke down and told Aja about the confrontation with Emmaline, that she'd left Donovan's house and that she hadn't heard from him since that day. She got emotional, thinking about the lengths Emmaline had gone just to ensure she and Donovan were apart.

Letting the tears fall freely, London lifted her shoulders. "So yeah. Second time this year I've been dumped like yesterday's trash." She sniffed, tired of acting like everything was ok. "I'm sorry, I know you probably think I'm the dumbest woman on the planet for falling in love with him. And you're right, I do make bad choices in men."

Without a word, Aja rose from the chair, grabbing tissues from the box on London's desk, and rubbed London's back. She wrapped her arms around London's shoulders then rested her chin on London's head.

This simple gesture from her cousin made London cry even harder. She'd missed this closeness with Aja more than she'd realized.

Wiping her face, she exhaled. "Aja?" She sniffed. "Sorry, I think I got snot on your sweater."

Aja rose, wiping a few tears from her eyes. Then she threw her head back in laughter. "Cousin, you really know how to kill a tender moment."

Propping herself on the edge of London's desk, Aja said. "Couple things. I don't think you're dumb. London, you are one of the smartest people I know. Why do you think I hired you? And I wanted to apologize for that comment I made to you. I said you still had bad judgment when it came to men. I shouldn't have said that and I don't believe that."

Aja crossed her arms. "I was angry, but that's not an excuse. Yes, your timing was bad but I think he's what you need after Derrick. Donovan is a good man and I think you two can work this out. He'll come around."

London wished she was as confident about Donovan as Aja sounded. "You think so?"

Aja nodded. "Yeah, I do. When he emailed me to get his final bill, I called him to go over everything. He sounded almost as bad as you do."

❦

LATER, LONDON SAT AT HER DESK, FEELING OPTIMISTIC about her life for the first time since moving to Atlanta. She was going over the notes she'd jotted down and saw the name Emmaline had mentioned when they were waiting on Donovan to return.

"Clayton," she said aloud. She didn't have a last name but it was a start. She would check Emmaline's blog and video channels first. Maybe this Clayton commented on one of Emmaline's blog posts or videos. London checked all of Emmaline's recent videos.

Nothing.

Most comments were from fellow cooks who wanted to try her recipes or had questions about ingredients. Emmaline's blog was very popular; there were lots of comments to review. Searching for "Clayton" yielded nothing.

She yawned, wondering what time it was. Glancing quickly at the time on her laptop, she realized it was nearly the end of her workday. Crossing her arms on her desk, London considered her options. She could pack up and head home before rush hour traffic hit its peak or she could follow her train of thought and scour Emmaline's older blogs and videos to see if Clayton had commented on any of them. She realized the office was deserted and quiet. Aja had gone home already. Zaria and Lavender were both working from home so she was the only one left.

London saw no reason to rush home.

Normally on Fridays, she couldn't wait for the end of the day and the start of the weekend, but she had no plans. If she went home now, she'd just sit in her room missing Donovan. She might as well continue searching, enjoying the quiet and solitude.

⚜

SOMETHING WAS GOING ON.

She knew this as soon as she pulled into the driveway. Donovan's car was parked on the street but the vehicle was empty. Was he in there talking to her father? About her, no doubt. The thought of her father interrogating Donovan like he was one of his firm's clients terrified her. She needed to get in the house fast. Checking her reflection in the overhead mirror, she fluffed her hair and quickly swiped on a coat of lip gloss from her purse. London's heart thumped as she got out of her car but she refused to get her hopes up.

Before reaching the door, London smoothed the sides of her long cardigan, wishing she could run upstairs to her room and change before seeing him. She hadn't put any effort into her clothes that day, opting to throw on a pair of dark wide leg jeans, a black ribbed sleeveless turtleneck and a black cardigan that was a leftover piece from her larger days. She knew she should let it go but hadn't had the heart, viewing the piece as her comfort food equivalent.

She unlocked the door and entered the house. Her heels clicking on the hardwood floors, London approached the den, the normal spot for entertaining guests, and found it empty. Further down the hall was her father's study, which is where her father must have taken Donovan. Must be serious if the men were in her father's domain.

London wondered how they were getting along. Her father had never liked her ex-fiancé and made sure London knew it. A sour look would pass over his face whenever she mentioned Derrick and she eventually only mentioned him when necessary.

Donovan would only be the second love interest of hers to meet her father. An urge to rush into the study pushed her forward but then she stopped. What was the point? She had no idea how long Donovan had been in their house. Any damage was likely already done. Still, the man hadn't left yet. Maybe that was a good sign.

The door to the study was open and London stuck her head in cautiously, as if she might catch her father standing over Donovan's bloody corpse. Ok, she might have read one too many mystery novels.

"Hey," The word coming out like a question, "what's this?" She motioned at the space between them.

There were two leather chairs with a large dark bookcase as a backdrop. Donovan and London's father were sitting comfortably in the chairs, enjoying glasses of brown liquor, she noticed. Maxie napped at her father's feet. The scene was cozy in a bizarre way and she half expected her father to offer Donovan a cigar as chummy as they looked.

"There she is!" Edward Lewis stood as soon as he saw London. "I was just telling Donovan here that you should be home any minute now."

London gave her father a questioning look and he grinned at her in response. Who was this man in front of her? "Yeah, I was wrapping up some loose ends at work."

"That's my girl, smart as a whip. London, I'll be heading out in a bit to meet a friend for dinner. Would you two like to join us?"

London wondered if this "friend" was the same woman her dad met at the cat café. Tempting as the invitation was, she needed to talk to Donovan alone. "Maybe next time. Is this your new cat loving friend, Dad?"

Her father grinned at her in response. "It is." He turned to Donovan. "We'll have to do this again sometime. I'll let you know when one of the suites our firm has access to is available. We can catch a game."

He left the room with Maxie trailing behind and closed the door.

London stared at the door then turned to Donovan.

She could tell he hadn't slept well lately but she still had to catch her breath at the sight of him. London wanted to fling her arms around him, tell him that she was miserable without him.

"I have so many questions, I don't even know where to start." She cocked her head at Donovan, fingering her silver hoop. "What are you doing here?"

Donovan rose from the leather chair. "I came by to see you." His voice was low, intimate. "I figured if I called or texted you to ask, you'd politely tell me to kick rocks, so," he raised his arms, "here I am."

"Looks like you won my dad over. Especially if he's inviting you to a baseball game." Her heart was racing. He was here hanging out with her dad while she had been drowning her sorrows in work.

"I mean, we thought you'd be home before now. I got to the door and he said I could come in and wait, you'd probably only be a few minutes getting home. Then we were watching the game and talking sports. You dad is pretty chill." He flashed a grin at her. The one he had to know made her knees want to collapse.

How was she ever going to get over him?

Donovan ran a hand over his locs. "London, I came over here to talk to you, hopefully convince you that I was wrong and plead my case. I emailed Aja and told her to send me the final bill... finding out who my grandmother is dating if she won't share isn't as important to me anymore."

He paced in front of the chairs, staring into the fireplace. "Every woman I care about is pissed at me right now. Gram is pissed that I hired you, you're pissed because, well, you have plenty of legit reasons to be mad at me. Even Val is mad because I screwed things up with you."

Donovan stopped pacing in front of London. "I've been miserable without you, replaying every dumb thing I did and said. But here's the thing. I'm sorry for my grandmother's behavior. If I had known all of this was going to happen, I would have still hired Exposé because otherwise, I wouldn't have met you and that would have been even worse."

Donovan turned, took London's hand. "I started falling for you the day we met. I just knew."

London hung on every word, hopeful.

"I know I'm asking a lot, I know I'm coming to the table with a ton of issues, including a meddling grandmother who doesn't understand boundaries. She also happens to have a key to my house that she likes to use, but I'm hoping you want me, want to give us a chance because now that I've met you and had you in my life, I can't imagine my life without you."

London closed her eyes, exhaling slowly, savoring the words she'd longed to hear but knowing they weren't enough. He said all this now but what if his grandmother made him choose?

Dropping her hand, Donovan slumped back into the chair. "Talk to me, London. Your silence scares me. I don't want to assume anything, because I'm laying all my cards on the table."

He let out a breath. "You have my whole heart in your hands, are you about to crush it and tell me it's all one-sided?"

London took the chair her father had used. "Donovan, I have been fighting my feelings for you the whole time because I, well, a long list of reasons that I concocted in my head out of fear. I can't deny that I'm in love with you."

Neither of them spoke. London's heart pounded, wondering how she might express her deepest fears.

Finally Donovan broke the tense silence. "I hear a *but* coming," he said tightly.

Crossing her arms across her middle, London decided to just say it. "Yes, you're right. I don't want to come between you and your grandmother. She clearly doesn't think I'm good enough for you and I think I started to believe that myself which is why I've been distant. I don't want you to choose me now then regret that decision if either of you decide that you can't come to an agreement and don't talk. I don't want to be the reason you no longer have a close relationship with your grandmother."

London looked across at Donovan, saw him thinking about that possibility. "I don't want you to resent me. I love you enough to let you go and choose her. She may need you more than I do." Her voice cracked. "So that's where we are."

As heavy as her heart felt, London had just lifted a burden from her shoulders. She had poured her biggest fears out to the man sitting beside her along with confessing feelings she'd long tried to suppress. Now that she'd said everything she was feeling out loud, could they make this work?

Maybe.

But she wouldn't get her hopes up too high.

Donovan said she had his heart, however, London could tell he hadn't really thought through what he would do without his grandmother in his life if she chose to turn her back on him.

She watched him, wanting to pull him toward her, offer a comforting touch, but he was in deep thought and she knew her actions would only be distracting.

He stood up again, offering his hand to help her up and said, "Which means we should fight for this. My grandmother may never come around; I will have to learn to live with that but it's her issue, not mine."

Once London was standing, Donovan pulled her closer, kissing her slowly, taking his time to make sure she understood he meant business. London hugged Donovan tightly, relishing the moment.

She decided that if she got nothing else out of their relationship, she knew what it felt like to be kissed properly. Everything else she'd experienced up until this man was amateur night. She felt that kiss from the top of her head all the way to her pinky toes. He released her lips and stared down into her eyes conveying all of the love he'd just professed. "Agreed?"

She nodded quickly, relief coursing through her. As if she was able to say anything other than *yes* at that point. Donovan could have just suggested they break into the Tower of London and steal the crown jewels and London would be all in.

He tilted her chin up. "What's going through that super brain of yours right now? I see you thinking." The gap-toothed grin, beautiful as ever, appeared.

"I was thinking...my dad might want to bring company home tonight. We should go to your place and pretend we're in Miami again."

"See, LL, this is why I love you."

⚜

LONDON WAS AT HER DESK THE FOLLOWING MONDAY, adding notes to Emmaline's case file. Would it hurt to give Emmaline's blog posts one last review to see if anything stood out? She shrugged, nothing to lose by trying. As she was scanning the blog posts, she recalled what Aja suggested.

Sending a quick text to Donovan, she waited for his response. Her phone vibrated a few minutes later. Donovan promised to check and get back to her in a few minutes.

While London waited, she reviewed more of Emmaline's older blog posts.

Scrolling through the website, London immediately thought Emmaline's pictures and posts reminded her of Martha Stewart in that Emmaline made her recipes and gardening look effortless.

London guessed that was the whole point. Making it all look easy for the average woman.

Maybe one day she'd give gardening a try. She could grow flowers or herbs. She discarded that thought almost as quickly as it formed. She didn't like dirt or things that crawled around in dirt. She'd stick to electronic digging for now.

Her phone rang.

"LL, you were right. There's a contact in her mailing list named Clayton who signed up about the time she had me install that app on her phone. His name is Clayton Rummel. You think that's Mr. Miami?"

London bounced excitedly in her seat. Aja was right, as usual. "Yep. I think that's our man. Let me see what I can dig up on him. I'll call you back later."

Eager to get back to work, London ended the call. Hopefully, the name Donovan found in Emmaline's mailing list wasn't a fake name. Somehow she didn't think it would be.

London rubbed her hands together, energy coursing through her. She was finally making some progress on finding out who the man was. She looked Clayton Rummel up on all of the current social media sites but only found him on Facebook. Even though the profile was sparse, she was able to determine that the Clayton she found lived in Miami. London raised a fist in victory, feeling 99.9% sure this was the Clayton she was looking for.

⚜

LATER, AS SHE SAT AT HIS DINING ROOM TABLE ACROSS from Donovan sharing Chinese takeout, she told him about her findings. He nodded, attacking his Sesame Chicken with vigor. London looked on with awe, wondering how he managed to pack away so much food so quickly.

"How'd you come up with the idea to check Gram's mailing lists for his full name?" he asked between bites.

She grinned. "Aja gave me the idea. We had a little heart-to-heart today. After suggesting I check comments on her blog, I saw that she had a mailing list that required first and last name.”

Donovan stopped eating. “What did you have a heart-to-heart about? She’s not letting you go, is she?”

“Nope. She actually said you’re a good man and that you’re lucky to have me.”

“Now that’s a smart woman right there. Good head on her shoulders.” He pointed a chopstick at her, emphasizing his point.

London’s eyes rolled. “You’re just charming my whole family these days. When did you two become besties?”

“We have an understanding. I went to your office looking for you right before we went to Miami but you weren’t there. I talked to Aja. She made me promise to take care of you. I told her I would.” He shrugged, as if his promise was no big deal. “So, I assume Clayton lives in Miami?”

“Yep. City of Miami proper.” London crossed her arms. She needed more detail about this tête-à-tête with her cousin. “So how did this conversation with Aja about me come up?”

“She was the one that let me in the office and told me you’d left for the day already. It was kind of a given that we’d be talking about you,” he said patiently as he dipped the remainder of an egg roll in a pile of sriracha sauce on his plate. “How sure are you that this is the man my grandmother’s been talking to?”

London crinkled her nose at the egg roll slathered with the spicy sauce. The two items didn’t go together in her world.

“About 99% sure.” She got up, intending to put her dirty dishes in the dishwasher, not ready to drop the Aja conversation. “I understand that you would be talking about me because you went there looking for me. What I’m wondering is how you all came to this understanding that I know nothing about.”

London sounded like a petulant child, she realized, which is exactly why, she assumed, they were talking about taking care of her.

“LL, you have people in your life who care about you. Why is that bothering you?” Donovan asked, ignoring his food and focusing on London. "I can't recall the last time I talked to my mother. I got tired of being the one to initiate contact thinking she'd call me but I'm still waiting. I guess if I was in another near fatal accident she might grace us with her presence but other than that..." Donovan shrugged. "You should be thankful for your family."

He was right. London sat beside Donovan, taking his hand. "I should get the Asshole of the Day award. That sucks and I'm sorry your mother doesn't get to see the amazing person she created." She smiled at him. "I do appreciate all of you."

He nodded, leaning in to kiss London. "Thank you. Enough about my mother. What else did you find on Clayton?"

London had practically memorized the man's background and was eager to share. "He lived in Atlanta at one point. After he did his time in the military, he worked in the financial services industry, then there was a four-year gap after which he started his own office cleaning company."

"He's on social media like that? Oh, you used that site for professionals, right?" I nodded. "Was he working in financial services while he lived here?"

"Yep. However, I think he moved to Miami during that gap in his employment. The cleaning service was based there. The firm he worked for here sounds familiar." London turned to Donovan. "Have you heard of Hudson Street Investments before?"

Donovan leaned back, rubbing his chin. "I think I saw it in that ledger Gena gave us. Did you bring it?"

Nodding, London rose from the dining chair to retrieve her tote bag from the living room. She dug the ledger out, thumbing through the worn entries. "Yep, here it is, I think. That looks like 'Hudson' doesn't it?" She tapped a finger on the entry she wanted Donovan to review.

He leaned in closer and confirmed it. "So, he worked with the con artist behind the Ponzi scheme." London typed the investment firm name into the search engine. The firm was no longer active but there was a link to a Department of Justice press release on the sentencing.

"Ok, this site gives details on Gene Dawson or whatever his name was." She clicked the link. London rubbed her hands together, eager to dig into all of the data in front of her. This was the part of her job that she loved. She read the press release then searched for the related cases. Gene Dawson along with two other men had pled guilty. London looked up each of the men. Clayton was not listed.

"Oh wow," London said, excited. "One of the victims filed a suit against the government saying that their victim's rights were denied because they weren't given an opportunity to speak at the sentencing hearing." She read on. "Since they had heard from victims in one of the partner's trials and had written statements, the judge felt hearing them speak again would have no bearing on sentencing."

London continued reading on silently then pointed at the screen. "Clayton Rummel is part of this lawsuit."

Donovan peered at the screen. "That means he was a victim, too?"

London and Donovan looked at each other, trying to put the pieces together.

London spoke first. "Your grandmother is dating the man who helped put his partner, who scammed a bunch of people, including your grandfather, out of millions of dollars, in jail."

Donovan nodded slowly, taking it all in.

Recalling the last time she'd broken bad news about Emmaline to Donovan, London tread lightly. "That cannot be a coincidence."

"What's your theory on this?" Donovan asked. He'd removed his hand from London's and now both hands rested in his lap.

London's heart thudded. He was already pulling away from her, she realized.

Taking a deep breath, she attempted to calm the rising panic in her body. "The mastermind of the whole scheme died earlier this year, in February. There was a video that detailed his crime and mentioned he had a partner, Clayton Rummel, who was never charged. When did your grandmother sign up for Silver and Sexy?"

Donovan ran a hand through his locs, thinking. "I want to say it was maybe March or so. I remember thinking it was cliché for her to seek out love in the springtime."

London shrugged. Spring was as good a time as any other for romance, but she shifted her focus back to the point she was attempting to get Donovan to see. "Ok. That video also alluded to roughly five million dollars that was never recovered."

Donovan sat up straight. "That wasn't love. She's after the money. That's why Gram was so secretive about the relationship. She's trying to take back what was stolen from her and my grandfather."

She nodded. Donovan had come to the same conclusion London had without her having to accuse his grandmother. "I don't think he has it. If he does, he's not spending any of it. He lives a very modest life. And think about it, five million dollars back in the early seventies is worth, what," she checked the conversion rate online, "about thirty million today. He has quite a bit of debt and he filed for bankruptcy a couple years ago. I'm sure he would have used the money to pay his bills."

## ❧ 20 ❧

# DONOVAN

Donovan sat at his desk in his home office deep in thought. He knew he needed to have a conversation with his grandmother as soon as possible, but he didn't know how to even begin the discussion. There was a possibility his grandmother would cut him from her life after what he had to say. She was stubborn and head strong, never liking to admit when she was wrong.

Later, they stood, Emmaline in the kitchen, near the sink, where she had hurried to put distance between her and Donovan under the guise of preparing a meal for him. Donovan stood in the doorway, wanting to give her the space she needed.

Awkward silence hung heavy in the air.

Donovan had just explained to his grandmother that he and London had figured out her end game with Clayton. He waited for a response, expecting a denial or deflection, or both if Gram was pulling out the big guns.

He glanced at a picture of the two of them from the competition in South Korea that she kept on her refrigerator door. She was beaming at the camera, the pride in her grandson evident. That trip had been more than a competition for him. Sure, the competition part was amazing, but he'd had the best time hanging with his grandmother and experiencing a different country with her.

Emmaline rinsed an already clean coffee cup that sat in the dish drainer and remained silent.

Donovan watched her, still waiting for something. "Gram... there's no money. Whatever you were planning to do, you can't do it."

He stepped into the kitchen, closer to his grandmother. He wanted to understand when she'd become this person he didn't know. From the prescription drug trafficking, to intentionally trying to hurt London, to catfishing a lonely man, he couldn't wrap his head around when she'd changed.

Maybe she'd always been this person and he'd been too blind to see it.

Suddenly Emmaline hurled the cup into the sink. Donovan flinched as the glass collided with the stainless steel then shattered. "Since you claim to know everything, do you understand what that man and his firm did to my family?" she said in a low controlled voice.

Donovan could feel the anger rolling through her in waves.

"When your grandfather and I got married, we had big dreams. We were going to buy one of the houses the White people abandoned during White Flight when they moved in droves out of the city of Atlanta. Cascade Heights was the place to be if you were Black and middle class, and I was waiting for the day when we'd have enough saved to put down on our very own home."

She closed her eyes briefly then narrowed them at Donovan.

"Your grandfather gave that man every cent we had saved up. Every. Cent." She tapped on the counter, emphasizing her point. "I was pregnant with your mother at the time. It's a wonder I didn't miscarry from all the stress."

Emmaline turned to Donovan fully. "We were stuck in that shithole apartment all the while driving past those fancy Cascade houses we could no longer afford. But you know what, Donovan?" she said with a humorless chuckle. "That wasn't the worst of it. Not only did they take our money, they took my husband's soul. He never recovered from that loss. I guess he felt like he was less of a man. So not only did I lose the house I wanted, I lost the man I loved."

Crossing her arms, she said defiantly, "They took everything from me and they owe me."

Donovan shook his head. "Gram, London checked Clayton's assets. There's no way he's got any money hidden away. We researched the case. He got swindled too. He's as much of a victim as you and Grandad were."

Emmaline practically spat. "That fat cow has you sprung. Why can't you see that? She's trying to tear our family apart and you're just accepting everything she says."

She stomped to the laundry room and returned with a broom and dustpan to clean up the remnants of the shattered cup. "Clayton Rummel was a partner in that firm and he didn't even get jail time. Well, now it's time for him to pay the piper. When I get done with him, he'll think twice about conning honest people out of their money."

"Don't talk about her like that." Donovan's arms were at his sides, fists balled. "I sat there with her and read the case. We looked at his bankruptcy record. He has medical bills in collection. He would have used that money if he had it."

He shook his head, trying to make his grandmother understand. "He doesn't have it!" He was yelling.

Donovan took a breath, then lowered his voice. "You are going to risk going to jail for nothing."

"Don't you talk to me like that! I'm still your grandmother. You watch your tone." Emmaline glared at Donovan.

"We lost everything," she said quietly. "*I* lost everything."

"Causing Clayton Rummel to lose what little he has isn't going to change anything. It's not going to bring Granddad back. My mom isn't going to wake up and say she wants to be a part of our lives again."

He relaxed his hands and took a tentative step toward his

grandmother. "Gram, hurting this man isn't going to heal our family. Don't do this."

"Donnie," Emmaline shook her head slowly, not accepting anything he'd said. "That woman has got some kind of hold over you and I don't like it. You aren't thinking for yourself anymore, plus you walked in and assaulted her fiancé for no reason. Can't you see she's no good for you?"

"No reason? Gram, he cleaned out her bank account and practically left her at the altar. I'm sure he didn't tell you all of that, did he?" Donovan crossed his arms. "And what did London ever do to you? Why don't you like her? You barely know her."

"It's what she represents that I don't like. She's so unhealthy. Just watch, she'll bring you down to her level and you'll be as big as her with high blood pressure and diabetes, sitting on the couch eating unhealthy junk food." Emmaline swept the floor in angry strokes as she spoke.

Donovan ran a hand over his locs. *Who was this person in front of him?* That feeling of having no idea who his grandmother had become struck him again.

"Gram, you always taught me to get to know people before judging them. Remember that? London's mother died when she was young and she had to deal with that loss. She decided to get healthy and she's lost over a hundred pounds. She does kickboxing and yoga and watches everything she eats. If anything, I am trying to get up to her level." He paused, getting emotional just thinking about London. "She's been through so much and she doesn't let it get her down. I am lucky to have her."

Emmaline pursed her lips but stayed silent. She'd swept the same spots about half a dozen times, Donovan noted.

Donovan squared his shoulders. He now knew what he needed to say.

He thought of London's worries about losing him when his grandmother forced him to choose. "I see that you haven't taken anything I've said to heart. It kills me to say this but if you insist on going through with whatever your plan is to get back at that man and you aren't willing to accept London, I can't be a part of your life anymore, Gram," he said quietly.

Emmaline stopped sweeping, propping the broom against the sink. "You're serious? You're choosing her over your own flesh and blood?" She snorted. "Well, suit yourself." She bent over to collect the broken mug pieces with the dustpan then brushed past him to dump them in the trash.

"You'll need me before I'll need you, grandson," she called out from the laundry room.

"Why can't we talk about this?" he asked as she made her way back into the kitchen.

"Sounds like you've said everything you wanted to say." She had her arms crossed again. "I'm going to my room."

Donovan watched her walk off, hoping she would turn around. The door to her room closed with a snap. Defeated, he took his keys out of his pocket, removing the spare key to his grandmother's house from his key ring.

He placed the key on the counter and walked out of the front door, willing himself not to look back.

"Those are cute! You should buy them," Lavender pointed at a pair of vintage gold earrings on the site London was scrolling. "You can wear them to the holiday dinner next month."

"I'm supposed to be buying stuff for other people on Black Friday, not shopping for myself," London reminded Lavender as they sat in London's office under the guise of collaborating on London's latest investigation.

"We're supposed to be working too, but you see how that's going," Lavender tapped the silver watch on her wrist, "the office is closing at noon, so we have exactly one hour to kill before we are sipping margaritas at the bar...no one is working hard the day before Thanksgiving."

The woman had a point, London nodded in agreement. The office was practically empty.

"Are you sure you don't want to come to Thanksgiving dinner with us?" London asked, looking over at Lavender, "there will be plenty of food."

Lavender shook her head. "I appreciate the invite but I'm looking forward to four days of braless binging on all the finest trash TV I can stand. You're welcome to join me." she put a hand under her chin, "Oh, this will be the first time Donovan meets all of your family, right?"

"Yeah, I've asked my grandmother to behave, but," she raised her hands in surrender, "she has zero filter."

London's phone, sitting on the edge of her desk, suddenly lit up, indicating she had an incoming call. She glanced at the display, raising her eyebrows when she saw who was calling.

"It's Emmaline, Donovan's grandmother," she held up the phone hesitantly, "should I answer it?"

"No, let her leave a message," Lavender shook her head urgently.

London's pulse quickened. As far as she knew, Donovan hadn't spoken to his grandmother since their confrontation where he'd returned her house key. What could the woman want with her?

Another disturbing thought hit her. "What if something's happened to him?"

The phone continued to ring.

"I have to answer." London exhaled, steeling herself. "Hello, Mrs. Roberson."

Lavender rose as if to leave but London motioned for her to stay. She might need her friend's emotional support after this call.

"Hi, London, how are you?" She rushed ahead before London could respond. "I know you're probably working so I'll make this quick. Can we meet for coffee today? I'd like to talk to you and it's best if we do it face-to-face."

London held the phone from her ear, staring at it in shock. Emmaline sounded unsure of herself, the confident swagger she'd displayed at Donovan's house when she called London out was gone.

"Um, I don't think..."

"Please, London, I will only take a few minutes of your time." The pleading tone was unexpected. "It can be after you get off work or later on, up to you; I'm sure you're busy."

"Tell her no!" Lavender hissed.

London wanted to say no, but her curiosity got the best of her. She eyed Lavender warily. "Our office is closing at noon today for the holiday, can we meet around 12:30 at Café Noir?"

Lavender's mouth dropped and London shushed her. She wanted to get the meeting with Emmaline over with, otherwise she'd obsess over it during lunch.

"Yes, I'll see you there. Thank you, London."

London ended the call and braced herself.

"So why exactly are you ditching me to meet that evil woman?" Lavender crossed her arms.

"Because I love her grandson who loves her even though they aren't speaking right now, and I feel responsible for that." London admitted. "If there's a way to get them to reconcile, I want to help." She sighed. "He's hurt by all of this."

Rubbing London's back, Lavender said, "I know and I get it, but what if she threatens you again? Do you want me to come? You know I have no problems telling her to fuck off if you want me to."

"No, I'll be fine," She put a hand on Lavender's arm. "Maybe we can meet later on? I will probably need a drink after I meet her."

"Yes, call me when you're done. Are you going to tell Donovan she called?"

"I don't know yet. I want to see what she wants first." London played with her hoop earring.

⬨

WHEN LONDON ARRIVED AT THE NEIGHBORHOOD coffee shop, Emmaline was already there, seated at a table near the door. She lifted a hand in acknowledgement and took a seat, studying the older woman.

Emmaline looked like she hadn't slept well in days. She was wearing more makeup than usual, causing London to suspect the woman was trying harder than ever to keep up the façade that all was well in her life.

Emmaline took a sip of her coffee. "Thank you again for coming, do you want something to drink?"

London declined, wanting to get to the point of this meeting.

"Ok, well, how's Donnie?" Emmaline asked.

London's patience was thin. "He's fine," she said, crossing her arms in front on the table. "Why am I here?"

Placing her cup down, Emmaline's shoulders dropped. "I need to apologize, London. I shouldn't have contacted your ex or said those horrible things to you."

She twisted her wedding band, not looking at London. "You were right...I hired a hacker to find Clayton's bank accounts and wipe them out. I wanted him to feel what I felt when his company took our life savings."

London started to speak but Emmaline held up a hand. "Let me get this out while I still can."

She took another sip of coffee. "I found out he signed up for that dating site from Facebook so I signed up and we connected. I was never interested in a relationship with him, which is why I didn't tell Donnie, but I didn't count on him being worried about me, thinking I was the one being, what's that word? Something about catfish, right?"

Nodding, London said, "Yes, he was worried Clayton Rummel was catfishing you."

Emmaline ran her index finger over the lip of her cup. "He's actually a really nice man, if I was in the market, which I'm not."

Her golden eyes met London's. London could see the pain in the older woman's face. "I broke things off with him, in case you were wondering, then I deleted that app from my phone."

She turned to glance out the window. "I couldn't go through with the hacker. Donnie told me taking that man's money wasn't going to fix me or my family and I realized he's right. Only I can do that."

London had to tell the woman what she knew. "Clayton

didn't take your money, Ms. Emma, they convinced him to invest so he would become a partner and he lost his money, too."

She nodded. "Donnie mentioned that. I told my friend to call the hacker off. Out of my two kids and cousins and grandkids, Donnie is the only one I can truly count on." Emmaline turned back to London. "When he dropped my house key on the counter, it broke my heart. I knew he meant it."

Emmaline put her hands in her lap. "I apologize for causing pain in your life and trying to keep you from my grandson. I can tell you're a smart woman who cares for him and I want to get to know you better, if you're willing."

Biting her lip, London debated with herself. Should she let the past go?

No. She was tired of running from her problems.

London squared her shoulders.

*Time to put everything out in the open.*

"I was in the restroom at Top Golf that night when you told your friends I wasn't good enough for Donovan because of my size and my skin tone."

The older woman sat back a bit in her chair, clearly taken aback by London's accusation.

"I did say that. And I will admit I assumed you weren't concerned with your health, as I have raised Donovan to be," she pursed her lips, "but Donovan has since enlightened me. I apologize for that as well. I shouldn't have judged you before I got to know you."

Emmaline stopped, appearing to consider her words carefully.

"About your skin tone, I come from a time when lighter skin was valued over darker skin and I believe to an extent this is still true today." She played with her ring again, looking at her hands, "If I'm being honest, I always wanted darker skin because many times people acted like I wasn't 'Black' enough or they assumed I was biracial, which I'm not."

The golden eyes bore into London. "I know I have some work to do on my beliefs and trauma regarding skin tone. But my grandson is a good judge of character and he's clearly got feelings for you so I'll adapt."

*Wow.* All London could do in response to the weak explanation was blink at Emmaline. She had no words.

London supposed that was as good as it got with the older woman. "Thank you for the apology, but honestly, I'm not at a point where I am ready for forgiveness yet, but maybe we'll get there."

Emmaline nodded. "That's fair. I understand. Thank you, London. Tell Donnie I said hello." She stood, turning up the last of the coffee, "Enjoy your Thanksgiving. We'll be at Nate Jr's if you and Donnie want to stop by." She placed a hand on London's shoulder as she passed to toss her cup.

London remained seated, thinking about Emmaline's words.

# EPILOGUE

## LONDON - CHRISTMAS EVE

"You know, this was a good idea in theory but I'm freezing my nuts off."

Donovan and London were huddled together on the porch swing at her house the night before Christmas. All the local weather forecasters had insisted there would be Christmas Eve snow, potentially giving Atlanta the elusive white Christmas they all thought they wanted.

"So dramatic. Ok, ok, I get the point, you're cold. But this was all your idea, Mr. I Want To See Snow As Soon As It Happens." She snuggled close, enjoying the scent of him. "But I'm pretty warm where I am."

"Well, come closer since you're so warm." Donovan put an arm around her waist, pulling her toward him. "And you're probably used to snow coming from DC. When's the last time we had a white Christmas?"

She exhaled a quick breath. "You know it's probably not going to amount to much even if it does snow, right? It will probably only be an inch, if that."

"An inch is plenty, I just want to see it fall," he said, dropping a kiss on her cheek. His warm lips on her skin sent delicious shivers through her. They may not make it to see any snow if she had any say in the matter.

"And this may or may not have been an excuse to get you out here so I could rub up against you," he said unabashedly.

She rolled her eyes. "We could be huddled up on the couch in front of the fireplace."

He'd convinced her that watching the snow from their spot, the porch swing on the screened in patio, would be fun, despite the temperature outside hovering around the freezing mark. They were pressed together like spoons in a drawer, bundled under a blanket with the porch heater on high while the anticipated snow refused to make an appearance.

"Yeah, but we could do that anytime. This is special. It's Christmas Eve and you just hosted your first Game Nite."

"*We* did. You and my dad made all the food. All I did was whip up some cupcakes from a box mix." Her heart was still singing from watching the two important men in her life laughing and working together. She had almost cried at the sight.

"You kept everybody on task though. But it was fun; we should make family game night our annual Christmas Eve thing."

He hesitated. "I think your grandmother was cheating."

She chuckled. "Yeah, that's why she wanted to play Uno. She cheats at Uno all the time. Nobody in the family will play with her anymore. She saw you and your grandmother as fresh meat."

London pulled the blanket tighter around them. Even though she was cold, she was thoroughly enjoying the moment. "Remember when I nudged you with my foot? I was trying to warn you when she suggested it."

"Oh, I thought you were playing footsie with me. I was about to make some excuse and drag you back to my place. We gotta work on our signals."

"I guess we do because I would've totally played along."

Donovan sighed. "I saw you and Gram talking in the kitchen. It looked serious, everything ok?"

Nodding, London shifted so she could see Donovan's face.

"Yeah, she told me she was glad I invited her over and that she's been talking to a therapist about her anger. She said she hopes we can be friends one day."

While they still had a long way to go before they could be considered friends, London decided to forgive Emmaline, more for her sake than Emmaline's. She saw first-hand how holding grudges and not being able to move on from past hurt wasn't good for her mental health.

"I'm glad you convinced me to invite her. It's been a rough couple of months and I don't know if we'll get back to the way we were before all this. But we're in a better place, thanks to you."

As if cued by his words, the snow started. Big, powdery flakes descended from the sky faster than she could count.

She grabbed his hand in support, wanting to freeze this perfect moment in time.


## THE END


Thank you for reading To Catch a Catfish! If you loved the story, please rate/review it
To get exclusive access to bonus scenes and a prequel, visit the Purple Peacock Press site.
Visit my Facebook page!


If you loved London's and Donovan's story, get Aja's story coming in 2024!
Aja Lewis has spent the last four years building her online dating investigation business from the ground up and is ready to take it to the next level but when the mother she never knew dies, she has to drop everything to investigate.

Life coach Del Parris has just lost his favorite client and good friend. Now the woman's outspoken daughter wants his help in getting to the truth. He doesn't want to get involved but what he wants and what he needs are two different things.
Aja's investigation takes her and Del to sunny Barbados, where the temperature isn't the only thing that's heating up.

Catfish in Paradise

# ACKNOWLEDGMENTS

I never thought I would get to this point where I've typed "The End" on this novel. But we're here! And I have tons of people to thank.

First, I have to thank my husband Steve for indulging me when I would randomly throw a scene idea or character trait at him and expect him to respond immediately. He knows me pretty well after twelve years of marriage but maybe he can't read my mind. We'll have to work on that.

To my partner in crime and Clubhouse hostess extraordinaire Satia Cecil, I couldn't have gotten this far without your help. I've learned so much from you over the years and I continue to be in awe of your creativity. I appreciate you and look forward to our next big thing together.

Thank you to Romance Writers of America for accepting me into their RAMP project where I was paired with the perfect mentor, S Cinders. She has taken my hand and gently led me down the proper path to becoming a successful indie romance author. She has connected me with other awesome authors and helped me make my manuscript so much better! And she laughed at a lot of the funny scenes which let me know that she gets me and my quirky sense of humor. S. Cinders, thank you, thank you, thank you!

Thank you to my Clubhouse family! I have learned so much from all of you....Judy, Celeste, Julie, Naomi, Bart, just to name a few. Thank you for helping make Sh*tty First Draft a go-to resource for newbies.

To my critique partners: Audrey, Anne, Judy and Shana....thank you all for the great feedback! I learned so much giving and getting feedback from you all. I wish you all much success and I'm happy to read for you anytime.

Silver Santa

A single dad with a newly empty nest.

A strait-laced guidance counselor with one birthday wish.

This Christmas, a steamy second chance romance twenty years in the making is about to ignite.

Sunshine & Silk Boxers

Gia and Winston's friendship is tested when Gia discovers Dre, her one-night stand from Nashville, has moved to Kissing Springs. With both men vying for her heart, will Gia choose her best friend or take a chance with a younger man?

This is a love triangle, age gap story that will set your summer ablaze!

***

<br>


Bourbon & Bordeaux

Tenacious new publicist Lovie Whitfield is eager to make her mark. She's about to land the opportunity of a lifetime—an exclusive book tour for an up-and-coming author with a provocative relationship book creating waves across social media. There's just one challenge: Saxon Mitchell, the owner of Kentucky's most sought-after bookstore and bourbon bar, must agree to host the book tour's debut.

Saxon, who is embracing his quiet small town life at The Book Barrel, refuses to entertain the idea of hosting his ex-wife's book signing. He values his privacy and endorsing a book that reveals intimate details about his life is out of the question. He dismisses Lovie's emails, texts, calls, and DMs, hoping she'll respect his boundaries and move on.

But Lovie isn't one to back down easily. In a daring move, she heads to Kissing Springs, KY to meet Saxon in person, setting off sparks that neither can deny.